SERVANTS

OF THE END

SHAWN FINN

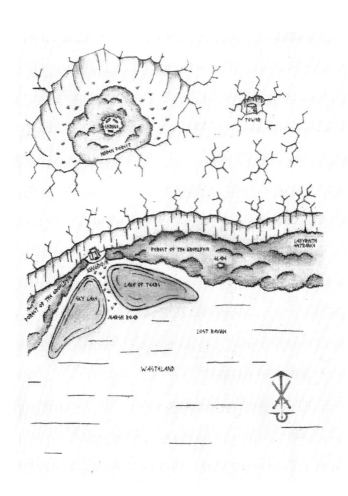

This book is dedicated to the memory of Janet Lueck

SERVANTS
OF THE END

SHAWN FINN

PROLOGUE

ain—white-hot—searing—all-consuming—
suddenly gone. The abruptness of its absence
resonated as a pounding drum that raced with
tribal frenzy and coupled with piercing shrieks. The
relentless barrage assaulted the senses at length,
becoming all that was known or real. Gradually, the
shrillness began to lose its desperate pitch and
dissolved into obscurity; the drumming, however,
continued on with forceful purpose despite the subtle
slowing of tempo. Its droning, rhythmic beating
continued ominously in the overwhelming isolation
that followed…

Perception seemed vague while floating in the void.
Distant feelings of self-detachment became evident as
he struggled to make sense of his surroundings. All
around him was absolute darkness, but he had no way
of knowing if his lack of sight was due to his own
blindness or rather the place to which he was confined
was devoid of light. Reaching out to confront
unknown obstacles, he discovered boundaries that
were yielding and strangely pliant. His instinctive

1

struggles against the elusive barriers brought about the realization that he could not feel his hands or control his movements with purpose. He sensed he was being held captive before he was even aware of the thought. His strength ebbed quickly, and he found himself unable to stay awake as the beating of deep, soothing drumming gently induced a long, comforting sleep…

There was no way to gauge the passage of time as he drifted in and out of consciousness. In the total darkness enveloping him, he was barely aware of his own body. It seemed as though he were floating on an endless void of nothingness. In his strange surroundings there was only one thing he perceived clearly—the slow, rhythmic beating holding him with a sense of calm well-being. The droning cadence subdued his will to try to rationalize its origin as again, its influence sent him into a deep, prolonged sleep…

He awoke disoriented—unable to differentiate up from down. His mind seemed barely capable of thought. He had an innate sense that he should be able to see or perceive *something*. Slowly, he became aware of his eyes straining with effort; then, he could feel his arms moving. The sensation was strange, almost as if it were the first time experiencing it. Unconsciously, he reached out for something—anything, but there was nothing, only the calming, hypnotic beats of endless, muffled thuds once again lulling him into the sanctuary of deep sleep…

Time continued to drift by in much the same manner. Occasionally, he would wake from slumber to find his surroundings unchanged, but he was beginning to recall his circumstances more easily with each waking moment. It seemed the fog was lifting from his mind, and he was able to hold his thoughts more firmly. He also discovered a tedious connection to his body which he was able to control if he concentrated, though the effort of it was exhausting. He could not understand why it would be so difficult to simply *move*. As he reached out into the darkness again and again, he was constantly reminded of the reason for the difficulty—the pliable yet unbreakable bonds. Frustrated, though undeterred, he continued seeking a means of liberation.

Through exhaustive struggles, he began to notice his exertions were slowly increasing his strength, both physically and mentally, but while his attributes continued to improve, he perceived the restraints were growing tighter against his efforts. Maybe it was imagined; perhaps, he just wanted to believe something was changing in his unalterable confinement—something that might reveal a means of escape. He was a prisoner; there was no denying it, but he could not recall how he had come to be in such dire straits. He was having a hard time holding on to his thoughts again, and the distraction of the endless drumming seemed to be getting louder, making it impossible to concentrate. Its captivating effect, combined with his constant exhaustion, enticed him once more into the ever-waiting arms of sleep...

He woke with a start; something had happened. He felt as though he had just returned from somewhere far away. He struggled to recall. There was a blinding light, and was it—pain? The longer he tried to extract he details of what had woken him, the more its clarity diminished, so he dismissed it from his thoughts and began to focus instead on his improving strength. Whatever had been sapping his energy was losing its influence over him, and the growing connection between his mind and body began to inspire hope in him. As his capabilities improved, perhaps too would his chances for escape.

He was certain his prison was becoming tighter and more restrictive, making it imperative he find a way out soon. Resolutely flexing his arms and legs, he began pressing with all his might against the unseen barrier and was alarmed to discover that he was met with immediate resistance. Where he had once been able to move against his restraints, he now found them almost completely unyielding. He tried again with the same result. Panic began to descend upon him. The oppressive confinement was choking him—draining his will to fight, and the unrelenting darkness was leading him to madness! He tried to scream, but there was no sound, only the ceaseless beating which no longer brought comfort; instead, it was a constant distraction making it almost impossible to think.

He was exhausted, and he knew if he were going to devise a plan, he needed mental clarity, so it was critical that he remained calm. Over time, he came to realize he only had a brief period in which to maximize his efforts before he had to rest, but he also noticed when he was forced to sleep, his vitality was restored. Rather than engaging in more futile attempts, he decided to rest and gather his strength. He would recruit every fiber of his being so when next he awoke, he would have the means to make his escape. Allowing himself to succumb to the mind-numbing drumming, he willingly submitted to slumber…

When he woke, it took several moments to remember where he was. He felt as if he had just returned from a foreign realm that was somehow familiar—a place with looming shadows and an overwhelming, unpleasant smell that made him feel unbalanced. He also recalled a blinding light and pain. He only had a moment to consider what he had experienced before the stark reality of where he was came crashing back. Once again, he could feel the unbearable restriction of his movements and hear the deafening thuds pounding relentlessly in his ears. He tried to fight down the rising panic as he recognized his confines had grown even more constrictive—almost to the point of breaking him. He strained against the vice-like grip, but the pressure continued to grow, and he felt as if his skull were being crushed. He tried to scream in desperation but still could not make a sound. His previous strategy of escape was abandoned as a blind instinct for survival took over.

He had been unable to discover the reason for his captivity, but it seemed his fate had been decided. Knowing he would not survive, he braced himself against a painful and imminent death when the crushing force vanished! He was instantly as light as a feather, and his movement was almost completely unfettered, but something still gripped him firmly yet gently.

His eyes fluttered open, and he realized the darkness was gone. He was finally able to see! Searching the newly discovered brightness, he noticed the light was not complete; there was an obstruction casting a towering shadow amid the wondrous illumination. Straining to find focus, the shadowy haze began to solidify as his vision became clearer.

The blood in his veins ran cold as he beheld his first sight—a pair of glowing, green eyes burning balefully—holding him fast within their unblinking stare.

A shrill scream pierced the warm night air. The newborn baby had found its voice at last!

CHAPTER 1

S kealfa waited impatiently outside the king's council chamber. He had received a summons from the king himself only a short time earlier. The young courier who had delivered it was out of breath when he handed over the rolled parchment bearing the king's freshly pressed seal; the urgency of its content was clearly displayed on his face. There was obviously a pressing matter King Bardazel wished to discuss since the hour was so late, yet still he stood, waiting. No doubt it had something to do with the recent attack the city had endured by the monstrous and bloodthirsty Grohldym. Their infrequent raids were nothing new; fortunately, the brutal attacks were sporadic with decades separating them. Skealfa had survived three such ordeals in his fifty-odd years living in the accursed city, and it was always the same. Life would go by peacefully enough in the kingdom for a time; some would even start to believe they had seen the last of the horrors. Then one day, without warning, the Grohldym would appear and rain destruction upon them.

Skealfa heard raised voices behind the heavy door of the council chamber; it sounded like some kind of argument, perhaps the reason for the delay.

The Grohldym—he spat with disgust as his thoughts returned to the foul creatures. They were murderous beasts, created from some sick design he could not begin to fathom. The hulking, sinuous beings were over three times the size of a man, and they were heavily armored with large, silvery scales. The burnished nature of their tough exterior allowed them to blend into their surroundings, giving them highly effective camouflage. They traveled low to the ground with amazing speed, and they moved silently with serpent-like fluidity. The reason they moved so well, he imagined, was because of the numerous limbs they possessed which allowed them similar dexterity to that of the centipedes he had observed as a youth, but these were no dumb brutes. They coordinated their attacks with military precision, and their methods of individual assault were highly unpredictable, making them virtually impossible to overcome. Their obvious intelligence was reflected in eyes that held a high level of reasoning. Skealfa had witnessed their unnerving gaze many times over the years as he led his soldiers in desperate attempts to repel the nightmare hordes.

Trying to spare the city as much destruction as possible had become the best that could be hoped for against a foe who had been confronted, but never defeated. The most recent recompense for his men had been death and heavy casualties. More personally to Skealfa, was the loss of his left eye and ear. The disfigurement itself was not a matter of concern to his vanity; it could be lumped in with all the other injuries he had sustained throughout his service to the crown. The king, however, had a vastly different view on the matter. He believed the loss of an eye and impaired hearing might compromise Skealfa's fighting prowess, putting him at greater risk for injury or worse, and since there was no one who possessed more knowledge of the tactics and abilities of the Grohldym than Skealfa, the king was reluctant to continue exposing him to unnecessary risks. There were rumors circulating that he would not be reclaiming his role as the army's battle-lord; instead, he would remain as chief advisor in all military matters. It would be a position where he would be less likely to engage in future battles as he formulated strategies from behind the city walls where his valuable experience would best serve the army.

Skealfa's anger boiled. He hated the Grohldym for all they had taken from him. As a young boy, his father, mother, and only brother had been slaughtered during one of the vicious attacks. Years later, after he had achieved the highest station in the king's army, the Grohldym claimed the life of his beloved wife, still carrying their unborn child; it would have been their first. Now, all hopes of a family were gone. Most recently, they had stripped him of his status and a good portion of his face, but the recent losses paled in comparison to losing those he loved. Desire for revenge was the driving force in his life. It was the only thing that had given him the will to keep moving forward during the dark days of despair when he had lost so much. Now, the opportunities to exact vengeance upon the Grohldym were in jeopardy, but he refused to let it end in such a way. There had to be justice against those who had taken so much from him! His personal code of honor decreed *he* must be the one to rid the land of this scourge and bring peace to the kingdom.

Skealfa began to pace as his agitation grew. The council chamber door still remained closed, and the Grohldym continued to plague his mind.

He was sure there must be a hidden lair somewhere within the twisted forest of madness surrounding the city, but searching there was difficult. There was a kind of creeping insanity that infected the minds of all but a select few who exposed themselves to the foggy mists swirling beneath the shadowed canopy. It was one of the reasons he had not been able to launch a successful campaign to root out the Grohldym, but he believed if he could assemble enough men who were resistant to the forest's effects and double their efforts, they might be able to track down and expose the nature of the creatures. Finding out what compelled them, or uncovering hidden weaknesses, could be the key to their ultimate destruction.

All were aware of Skealfa's unique understanding of the forest. He was one of the few people in the kingdom who could linger in the dark woods and maintain their reasoning, and he was the only one whose physical attributes were altered positively while remaining there for extended periods. Upon entering the forest, he became stronger and more keenly focused which is why he had been able to spend considerable amounts of time exploring its dark recesses. Now that his status had been reduced to "advisor", he was not sure if he had enough influence to persuade the king to let him lead another party to attempt further pursuit. It would be especially difficult after the recent loss of lives and resources. *"Maybe an opportunity to broach the subject will present itself when I speak to the king,"* he thought. *"What is taking so long?"*

Skealfa was sure he had been summoned to report on the current state of the kingdom. His account would be similar to many others that had been made following attacks in years past. The ancient parts of the city had not suffered any real damage, and the newer structures that were destroyed could be rebuilt, but it was evident the Grohldym's intentions were focused mainly on laying waste to humanity. Seventy-one soldiers had been slain defending the city and over twice that number had been gravely wounded. Civilian casualties were much higher; several hundred unarmed men, women, and children had been slaughtered in the city streets and outlying homesteads—torn to pieces by the Grohldym as they descended on the kingdom. Dozens were taken as well; the exact numbers and identities were still being determined.

The vicious cycle was the same as it had always been, except for one thing; someone who had been taken by the Grohldym during the attack had returned—a woman. Stranger still was the fact that her dress appeared to be soaked with her own blood, yet she showed no sign of injury. She had not spoken a word since her discovery in the desolate, ancient ruins on the outskirts of the city, but her empty stare bespoke of horrors too terrible to comprehend. Skealfa shook away the dark thoughts that began to creep into his mind—thoughts that plagued him endlessly without mercy.

The voices in the chamber grew louder, pulling him back from his ruminations. Despite the absence of his ear, he could clearly hear the voices of the king and his son, Prince Nieloch, raised in anger as they argued. They were locked in a heated debate—the reason for the delay, no doubt.

CHAPTER 2

King Bardazel had planned to meet with his chief military advisor, the once great battle-lord, Skealfa. He wanted to hear more of his thoughts on the recent attack and get an accounting of damage to the city, but there was something even more pressing on his mind. He had been unable to sleep since learning that a woman had mysteriously found her way back from the Grohldym's capture several days earlier. It was a significant event, and he was confounded by what it might mean. As ruler, he was quite familiar with the history of his kingdom. He had studied many of the records in the palace archives extensively. The scrolls and tomes contained there went back thousands of years and documented all that had been learned by those before him. By all accounts, his people had been cursed to live in fear of the creatures, unable to escape their whims since time immemorial. He could find no evidence that anyone had ever returned from their clutches, so if a woman had managed to elude them, perhaps there was a way for all to escape their oppression.

The king's ancestors would have long since fled the region, if not for the geography of the world around them which was remarkably cruel; it held everyone who dwelt within the kingdom captive.

A massive range of mountains spanned the entire length of the city at its back, stretching far beyond it in either direction. The mountains were impassable, being comprised mostly of sheer cliff faces that towered high into the clouds, and their composition was such that no tool could mar them.

The Forest of the Grohldym sprawled thickly at the foot of the mountains on both sides of the city and had no end in either direction as far as anyone knew.

Directly in front of the city's main gate were two immense bodies of water that appeared to be mirror images of each other, but they were vastly different. The eastern body, known as the Lake of Tears, was comprised of warm, murky, salt water. The western body, referred to as Sky Lake, was a seemingly bottomless lake, filled with crystal-clear, fresh water which was icy cold.

Dividing the two mighty lakes was a marshy swath of land identified simply as the marsh road, and beyond that lay an endless wasteland broiling under an unrelenting sun.

Many attempts had been made to find a way beyond the kingdom, without success, but Bardazel was convinced there must be a way to escape, and he obsessively searched for clues that would show him how.

When the king summoned Skealfa, he had been anxious to devise a plan that would allow his forces to capitalize on recent events. He speculated that something extraordinary must have happened in the forest which had presented an opportunity for one of the captives to escape, and he wanted Skealfa to organize a scouting party to discover what it was. He had a simple, straightforward strategy in mind that he was about to set in motion, when the prince burst into the chamber unannounced, throwing his plan into disarray.

The king struggled to regain his composure, stunned by what his son had revealed to him moments earlier.

"I will not have it!" Bardazel shouted. "I will not have the heir to my throne risk his life searching for a newborn child that is surely dead—a child that you believe to be your own?"

"The child *is* mine!" Prince Nieloch responded vehemently.

"Preposterous! It is bad enough you carried on an illicit relationship with some peasant girl, but to believe the child she carried was *yours*—"

"Her name is Glithnie!" Nieloch retorted, "and yes, the child is mine."

"How can you know that for sure?" the king pressed.

"We are in love! Neither she nor I have known the embrace of another."

"You are naive in your youth, I am afraid." Bardazel words were laden with condescension. "She would not be the first woman to use her whiles to improve her situation by spinning lies!"

"She cares not for my title or my position. It has been nothing but an obstacle for us!" The frustration in the prince's voice made it clear that it was a sore subject for him.

Bardazel decided a change of tactics was in order. "So, let us assume the child *is* yours and I agree to let you jeopardize your future in this mad pursuit. What would the people think if I allowed my only son and heir to risk his life searching for a commoner's missing child? Since you do not possess the skills of a soldier, they would certainly draw conclusions as to the reason why, and I cannot allow them to know that the royal line has been corrupted by the blood of a peasant! The scandal of it would shake the kingdom!" The king was trying to remain calm, but as he spoke, the impact of his own words was making it difficult.

"I cannot just stand by and leave my child to an unknown fate without even trying to save it! The baby may end up being all I have left of Glithnie if she does not survive. Surely, you can understand what that means. You *know* what it is to lose the woman you love! I have to believe the loss of mother caused you more pain than you showed." The prince drew a deep breath. "I know you are ashamed of my actions, but it is your grandchild. Does that not matter to you at all?"

"The fate of those taken by the Grohldym is death," the king stated coldly. "How can you think a newborn would fare otherwise?"

"How can you know for sure that all who were taken have died?" Nieloch argued. "Glithnie survived *and* returned."

"That is true." Bardazel considered his son's words for a moment. "Unfortunately, she is unable to shed light on the matter since whatever she endured has driven her mad. She has not spoken a word since her return. She does not eat or sleep. It is likely she will not last much longer. It seems anything we might have learned from her will be lost. If she had been able to tell us *something* that could have helped your cause, perhaps I would see the matter differently. As it is, there is no way I will allow it."

"There is another who may be willing to help me." Nieloch spoke with reluctance. "Before the attack, Glithnie told me of a strange, old man who is not of this city that she met in the forest. She said he was ancient and wise, and she was convinced he possessed mystical abilities."

"Impossible!" Bardazel exclaimed. "None but the Grohldym live in the forest, and while it is true that there are some who can withstand its influence, they cannot linger there, much less reside."

"She said that he did not live there, only that he occasioned the forest in pursuit of his mystical studies."

"And how is it that your 'Glithnie' came to know of him? How did a simple peasant girl enter the forest at all? Is she somehow immune to its mind-twisting effects?"

"She told me that she first met him when she was a young girl living at her homestead on the shore of the eastern lake. When her parents were preoccupied with their daily labors upon the waters, she would sneak away to gaze at the forest despite their stern warnings to stay close to home. She was intrigued by the strangeness of the dark woods but was too afraid to enter. She had overheard her father speaking in hushed tones about the murderous beasts that lived there, and though she had never seen evidence of their presence, she knew the people of the kingdom avoided entering the woods. She became even more curious when her parents learned of her interest in the forest and forbade her to go anywhere near it."

Bardazel raised an eyebrow meaningfully at his son, but the prince ignored the innuendo.

"Glithnie did her best to respect their wishes, but she continued to find herself drawn to the forest again and again. When she finally gathered the courage to go in, she was fully unaware of the curse within its shadowed canopy. She suffered no ill-effects, but her mind was surely being influenced. There was something enticing her to go deeper each time she entered the gloom of the forbidden woods. She told me that being there felt like 'home' even though she was filled with dread at the same time. It was an odd sensation that corrupted her mind like an addiction. She always felt a sense of relief when she left the forest and returned to her cozy farmhouse after her secret ventures, but at night when she was lying safely in the comfort of her bed, her thoughts would always go back to the cool silence of the strange woods, and she yearned to return when next she could get away.

"One day, she happened upon a small clearing in the dense forest where the sun shone brightly on the lush forest floor. There was a trickling brook that fed a deep pool of crystal-clear water. The feeling of dread that she usually felt in the rest of the forest was absent there; instead, she felt calm tranquility. It was the feeling of 'home' that had been drawing her in. The small clearing became her own secret place that she would return to many times over.

"She never expected to encounter anyone else in the forest and was shocked when the day came that she was approached by a strange, old man in the clearing. She had been lost in thought, picking small flowers that she would add to the secret collection beneath her bed. When she looked up, there he was, standing motionless at the edge of the clearing, staring at her intently."

"What makes you believe the old man is not one of the many residing in the city?" Bardazel interrupted.

"A young peasant girl living in one of the lake villages would have no way of knowing."

"I thought the same thing, so I asked her to describe him to me. Her description was vivid. She said he wore strange robes that shimmered when he moved, and his long, flowing hair was radiant white. He also had a strange accent that she had never encountered on her visits to the city. She was mostly taken by his intense eyes which were a brilliant green color unlike any she had ever seen. I asked some of the palace guards to make inquiries among their numbers to see if anyone matching his description could be located, and I was not surprised when they told me that no one bearing a similar resemblance could be found anywhere in the kingdom."

"Someone like that would surely have been noticed after all these years," Bardazel pondered. "If he does not live in the city or the forest, then where could he come from?"

"She claimed he never told her."

The king began to pace the room, stroking his beard excitedly. Nieloch noticed his father's enthusiasm, hopeful it would lend to his cause.

"He does not live in the city or the forest," the king mused. "The marshes seem as unlikely a place as the others, and they have been traversed well enough over the centuries; he would have surely been discovered living there if that were the case. The wasteland cannot sustain life for long; countless failed expeditions to cross its endless, scorched sands have proven that. He must have come from somewhere beyond the wasteland. That means there must be a way to traverse its bleak horizon—a passage that has been overlooked! We must find this man. He may well hold the key to the salvation of the kingdom!"

"He may also be able to help find my child," the prince reminded his father.

"Yes, of course." The king's response seemed to come as an afterthought. "Now, you must go to Glithnie at once," he continued excitedly. "Do your best to get her to break her silence. Let her know that I will exhaust every resource to locate her lost child. Try to get her to produce some shred of guidance that could aid us in locating the old man. I will call for you after I have consulted with Lord Skealfa to strategize on the best course of action. We will see then how much involvement you will have in the campaign.

"Guards! Bring Lord Skealfa inside."

CHAPTER 3

S kealfa bowed to the prince as he exited the council chamber and did his best to conceal his agitation for his delayed admission. The battle-lord was an imposing man who stood head and shoulders taller than all others in the kingdom. He was powerfully built with a deep, broad chest, and his arms and legs were heavily muscled, hardened from years of training. Campaigns and vicious battles with the Grohldym kept him committed to a constant state of readiness, so he moved effortlessly in his heavy armor, owning the prowess and agility of a highly efficient predator. The scars crisscrossing his face and body were earned in hard fought battles, and due to his most recent encounter, he wore a helmet that shielded half of his face from sight. The eye he still possessed smoldered with burning intensity, reflecting his constant desire for revenge.

As Skealfa entered the room, he noticed the king's demeanor which alluded to his excitement despite his mask of practiced composure. Bardazel gave a brief apology for the delay, offered with respect to one who had so valiantly defended his kingdom, but he was anxious to get to the matter at hand.

"How may I serve the kingdom?" Skealfa asked.

"As you always have, Lord Skealfa, bravely and with honor," the king replied graciously. He paused briefly before continuing. "I know that you have endured many hardships throughout your lifetime, and I am aware that many of those hardships came as a result of the Grohldym's vile actions. Your desire to lay waste to our ancient enemy is well known, and I can appreciate your position. Standing as battle-lord, you have proven your devotion to that cause by fearlessly risking your life defending this kingdom against the foul creatures time and time again. You have done so in the streets of the city, and even within the palace walls. You have also pursued them relentlessly in the forest, tirelessly seeking them out with hopes of learning the secret of their existence or discovering their inexplicable origins. Alas, those mysteries remain unsolved, and now your capabilities have been diminished if not your valor."

It galled Skealfa that the king now regarded him in this way. He knew that he was still the most capable warrior in the kingdom despite his recent injuries. His anger boiled, but he held his tongue behind clenched teeth as Bardazel continued.

"When I summoned you, I wanted to hear more of your thoughts on the recent attack. I hoped you might have new insights on how the woman managed to escape the Grohldym. Perhaps something distracted them, causing them to lower their guard. Maybe, it was something that could be exploited if we were to act quickly. I was considering having you organize a small reconnaissance party comprised of your most capable, elite soldiers to further investigate the Grohldym's last known location. I was not planning on having you lead the expedition, however. Your recent wounds are grievous and may compromise your ability to withstand another encounter so soon, and I do not want you to take any unnecessary risks since your knowledge of these creatures is invaluable to the kingdom. As you may be aware, I have been contemplating keeping you within these walls in an advisory role, but I have received new information that supersedes my previous plans. I have decided on a new course of action, and it is imperative that it is successful, so I will need my most capable and trusted agent to carry out my will." The king regarded Skealfa seriously. "I must ask that you put yourself in harm's way yet again. The future of the city itself may well rest upon your shoulders."

"I am honored to serve as you command," Skealfa replied enthusiastically. "My injuries have not diminished my desire to spill the blood of our enemy, and I assure you, I am still *more* than capable of doing such. What would you have of me?"

Bardazel lowered his voice. "What I have discovered is of a delicate nature to the crown. There are facets of the mission that must remain hidden. This will not be a simple matter of reconnaissance. I need you to find someone—a stranger who is not of this kingdom."

"An outlander?" Skealfa said with surprise. "I thought there were none beyond our borders."

"As did I, but my son has just told me of a strange, old man who is not of this kingdom. He was encountered in the forest by the woman who returned."

"So, she has spoken?"

"Unfortunately, she has not, but the prince is familiar with the woman. She informed him of the man's existence some time ago. Apparently, he tried to track down the old man himself, but he was unsuccessful."

"I'm not surprised," Skealfa snorted. "Prince Nieloch has rarely been beyond the walls of the city, but can we be certain that such a person actually exists?" he asked with skepticism. "What if this story is merely some mad fantasy?"

"I'm willing to explore the possibility that the man exists," Bardazel replied resolutely. "I will pursue any and all leads that could liberate my people from the confines of these lands. I will not submit to the whims of the Grohldym and endure the same fate as my forefathers. I will find a way beyond these lands, and I will not turn my back on any prospects to do so no matter how unlikely they may seem, even if others do not share my vision." The king cast a meaningful look to emphasize his point.

"Of course, majesty," Skealfa conceded quickly before continuing. "The forest would be an unlikely place for an outsider to reside; it is dense and treacherous, but it might be possible for someone to live there if their mind remained unaffected by its influence."

"The woman claimed that he does not live in the forest. Apparently, he never told her where he came from, and since the marshes are traveled with some regularity, it is unlikely he could remain hidden there." Bardazel paused and stroked his beard. "He must come from the wasteland or somewhere beyond. What do you think?"

Skealfa considered the king's words. "The wasteland is vast and largely uncharted. I suppose it might be possible for someone to live there undiscovered, but it is hard to imagine anyone could survive in such hostile and desolate surroundings for long."

"True," the king replied, "but I believe our best chance of finding him would be to start in there. You have made many journeys into the wasteland so you are familiar with the landscape, and you know what you might encounter there; still, I think it would be advisable for you to review the routes that have been recorded in the archives before setting out. See if you notice anything unusual in the notes. Also, take a moment to study the courses of parties that never returned and were presumed dead; there may be clues or odd patterns in those areas of exploration as well." Bardazel moved closer to Skealfa as he continued. "Crossing the wasteland has proven to be impossible for us, but perhaps this outlander has fared better. The woman suggested that he has mystic abilities, perhaps he is capable of finding success where we have not for that reason. I imagine discovering if that is the case will be crucial."

"If we are to learn anything from him, we must first locate him," Skealfa said, then he paused for a moment of consideration. "I agree that the wasteland is the best place to start, but I think it makes sense to concentrate our efforts in closer proximity to the forest rather than following typically patterns. Past excursions seemed to focus on traveling as far from the city as possible. The parties I have led were able to cover no more than three days distance before having to return. If this man regularly visits the forest, I cannot imagine he would cross the vastness of the wasteland each time. Perhaps some of the terrain nearer to the city merits closer scrutiny."

"I will leave the finer points of the search method to your discretion. I am confident that your instincts will bear fruit." Bardazel looked intently at Skealfa before continuing. "There is another matter we must discuss. Aside from learning about the existence of the outlander, it was also revealed to me that the woman who returned was heavy with child when she was taken by the Grohldym. As you have seen, that is no longer the case, but the blood that covered her dress appears to confirm this claim. It is likely the infant has perished, but if by some miracle it has survived, retrieve the child. Be aware of the possibility of its existence as you search for the old man, but do not deviate from your primary objective. Finding the outlander is of the utmost importance. Do not compromise the success of that mission in hopes of finding a missing child who is most likely dead." The king placed his hand on Skealfa's arm. "Know this: If you can locate the old man and deliver him to me, you will have proven that your abilities remain undiminished, and you will retain your position as battle-lord."

"I am grateful for the opportunity my king." Skealfa's spirits soared as his hopes for revenge were rekindled. "I will find the old man and return him to you at all costs."

CHAPTER 4

S kealfa commenced with the inspection of the five elite soldiers who stood before him in the barracks. Varthaal, Brilldagh, Crel, Toric, and Hreydol had all been selected by Skealfa himself for the current mission. They had been chosen for their skill in battle as well as their unflinching loyalty to him.

Varthaal was the unspoken leader of the five. He was a fair amount older than the others, and he had accompanied Skealfa on many exploits. His good judgement and level-headed nature made him a valuable commodity during high-stress situations where his sword and shield had been essential.

Brilldagh was a solemn man who stood far taller than most in the kingdom, yet he was still dwarfed by Skealfa's massive stature, and while his unusual leanness only emphasized the difference, it did nothing to diminish his virulent skill with the long spear he wielded with deadly precision.

Crel was quite the opposite. Barrel-chested and jovial, the good-natured soldier's rotund appearance disguised unexpected speed and power which he used to inflict devastation upon his enemies utilizing his heavy mace and battle-axe in tandem.

Toric also employed the use of two weapons against his foes. The audacious style in which he implemented his dual swords reflected his brash, and apparent, reckless enthusiasm in battle.

The most recent addition to the ranks of the elite soldiers was Hreydol. Soft-spoken and thoughtful toward his purpose, his proficiency with a bow made him a unique and beneficial asset as his ranged attacks had the ability to disrupt advancing enemies. He was also very capable with his short sword when close quarters fighting was unavoidable. Being the newcomer, he was eager to prove his worth among his peers.

In addition to the men's outstanding combat abilities, they also possessed exceptional resistance to the ill-effects of exposure to the forest and wasteland. Their ability to tolerate extended periods in both regions was not as developed Skealfa's own, but they had all proven themselves to be valuable assets on past expeditions and skirmishes in both locales.

Since the recent attack on the city, the number of elite soldiers had been reduced drastically. Skealfa hated the idea of risking more of these unique soldiers, but his expectations of entering the forest would be limited to necessity. His main course of action would be trekking into the wasteland where the adverse mental effects were not as severe.

King Bardazel had made it clear to Skealfa that locating the rumored outlander was of the utmost importance to the kingdom. Not only had he been tasked with finding him, but he also had to convince him to return to the city and meet with the king. Bardazel had authorized Skealfa to entreat the mysterious, old man with various enticements from the royal treasure chamber that might appeal to him. The king was emphatic however, that he should retrieve him one way or another. The man was not to be harmed, but it had been made abundantly clear to Skealfa that if he wished to retain his station as battle-lord, he must deliver the stranger to him.

Skealfa was not entirely certain this alleged person was even real; his existence was confessed through a secondhand account, obtained from a woman who had recently been driven mad. It was not the most reliable evidence to be sure, but if there was a person haunting the wastelands, he would be the one to bring him before the king in order to solidify his rightful station.

The soldiers appeared to be well prepared for the expedition. Their weapons and armor had been repaired and restored to gleaming perfection. The injuries that had been sustained among them were mostly superficial, but Skealfa examined all mending wounds to verify that infection would not become a complication when they were far afield in unknown and potentially hostile terrain. He could see the men were well-rested and craving action. There was vengeance burning in their eyes for their fallen brothers-in-arms and for loved ones who had also been claimed by the Grohldym's brutal assault.

The men were aware of the rumors circulating through the ranks that Skealfa had been slated for removal as battle-lord after the recent raid. Supposedly there was concern from the king that his wounds might compromise his effectiveness in battle. There had been no official announcement to confirm the rumors, but as they looked upon his grim countenance, some wondered what was truly at stake. If there was any truth to the rumors, they would not be the ones to fail him. They were willing to go to any lengths to ensure that King Bardazel had no reason to doubt the proficiency of their esteemed commander.

The men had always admired Skealfa's intractable focus and relentless efforts to rid the land of the Grohldym horde. He was ferocious in battle and had saved countless lives of citizens and soldiers alike throughout his impressive career. Many in the army had never served under anyone other than Skealfa. As children they had been told stories of his might and bravery in battles against the Grohldym. He was by far the youngest soldier in history to achieve the position of battle-lord, attaining the esteemed title at the age of his sixteen. He was loved by the people and revered by soldiers young and old who could not imagine being led by another.

Skealfa was impressed by the readiness of his men, but he had expected no less from them. He knew the hardened fighters standing before him would be anxious to pursue their ancient enemy, and he could see they were eager to inflict pain and devastation upon them as they sought to balance the scales. It was time to tell them the true nature of the mission before the flames of vengeance burned out of control.

"I see before me, five of the most capable warriors it has been my honor to lead," Skealfa began. "You have proven yourselves courageous and competent in battle, and you have been steadfast in your defense of the city against the perils of the forest, disregarding your own well-being. We all share the losses wrought by the foul Grohldym, and they weigh heavy in our hearts. Desire for revenge calls upon our honor to seek out these murderous beasts and lay waste to their entire population. I long to see the day when they have been annihilated so they may never again lay claim to the lives of those we hold dear. We must ensure that their deaths are brutal and painful and that the violence we rain upon them will be unrelenting as we send them into the abyss, erasing their foul race from the minds of future generations because we have so completely and utterly eradicated them!"

The men raised their fists and shouted with enthusiasm at Skealfa's infectious furor.

"It will be so upon a day, and I will be the one to lead you to their slaughter," the battle-lord assured them. "However, the course that will take us to that glorious end is not a straight one. There is a side road we must travel in order to reach our desired destination. Before we can fully commit to the pursuit of the Grohldym and deal out their fate, we must first venture into the wasteland to discover the whereabouts of a strange hermit who is said to reside there. The king has tasked us with finding this person and bringing him to the palace." Confused looks passed among the men as Skealfa continued. "The man is not of this city and his origins are unknown, but the wasteland seems to be the most likely place to find him. You are all aware of the king's determination to discover a way beyond the confines of our borders. He believes this person may be valuable in that regard. He is hopeful the outlander possesses knowledge of civilizations other than our own, and he wishes to discover if this man will be able to offer counsel that could free our people from the perpetual torment inflicted by the Grohldym. It is our duty as loyal soldiers to serve the crown and deliver this person to King Bardazel but finding him will be difficult. Until now, nobody has been aware of his existence. It is only through extreme circumstances that I have been given knowledge of his presence in our kingdom. He clearly does not wish to be discovered otherwise he would have most likely been encountered on past excursions. With that being said, the sooner we find him, the sooner we can return to our pursuit of vengeance while the king seeks his answers." Skealfa paused. "Is everyone clear on our mission?"

"We understand, and we will serve the king as he commands," Varthaal replied ardently on everyone's behalf. "Where you lead, we follow, always."

"Your commitment and loyalty are well received," Skealfa replied warmly. "Do not be disheartened by this turn of events," he added. "We may still find opportunities to engage the Grohldym in our pursuit of the outlander. He has been known to enter the forest on occasion, and we may find the need to seek him out there. We will follow our leads as we find them, and if we find ourselves at odds with the accursed beasts along the way, so much the better."

"Aye!" sang the men in unison.

"Now, let us commence with the task at hand. Dawn will be upon the city before long, and I would have us depart without being noticed. We will undertake this mission in secrecy. I do not wish to alarm the citizens after the recent bloodshed."

With the meeting at an end, the men collected the rest of their provisions and followed Skealfa out of the barracks. They passed through the outer courtyard and entered the still sleeping streets of the city moving swiftly and silently until they reached a seldom used access gate that led outside the city walls. Skealfa unlocked the heavily barred gate allowing his men passage, then locked it securely behind him. There were several of the small access gates located at various points along the length of the city walls, and they were typically left unguarded when the city was not under attack. Since only select members of the royal house and the battle-lord had the keys to unlock them, they were rarely opened and mostly existed as maintenance access to monitor the state of the walls or as emergency escape points. In the shadows of the dwindling night, the gate provided a convenient means to leave the city without having to pass through the main gate and being observed by the guards posted there.

The king and Skealfa had agreed it would be best if citizens and soldiers alike were unaware of the urgent mission until it was no longer possible to keep it from them. There seemed to be no point in creating unrest in their minds over rumors until they had solid evidence the king's speculations could be justified.

The small party made its way quietly along the outer wall, passing by several of the small fishing camps that dotted the shores of the great lakes. There were stirrings in some of the huts as early rising fishermen prepared for the labors of the day, but the group avoided notice and quickly put the camps behind them.

Soon they were moving through the marshes, creating distance between themselves and the main gate as they worked their way along the marsh road. The passage between the lakes was not so much a road as it was a wide, muddy stretch covered with tall grass that stood as high as a man's shoulders. The slimy ground that snaked between the roots of clumped grass made traveling in the dark challenging, as the lightly used avenue leading to the wasteland was typically overgrown with disuse. The fishing folk had little use for it, since they resided mostly on the shores near the forests and city walls where they launched small fishing vessels from the docks which had been constructed there. It also served no purpose for the harvesters since the rice they collected grew on the opposite shoreline of the western lake. Besides those making occasional trips to gather salt from the barren flats stretching out from the wasteland border of the Lake of Tears, the soldiers were the only ones who used the passage between the lakes to access the wasteland, carefully avoiding the distant shore of Sky Lake where a careless step could be fatal in its deceptive shallows and treacherous quicksand.

The waning moon hung low in the clear, night sky, its light reflecting like glittering jewels upon the water of the lakes on either side of Skealfa and his men as they traveled. The effect created a swath of darkness before them that slashed between the lakes, marking the unmistakable route, and eliminating the need for torchlight. All of them had passed through the marshy grassland on previous occasions, so they had no great difficulty navigating their way along the tricky path.

By the time the morning sun was clearing the horizon, the ground beneath the group was firm and dry. The expanse of tall grass had been replaced by sharp, broken rocks and sparse brambles. Skealfa stopped within sight of the twin lakes and gathered his men to explain the method they would employ to search for the outlander.

"All of you have accompanied me into the wasteland on past exploits as we have sought to discover a passage beyond its bleak horizon. On this occasion, that is not the case, so we will be executing a different approach to accomplish our objective. Since we are seeking an individual that may be living in these harsh climes, we will be focusing on areas in closer proximity to the forest where he has been seen. I imagine he resides within reasonable traveling distance of the twin lakes, relying on them as a resource for his survival. It is a commonly held view that human life cannot be sustained deep in the wasteland, and past exploits have failed to uncover another source of drinking water beyond Sky Lake, so I believe we will find the outlander at a location that is within a few days journey to the lakes.

"In order to cover as much ground as possible, we will space ourselves apart as much as we can while remaining within sight of each other. One by one we will separate deeper into the wasteland, creating a line that will run as far as our visual connection will allow. Since the landscape is mostly flat, we should be able to keep a fair distance between us. It will also help that the wind rarely stirs, so windswept sand and dust should not obscure our vision. We will move as a unit along the lake to where the eastern shore meets the forest, then we will continue on until nightfall. If anyone sees something that would indicate the presence of the outlander, that man will signal with his horn twice. The signal should be repeated down the line and we will go to that location to investigate. If at any time, someone becomes lost from sight for an unseemly duration, sound your horn in three short blasts. The alert should be repeated down the line and we will all work our way to the first sounding until a clear line of sight is re-established or the reason for the loss of visual cohesion is discovered.

"If we do not find the outlander throughout the course of the day, we will regroup at my position near the center of the line just before dark. In the morning, we will return to our positions and continue for another day. If we discover nothing in that time, we will move the line deeper into the wasteland and begin working our way back to where we are now. Once we return to this position, we will replenish our water supply and resume our search in the opposite direction.

"We will make four sweeps in both directions. If this person is out here, I believe we should be able to locate him within the next eight days. If we have made no discoveries by then, we will have no choice but to return to the city to fully replenish our supplies. I will report our progress to the king at that time and see what is decided.

"Now, Varthaal will remain here while the rest of us move to our positions. Once the last man is at the furthest point, he will sound his horn one time. The signal will be repeated down the line and back again, then we will proceed. Is everyone clear on the structure of the search?"

The soldiers nodded with steadfast resolve.

"I know journeys into the wasteland are grueling affairs that often claim lives, but you men have been tempered by the perils of a harsh world and you possess the mettle you will need. Now, let us begin."

CHAPTER 5

Czarstostryx emerged from the cool silence of his reclusive dwelling and stepped into the oppressive heat. He paused briefly, raising his hand to shield his eyes from the blinding sun. After taking a moment to adjust to the harsh light, he scanned his surroundings to confirm he was alone. He doubted he would encounter intruders in such an inhospitable and remote location, but steadfast caution had kept his existence a secret for well over a century.

Although soldiers from the city ventured into the wasteland on occasion, he knew they would never discover his shrouded home. Even if they were to be found in close proximity, it would be purely coincidental since they only seemed interested in discovering a means of crossing the endless span of scorched earth. He noticed several of their failed attempts throughout the years.

Some of the expeditions made it quite far before being forced to turn back. Others had not been so fortunate and perished deep in the wasteland. He verified these failures by periodically tracking groups that did not return, discovering their emaciated bodies littering the burning sand far afield. His observations were more out of curiosity than anything, and they afforded him a chance to gather useful information about the strangers he sometimes observed from a distance, up close.

Czarstostryx knew the people of the city would never find safe passage across the endless sands. The wasteland held a strange enchantment; one could not simply walk beyond it, there were secret paths that had to be negotiated in order to find a way through. He knew this from his own exploration and studies which he had remained committed to for as long as he could remember. He had developed an acute understanding of the various regions' peculiarities as a result.

The wasteland's influence served to confuse one's sense of direction, making it virtually impossible to navigate a true course, but he had developed an ability to shield himself from the affect, so he was able to travel successfully through its barren climes. He had journeyed extensively through the arid wilderness, and he knew the vastness of the seemingly endless desert was beyond even his skill to overcome. The soldiers, not possessing the ability to resist the wasteland's influence, had no chance at all. He supposed after all their failures, they must realize this for themselves, but he understood their desperation to leave the hostile land that held them captive, and since they always seemed to become more determined to escape after the Grohldym raided their city, he expected they would be entering the outlands again soon.

After walking a short distance, Czarstostryx turned back to assess the narrow ravine that marked the entrance to his home; it would be easy to escape one's notice even if they *did* know where to look. Still, he was not willing to take any chance of it being discovered while he was gone. Clearing his mind, he focused his will, and with a few muttered syllables and a slight gesture of his hand, it was done. Confident his dwelling would not be discovered in his absence, he set out for the Forest of the Grohldym.

As he walked, he considered the connection between the Grohldym's activities and the nature of the landscape itself. Over the years he recognized that the devastation the creatures wrought upon the people of the city had a ripple effect throughout the landscape, and he was curious to see what new discoveries he might make in the wake of the latest invasion.

He remembered vividly the first time he had seen the Grohldym attack the unfortunate inhabitants of the city. The soldiers had mounted a well-organized defense, but they were far outmatched by the ferocious beasts who seemed to be systematically slaughtering anyone they encountered. He had wondered why the creatures would behave in such a way since they were not consuming any of their victims. Afterward, when the Grohldym withdrew, he witnessed the creatures dragging captives into the forest for some unknown purpose. Hours after they vanished into the trees, thunder began to echo ominously in the distance, yet there were no storm clouds on the horizon. He had been quite intrigued by it all.

After seeing a recurrence of the same events several decades later, he decided to investigate the matter, curious to discover what became of the unfortunate thralls, but his concern for the welfare of the people was secondary to his own personal interest. Utilizing all of his skill and craft, he managed to track the creatures deep into the woods. He used extreme caution to avoid detection and mindfully kept his distance as he followed. Eventually he lost their trail, and since most of the time they were out of his line of sight, it was hard to know exactly how they had been able to elude him. As he stood pondering the situation, a violent clapping of thunder shook the ground. It was not in the distance as before, but all around him with deafening intensity. Uncertain of what it all meant, he fled the forest, leaving the questions that had led him there unanswered.

It was many years later before he was able to try again, but when the creatures inevitably returned, he fell into pursuit as he had before, hoping he would be able to find his answers. Pursuing them a second time, he noticed they were following the same heading through the forest as before, traveling along the base of the massive cliffs far away from the city. As he approached the region where he had lost them previously, the ominous thunderclaps again shook the forest. Expecting as much, he maintained his resolve and continued to press on, making his way eventually to his projected destination. When he got there, the Grohldym and their captives had once again vanished. He decided to linger and investigate further.

It was exceedingly difficult to know for sure where they had gone because the forest was widely traveled by the creatures and evidence of their passing was abundant. Knowing for certain where one trail ended, and another began was not as simple as he had hoped. The trees of the forest crowded close to the cliffs making it difficult to see very far in either direction, but he knew he had to be in the general vicinity of where they had disappeared. He made a choice at random and began moving slowly along the cliff's sheer surface, scrutinizing every detail. He knew the Grohldym might appear again at any moment, but he forced himself to dismiss his concern over the matter. He *had* to know what had become of them!

He had not gone far, when a momentary flash of light emanated from the cliff face just ahead of him. Quickening his pace, he approached the spot where he had seen the brief illumination. There did not appear to be anything unusual at first, then he noticed a narrow crack that was wide enough to pass through. Apparently, the sunlight from high above had shone at a precise angle just long enough to reveal the interior. Upon further investigation of the area, he noticed evidence of a commotion on the ground directly outside the small opening. It seemed likely he had uncovered where his elusive quarry had gone. Cautiously, he peered inside the gap and was surprised to discover the ground inside was undisturbed. There also appeared to be a path leading deeper into the cliffs beyond what he could see. He did not dare risk losing his best chance of solving the mystery, so he warily crept into the dark opening, unsure of what he would find…

It had been many years since Czarstostryx first discovered the mysterious path leading into the canyons. As he walked, he continued to contemplate all he had learned.

Plumbing the depths of the seemingly endless labyrinth of narrow canyons within the towering mountain range required a large investment of time. During his first expedition he quickly ascertained that the mind-altering effects polluting the forest also corrupted the core of the mountains but to a much greater extent. His resistance to the forest's influence had allowed him to make great strides in its exploration, but he could not linger in the shadows of the oppressive canyons as easily. His tours became brief affairs as necessity forced him to leave the narrow confines often to clear his thoughts. Unfortunately, in order to restore his senses, he had to remove himself from the forest as well and return to his home in the wasteland to fully recover from the extreme mental fatigue. This unavoidable obstacle made his progress painfully slow, but he would not be discouraged. He knew there must be something immensely powerful within the canyons to impose such extreme deterrents, and he became even more convinced of his theory when the entrance disappeared unexpectedly after a full cycle of seasons had passed. He came to learn it would not return until the next time the Grohldym fell on the city to wreak havoc.

There was only one year in many to search for the hidden secrets within the canyons. He recalled bitterly how much time had been lost, but he did not allow the limitation to hinder his progress unduly. When he could not enter the labyrinth, he spent a great deal of time pouring over the books and scrolls in his home. There was a wealth of information referencing the flora and fauna found in the world around him, and his examinations of their properties greatly improved his ability to survive and even thrive in unusually harsh surroundings. There were also arcane tomes within his dwelling he had learned to decipher after years of study. Their contents described powerful magic and lost rituals meant to evoke a powerful being from an unknown realm who could bestow god-like power upon its devotees.

Czarstostryx became obsessed with mastering all he discovered in his research; consequently, his diligent pursuits had afforded him an unusually long life and unmatched talents. He knew that in order to uncover the revelations within the canyons, the attributes he had developed were an absolute necessity. He had already spent the equivalent of several lifetimes trying to expose the secrets hidden there, but as the long years stretched on, he knew he must face the fact that he was not immortal, not yet anyway, and time was not an unlimited commodity.

Czarstostryx was hardly aware of the oppressive heat as he continued to reflect on all the time and effort he had invested.

He had meticulously mapped and documented all the details of his exploration in the canyons, and the more he did, the more he came to realize that there was a direct correlation between his notes and what he had read in several of his books regarding the location of a powerful being who could be found there. Over time, he learned to interpret the meanings of scattered, abstract references found in several of the more obscure books at his home. Some were narratives describing the rituals that could be performed to draw the attention of the hidden deity, and others referenced locations he had never before seen. As he penetrated ever deeper into the canyons, he knew the hidden places must be within the labyrinth, and as his ability to navigate improved, he was able to recognize indications that he was getting close to reaching his goal.

Czarstostryx was filled with excitement as the thoughts raced through his mind, causing him to quicken his pace.

The burning sun had begun its slow descent when the shimmering reflection of the great eastern lake appeared in the distance. The scattered fishing camps on its outskirts that usually bustled with activity appeared to be abandoned in the wake of the recent attack. Czarstostryx cautiously gave the lake a wide birth as he made his way toward the forest bordering its eastern shore. If patrols had been dispatched into the wasteland, they would most likely be using the marsh road which was much further from his position, but there were no guarantees they would not set out from the outer shores of either lake, so it was prudent to avoid the area altogether.

Czarstostryx was relieved he would soon be leaving the burning sands behind him to enter the cool shadows of the forest. It would be a welcome transition that would allow his passage to be far more covert. He preferred not to traverse the wasteland in the daytime when being exposed to curious eyes was a constant concern, but it was important he reached the forest at the right time. Experience, and several close encounters with the Grohldym, had taught him the most opportune times to pass through the forest unmolested. There was a remote chance soldiers would be scouting in the woods when he arrived. He was aware they patrolled the forest from time to time, but it was a rare occurrence, and they could be easily avoided.

Aside from the occasional scouting parties, he had only seen one other person in the forest—a remarkable young woman encountered in an unusual glade at the heart of the forest. Over the course of several years, he quietly observed her visits, watching as she grew from a curious girl into a fine young woman of striking beauty. He was not inclined to reveal himself to her at first, but her ability to conceal herself as she moved through the forest was truly impressive; where he used mystical means to shroud himself, she had an innate ability to blend into her surroundings, becoming almost invisible with her stillness. She also seemed to have a natural resistance to the forest's mind-altering influence, which was highly unusual. He eventually decided it would be useful to find out more about her unique abilities, so he introduced himself to her. He smiled briefly as he recalled the memory. She was with child when he had last seen her, though she was not showing any noticeable signs, and it had surprised her when he commented on it. She seemed saddened at the prospect of having the baby but had chosen to remain tight-lipped on the matter.

It had been quite some time since their last encounter, and Czarstostryx presumed the baby would have been born, if not, very soon. He typically had no interest in the affairs of kingdom's inhabitants, but he had developed a kind of fondness for the woman. She had a soothing presence, and her peaceful nature was something rarely encountered. He found himself enjoying the bits of time he spent with her more than he realized it seemed. He hoped she had fared well in the recent attack...

The low-hanging sun cast ominous shadows among the trees as Czarstostryx closed the distance on the canyon labyrinth. He was anxious to reach his destination, but before he did, it would be necessary to enter the glade to gather a few necessities. He half-wondered if Glithnie would be there but considering the recent stirrings of the Grohldym and her delicate condition, he doubted it.

As he approached the familiar clearing, he took a moment to pause and study the small glade before emerging from the shadows. It was a unique spot in the gloomy forest—a place where the sun penetrated the twisted canopy and shone warmly throughout the day which likely contributed to the minimization of the mind-altering effects found there. Lush ferns and large, smooth stones heavily cushioned with thick moss, surrounded a deep pool of crystal-clear water which was fed by a small, trickling stream that glistened in the light of the setting sun. It was a scene of utter tranquility. Perhaps, it was why the young woman had been attracted to the site in the first place.

Czarstostryx stood silently, watching, and listening intently, but daylight was fading fast, and the growing shadows were threatening to deceive his perception. There was no time to linger at any rate if he wished to reach his destination before nightfall. As he prepared to advance and collect the required items from the glade, he saw movement at the far edge of the clearing—just a tiny shift in the shadows. Then, he saw it again. His breath caught in his throat as he observed a small, naked boy cautiously emerge from the tree line on the far side of the glade. The child moved with uncanny stealth and agility as he made his way to the edge of the pool.

Czarstostryx's heart pounded as he drew a quiet breath. *"Who is this? How did a child come to be here?"* The questions loomed large in his mind. He had to find out! He considered removing his mystical camouflage to make his presence known, but just as the thought entered his mind, the boy's eyes fell directly on him. The hair on Czarstostryx's neck and arms stood on end as he felt a familiar stirring of energy. The child vanished—disappearing into thin air. The immense surge of power marked the boy as a highly magical being, and Czarstostryx suspected trying to locate him would be an exercise in futility, but he spent a modicum of time looking for traces of his whereabouts regardless. Unfortunately, he could find nothing to indicate what had become of the boy.

It was a puzzle he would have to solve another day, and he had already lingered too long as it was. He would make it a point to investigate the matter further when he was not pressed for time. Hurrying on, Czarstostryx made his way to the canyon labyrinth.

CHAPTER 6

The child was shocked by the sudden appearance of the strange, old man, and his heart was beating fiercely from the encounter as he ran like a shot through the forest. He *knew* something was amiss when he approached the small clearing; there was a strange feeling in the air similar to that of an approaching storm, but it was more concentrated. He had been uncertain what it might mean, but the need to quench his thirst had compelled him to proceed. When he noticed a fluctuation in the unusual energy, he immediately spotted the old man concealed among the trees and nearly jumped out of his skin at the sight of someone silently regarding him who could influence his surroundings in such a way.

Running as fast as his legs would carry him, the boy navigated quickly and silently, never looking back until he reached a grove of unusually large trees. Slipping between the massive trunks, he worked his way to the center of the stand where the largest, most ancient tree stood. There were no low-lying limbs or handholds near the ground, but it did not prevent him from finding his way upward. Raising his eyes to the canopy high above, he confirmed where he wished to be, and clearing his mind, focused his thoughts on elevating himself to the giant branches far beyond his reach. He began to rise from the ground, floating weightlessly toward his objective. Shortly thereafter, he stepped lightly onto an enormous branch and followed it to a large hollow in the trunk.

The tree had been damaged by lightning many years earlier, and a large portion of it had been blasted away. Over the centuries, the tree had slowly healed around the wound, creating a spacious cavity where the boy found shelter, and with the addition of dry moss and leaves, he had created a warm, comfortable place to sleep. The cozy nook was also a sanctuary from the dangers that lurked below. None of the creatures who roamed the forest floor would climb the gigantic tree, so he did not need to worry about them while he was nestled safely within the ancient chamber. It was quite by accident that he first discovered his hidden refuge. He recalled the events leading to its discovery as he settled in.

Before finding his sanctuary, he was primarily living in dense thickets of undergrowth where he foraged for insects and small creatures to sustain himself, but through the cautious exploration of his surroundings, he eventually discovered a glade with a clear stream running through it which had become his key source of water. The small clearing was also filled with ferns bearing tender shoots that provided sustenance far tastier than the insects and grubs he had grown accustomed to.

When he was in the glade, he noticed an unusual sense of peace. There was something familiar and calming about the place that put his mind at ease so he spent a lot of time there, but he felt overly exposed in the warm, sunlit clearing, and he knew he must stay ever vigilant against the strange, shimmering creatures that moved through the dark woods.

He managed to remain unharmed by the frightening beasts, mostly because of his acute hearing which was keenly attuned to the sounds of the forest. It was not difficult for him to perceive the creature's movements when they drew near, and he always avoided discovery by remaining motionless and silent until they were gone. There had only been one time when his advanced senses had failed him.

When he first discovered the grove of giant trees, he was captivated by their sheer size. He remembered gazing in awe at their towering height and marveling at the enormous branches that disappeared from sight as they stretched ever higher. Peering upward, he had become mesmerized by the subtle movement of the leaves stirring in the lofty breeze high overhead. The effect was hypnotic, and he lost himself in a pleasant daydream guided by the wonderful trees.

He had no idea how much time had passed when he was suddenly struck by a sense of imminent danger. He quickly spun around to confront the unknown threat, which to his horror, turned out to be three of the dreaded beasts bearing down on him. It was too late to run, and there was nowhere to hide, but somehow, he had to get away! His mind locked onto the branches high above his head, and he recalled the pleasant feeling of tranquility he had just been experiencing. He wanted to *be* there. The sublime sensation and his desire to attain sanctuary converged instinctively. Immediately, he rose above the forest floor and swiftly ascended to the safety of the canopy, settling lightly onto one of the massive branches just in front of a mysterious opening in the tree.

Far below, he saw the monstrosities raging at being denied their quarry, but they had a strange aversion to the ancient tree and would not approach it; instead, they tore at the ground around its base with their razor-sharp talons. He had narrowly escaped their grasp, and they would not follow him, but he continued to watch their frantic unrest to be certain he was out of danger until it became clear they would not be able to reach him. Before long the creatures relented and retreated into the shadows of the forest.

Convinced the danger had passed for the moment, he turned his attention to the strange fissure in the tree. The narrow opening seemed inviting to him somehow, and since he had no idea how he was going to get back to the ground safely, it seemed he had little choice but to investigate.

He crept cautiously into the dark cavity which was surprisingly spacious and quickly realized it would provide excellent protection from the elements. Transitioning to his knees, he began searching with his hands in the darkness, discovering the interior surfaces were smooth and dry. Further exploration revealed a narrow alcove along the left side. He traced its contours with his fingers as he stretched his body along its length and soon found himself lying in a remarkably comfortable position. The hollowed space fit his form perfectly as if the tree had grown that way to accommodate him. He barely noticed the solidity of the tree's composition as he lay cradled in the cozy compartment. He took a deep breath and began to relax, feeling the tension melt from his exhausted body. He grew drowsy in the quiet space, listening to the beating of his heart in the calming stillness. For a moment he had an overwhelming sense of deja vu, but overcome by fatigue, he fell into a fitful sleep wondering if the heartbeat he heard, in fact, belonged to the tree that held him close within its protective embrace...

The boy woke with the realization that he had fallen asleep while reminiscing. As the remnants of his dreams dissolved, he recalled the sudden appearance of the strange, old man who had caused him to retreat to his haven. It was a disturbing event, and he was still shaken by the encounter. He knew there were others living beyond the forest; occasionally, he would watch them from the shadows of the forest as they busied themselves with various tasks throughout the day. Some of them lived in small clusters of houses scattered along the base of the towering mountain range near a large body of water, but the majority lived behind a large wall where many of the giant structures appeared to be part of the mountains themselves. He was curious about those he saw and often marveled at the strange coverings they wore. Some of them were shiny and reflective like the hides of the monsters living in the forest, and some were long and flowing, cast in an array of vibrant colors he had never seen. Through time spent observing them, he realized they never entered the forest; they seemed to avoid it in fact, so he never expected to find himself being spied upon by one of them in the glade. It had been a terrifying experience, but the truly troubling thing was how close the old man had gotten before he had noticed his presence. The boy was very adept at identifying potential threats, yet somehow this individual had managed to avoid immediate detection.

His instinctive, panic-induced response allowed him to get away, but he did not want to be taken unaware a second time. He decided it would be prudent to learn more about the one who had invaded his home and discover why he would intrude where others would not.

Exiting his sanctuary to stand on a large bough, he scanned the forest floor. There were no signs of anything amiss, so he stepped from the branch and drifted as lightly as a feather to the ground far below.

CHAPTER 7

Czarstostryx was baffled by the unexplained appearance of the child, but he resolved to put the matter behind him for the time being. With twilight descending, it was necessary to focus all of his attention on finding the canyon entrance. Opportunities to penetrate the depths of the labyrinth were few and far between and the forest had undergone many changes in the subsequent years, making navigation tricky at best. Czarstostryx considered it fortunate the position of the elusive entrance remained consistent, and he was relieved he had not crossed paths with the Grohldym as he traveled. Even though he possessed the skills to protect himself, he preferred to avoid a confrontation in the gathering darkness, but it would not be a matter of concern for much longer. He was nearing the labyrinth— a place where the Grohldym did not enter.

Night had fallen by the time Czarstostryx reached the entrance, but he had no difficulty locating the narrow crack in the cliff face; it stood out in bold relief against the pale stone, and an oppressive darkness radiated from within its depths. Stepping into the confines of the canyon path, Czarstostryx brought forth light by striking his walking stick upon the rocky path and speaking the required word of power which produced a phantom flame that rose from the ground and traveled the length of his staff until it hovered just above it. The gloom of the labyrinth seemed to smother his illumination, allowing only a diminutive radius in which to see, but it was not a significant issue considering how the trail snaked through the canyons. There was rarely a straight path that would have allowed the light to travel very far even if it were able to. Within the limits of the warm, yellow glow, a narrow trail was revealed which Czarstostryx began to follow.

The time constraints placed on the expeditions weighed heavily on his mind as he hurried on his way. In the long years when the entrance was sealed, Czarstostryx spent his time diligently studying his books and practicing his craft, constantly looking for ways to increase the length of exposure he could endure when he had access to the labyrinth. He had gotten to the point where he could withstand several days within the maddening maze before its influence began to plague his mind beyond his skill, forcing him to withdraw and recover.

During his time inside the canyons, he meticulously mapped his progress, utilizing every moment to push himself as far as possible to find out where each new path would lead him. He had documented miles upon miles of twisting, branching trails, utilizing a painstaking process of elimination while working his way through myriad dead ends and redundancies, gradually closing in on his objective. After years of unrelenting industry, he knew he was finally getting close to reaching his goal. He could feel it in his bones.

Czarstostryx had committed to memory the course that would take him directly to the first significant area he sought which was a large cave not far from the entrance. It was a convenient place to stage supplies, make preparations, and review his maps before setting out to plumb the greater depths of the canyon maze. Excitement filled him as he stepped into the familiar cavern. After years of anxious waiting, he had finally returned. He checked the protective ward he placed decades earlier and found it was still intact. The fact that it was unbroken confirmed he would not be taken unaware by anything unseen lurking in the shadows.

Making his way deeper into the cavernous chamber, he located a small pit where he prepared a fire using kindling he had gathered travelling through the wastes. After igniting the dry wood with a gesture, he extinguished his phantom flame. As the fire blazed warmly, he pulled a small kettle from his pack and poured a bit of the water collected from the crystal pool into it. To the water, he added several tiny mushrooms, also harvested from the glade. He then placed the kettle into the pit among the developing coals.

While the brew was heating, Czarstostryx withdrew several rolled parchments from his pack, spread them out on a large outcropping of stone, and began studying them by the light of the fire. Choosing several of the maps, he placed them together in sequence so his chosen path would be shown unbroken. Although he had memorized every twist and turn penned to the parchment, it was necessary to see the route he planned to travel in order to perform the intended magic. While focusing his will and chanting secret words of power, he traced a course on the map with his finger, starting from the cave entrance and continuing to the furthest, uncharted point on the map where he wished to go. With the prescribed thaumaturgy completed, he carefully rolled up the maps and returned them to his knapsack.

Kneeling beside the dying fire, he retrieved the kettle and raised it to his lips, blowing lightly upon its contents. With a large gulp, he swallowed down the concoction that would help shield his mind, then he slipped the kettle into his pack along with the maps. He took a moment to position the satchel on his back before reaching into a hidden pocket within his robes to confirm its contents.

His hand found the precious item he sought—a small artifact discovered in the cave almost a century earlier. He carried it with him every time he returned, sure that its significance would someday be revealed. The artifact was made of the same stone as the cavern walls, though it was highly polished and possessed unusual geometric shaping along with deeply etched markings. The strange symbols were similar to some he had found in his research, but he had not been able to decipher their meaning. He felt energy radiating from the small relic as his hand closed tightly around it; the intensity would fluctuate as he explored depending on his location within the canyon's winding corridors. The tangible connection between the artifact and his hidden objective had proven to be quite useful in his exploration of the labyrinth.

Having accomplished the necessary preparations, Czarstostryx made his way back to the cave's entrance and stepped into the cold, night air. There was now a faint glow emanating from the ground just outside the cave which illuminated the path between the towering canyon walls. In the black of night, deep within the labyrinth, the dim light appeared in stark contrast and cast long, eerie shadows through the corridors of stone. Czarstostryx set out with haste, following the path of light along his chosen route. Even though he was familiar with the course he was traveling, he did not want to take any chance of making a wrong turn and losing precious time. The corridors of the labyrinth were deceptive, but the spell he had cast would guide him unerringly along the chosen path of his previous exploits, taking him quickly to uncharted regions where the object of his ambition would surely be found.

He moved with as much speed as his body would allow, but the increasing difficulty of the journey troubled him as he hurried on. Long years had passed since he first discovered the obscure canyons, and those years were beginning to take a toll on his body; his mind, however, remained sharp and focused, improving exponentially with the passing of time. It was a cruel design, but he was not going to let it hinder his ambition. His indomitable spirit and accumulation of mystic wisdom had allowed him to overcome the limits of the flesh far longer than ordinary men.

The night air crackled with electricity, and Czarstostryx could feel the hidden source of power stirring within the canyons. It was a sensation much the same as what he experienced when undertaking all magical endeavors—an intoxicating surge of raw energy weaving itself into his very core, making him a part of something everlasting and unbreakable. He strove to be forged by that power—to surpass the weakness of the flesh and achieve ever-higher levels of consciousness. He had no doubt in his mind if he could locate the source and tap into it somehow, the possibilities of what he could achieve might be limitless; perhaps, he could even find the means to overcome the flesh altogether!

The excitement of his thoughts had momentarily distracted Czarstostryx from the stabbing pain growing in his side. His breathing was becoming labored, and his knees were aching from the moderate jog he had been maintaining. He knew it would be nearly dawn before reaching the limits of his charted advance and it was critical that he utilize the benefits of the mapping spell before the rising sun could dilute its effect, so he grudgingly slowed his pace to ensure he would be able to continue without stopping to rest.

Czarstostryx continued his dogged pace along the glowing path, moving as quickly as his aching limbs would allow. He did not allow himself to become sidetracked by the alternate avenues that presented themselves in the surreal landscape; he had already traveled those narrow corridors in previous years, and he was clear to his purpose, but he was finding it difficult to contain his growing excitement despite his best efforts at restraint. He was aware that it was important not to push himself beyond his physical limitations, but the potency of the cool night air fueled his enthusiasm, spurring him onward, driving him to push ever harder into the canyon labyrinth as every step he took brought him closer to the unseen prize that had eluded him for so many years.

As he trekked through the night, Czarstostryx felt the resonance within the artifact growing stronger. He could also feel the ambient energy in the air gaining intensity, surrounding him, infusing him with the strength to travel beyond the limits of his past excursions, but dawn was fast approaching, and the guiding illumination was beginning to lose its intensity.

Turning his gaze upward, he could barely see the first hint of morning light cutting through the blackness of the cliff tops high overhead. The only time he had ever seen the sunlight penetrate the depths of the labyrinth was on the day he discovered the hidden entrance, but he knew it could not reach the canyon floor where he stood, though it would still create enough light to disrupt his navigation spell. Returning his attention to the path before him, he realized it was no longer a matter of concern. He could see the termination of the guiding light just ahead of him severed by the yawning blackness of two menacing avenues. The foreign intersection was as far as he had ever been.

Czarstostryx collapsed on the ground just as he reached the junction, exhaustion finally claiming him. He slumped against the canyon wall, taking a moment to recover and catch his breath. His mind continued to race as he steadied his breathing and attempted to regain some of his strength, but he would not allow the demands of the flesh to hinder him one moment longer than was absolutely necessary.

CHAPTER 8

Czarstostryx felt as though his legs were on fire as he steadily climbed the steep path, but he continued to push himself mercilessly despite the terrain. He could not help feeling a modicum of regret for having chosen the path that was likely the more arduous of the two, but his systematic method of selection did not account for unexpected inconveniences. Whenever he encountered a fork, he always chose the avenue on the left to examine first. Having done so, he quickly noticed the new route was unlike any other he had traveled before. After a short distance, it began to pitch steeply upward. Typically, he was faced with a confusing series of twists and turns that required careful mapping and patience to navigate, but the meandering trails always remained on a relatively level plain, never rising, or falling to any great degree. The recently discovered progression upward was vexing.

As Czarstostryx ascended, he periodically paused to chart his progress on a fresh scroll, but he kept the intervals as short as possible, and even though his aching muscles screamed in protest, he doggedly pushed himself, his mind racing with the prospect of what might lie ahead. The trail appeared to be leading him to the very tops of the canyon walls. His excitement grew as he considered the possibilities of what he might be able to see from such a vantage.

As the gloom of the canyon's depths receded, the morning sun shone much brighter, and its warmth began to melt away the constant chill from Czarstostryx's aching bones. A broad smile formed on his lips as he anticipated the fruition of his lifelong endeavor. The peaks of the canyon walls were only a stone's throw above him. He would reach the top shortly and bear witness to what lay beyond— something no one had ever seen. More importantly, he would finally discover the source of power that lay hidden within the canyon labyrinth.

The artifact seemed about to burst in his hand; its agitation had increased exponentially as he had climbed. He was nearing the utmost heights of the canyons when he rounded a sharp turn and froze in his tracks. The artifact suddenly went still. The path ended abruptly just a few paces ahead of him, transitioning onto a small ledge that stood above a sheer drop going straight down into the darkness below. Czarstostryx's eyes grew wide as he looked beyond the gaping chasm. Glistening in the gathering light stood a towering monolith just below the tops of the cliffs.

The massive structure appeared to be hewn from the surrounding mountains, but it was separated and isolated, standing centered in their midst. He recognized instantly that it was not a natural formation; it had the same polished appearance as the artifact and similar characteristics to some of the ancient structures of the city that were carved from the mountains. He had spoken to Glithnie about the city's architecture and gained a surprising amount of insight from her regarding it. Between her accounts, and his own impressions, he could see that the tower standing before him was clearly a kindred formation despite its specific uniqueness, but why was it so far flung from its counterparts, and why would it be built just below the height of the surrounding cliffs and not tower above them? Czarstostryx was unsure of the answers to the questions filling his head.

Slipping the artifact into a hidden pocket within his robes, he cautiously approached the cliff's edge and peered into the chasm that lay between himself and the massive tower. His eyes followed the smooth surface of the tower as it descended into the darkened depths. There were no visible openings affording a glimpse of what was inside. His gaze returned to study the upper portion. The top of the tower was perfectly flat and nondescript, offering no clues as to the relevance of its construction.

Czarstostryx thought it might be possible to gain some perspective on the tower's design if he had a better view, so he considered trying to find a way to climb higher. Probing the walls on either side of the path, he hoped to find a crack or handhold of some kind, but there was nothing. He quickly realized climbing higher would not be an option, noticing the surface of the cliffs at his current elevation had been worn smooth, possibly caused by the force of the elements being driven by millennia of storms. It appeared there was no way to reach the tower from where he stood. There was nothing available to span the gap, and the distance was far too great to leap across. Even if he returned with a rope, there would be no way to secure it to the tower.

He continued to scan his surroundings, scrutinizing every detail, searching for anything unusual that might offer a means of reaching the tower that loomed so near yet remained utterly unreachable. Again, he traced the contours of the cliff walls on either side of him. Then, he dropped to his knees and carefully felt his way along the ground. He lay flat on the path and crept to the edge of the bluff, looking over the edge to examine the sheer drop directly below him. Still, he could find nothing to indicate advancement on the tower was possible.

Frustrated, he stood back up wondering at the significance of the location he had discovered. There had to be a reason the trail ended so near to the spire of the isolated tower. The great monolith was surely the source of energy which had drawn him in, but now that he had finally reached it, he was being denied any means of unlocking its mysteries!

He had been so overcome by his fuming that he had not thought to inspect the artifact that had quieted so suddenly in the presence of the tower. The two were obviously linked, so a closer look might reveal the vital clue he was missing. As he drew the relic from his pocket, he noticed it felt heavier than before. It seemed to be pulling his hand downward. Holding it before him, he loosened his grip to see if there were any other changes of note. Before he could react, the artifact was torn from his grasp by an unseen force. Diving to the ground, he clutched for it in vane as it sailed over the edge of the cliff and plummeted into the gloom.

Czarstostryx stared in astonishment, listening for its impact on the ground below, but there was only silence. The precious artifact he had possessed for so many years was gone. It was a vital component to unraveling the mysteries within the canyon, and he knew he must retrieve it. Since pursuit over the edge of the cliff was beyond his skill, he knew he would need to find another way. His only option was to backtrack and try the other path at the fork.

He had chosen to follow the left path as a matter of protocol, but it appeared he had exhausted its potential to further his objective. Apparently, it was just another dead end in a long series—a unique dead end to be sure, but a roadblock none-the-less. Pulling a scroll from his pouch, he made careful notes and sketches of his surroundings. He was anxious to get below to the fork, but it was critical that he documented his discoveries before moving on while the details were still vivid in his mind. Once he was confident that he had recorded all pertinent information regarding the path to the tower spire, he rolled the parchment and carefully stowed it in his satchel.

Driven by a keen sense of urgency, Czarstostryx began his descent, and traveling downhill, reached the junction in far less time than it had taken to move beyond it. Standing at the fork in the path, the chill within the murky underbelly of the labyrinth once again settled into his aching joints. He had been in the labyrinth less than one full day, maintaining a vigorous pace the entire time; physical and mental fatigue were a factor on their own, but he could also feel the effects of the canyons trying to infiltrate his mind, and though he had managed to improve his resistance, he was not immune. Haste was critical, and he still had a day's journey just to get out of the canyons, but he did not even want to consider leaving without first retrieving the artifact. He was too close to finding that which he sought, to risk leaving it behind.

Because the entrance had just reopened, he was fairly certain he would have access to the labyrinth for a full cycle of seasons since that had been the case it the past, but there were no guarantees, and he could not afford to take anything for granted. He was not as confident as he once had been that he could survive several more decades if he missed another opportunity. Likely, this was his final chance to unlock mysteries that might render mortality obsolete.

Producing a fresh scroll to catalogue the specifics of the alternate route, he set out with grim determination. By the light of his phantom flame, he carefully mapped the details of the new path. He moved as quickly as possible but made sure he did not miss any critical details in his haste. Fortunately, the new path was unremarkable as it wound its way along the canyon floor, so he was able to make excellent progress.

After a bit, Czarstostryx noticed the trail was widening, and it continued to do so as he pressed forward. Maintaining close proximity to the wall on his left, he observed the opposite side slowly fade from sight as it became obscured by darkness. He thought about referencing the distance between the walls as he continued onward but then realized he had entered a vast gorge. Stepping away from the wall, he moved cautiously into the black unknown.

After venturing a short distance, the phantom flame began to illuminate a massive form slowly materializing before him. His heart began to beat loudly in anticipation as he approached. It appeared he had found his way to the base of the mighty tower observed from the heights. He considered the possibility it might be a different formation. The landscape was expansive; who knew what mysteries the labyrinth held? He had to know for sure. Excitement filled him as he closed the distance.

Nearing the towering structure, the light of the phantom flame was reflected brightly against its surface, revealing it was polished like the artifact he had lost. Gazing upward he could just make out the distant sunlight cast upon the towering spire far overhead. It was impossible for him to make out the details of the surrounding cliffs at such heights, so there was no way to verify his previous vantage point, but odds decreed it was the tower he had discovered earlier, and it certainly seemed to outweigh any other possibility. If it was the same tower, the artifact would have to be somewhere nearby.

Czarstostryx began to survey the perimeter of the massive structure, inspecting the ground closely as he began working his way around its base. The distance between the canyon walls and the tower itself was at least ten times greater than most of the paths he had explored, so he had to zigzag along the open space as he moved around the tower, making certain he did not overlook any area the artifact may have come to rest. As he methodically made his way, he began to perceive a barely audible hum coming from somewhere in the distance. The sound became increasingly noticeable as he rounded the base of the huge tower, and by the time he had reached the halfway point, he was able to pinpoint the origin of the sound just ahead of him.

The hair on his arms and neck stood on end as he closed in on the source. What he had suspected earlier was now confirmed; it was indeed the tower he had seen from above. The artifact that had liberated itself from his grasp appeared before him, suspended in midair at shoulder height, a hands-breadth from the surface of the tower. It hummed loudly as it floated, radiating with energy beyond anything he had previously observed. As Czarstostryx drew closer, he could see a shadowed recess in the tower's surface which mimicked the contours of the artifact precisely. The artifact appeared to be a missing piece of the tower itself, misplaced somehow through the years, perhaps yearning to be reunited within its rightful station.

Czarstostryx raised his hand toward the artifact, then paused a moment to consider the unknown consequences of what he was contemplating. The artifact was a piece of everything he had devoted himself to. All of his research and ambition for power were linked to it, and so was the tower standing before him. The impetus of his mortality touched his thoughts briefly, but he would not let the possibility of death stand in the way of a lifetime endeavor. The artifact resonated wildly. He could feel its energy engulfing him, exhilarating his senses. He felt supremely alive and fearless. Caution be damned; he would have his answers! Slamming the artifact home, he braced himself for the outcome.

There was a flash of brilliant light as the tower received its missing component. A powerful shockwave hit Czarstostryx full in the chest with the force of a charging beast, sending him through the air to land unceremoniously on his back. The entire tower began to pulse with raw energy and the ground began to rumble, echoing deeply throughout the gorge.

Czarstostryx's eyes remained fixed on the tower as he regained his footing. There was a resounding clanging from within the tower; then, what appeared to be streaks of lightning, outlined a doorway. The surface of the tower within the perimeter of lightning began to draw inward, revealing an opening. The stark blackness within the newly formed doorway seemed to devour all the light. Czarstostryx felt an irresistible pull drawing him inside, and he did not hesitate as he stepped through the doorway. He would have his answers at last!

CHAPTER 9

King Bardazel stood brooding in the treasure hold, gazing upon the collection of artifacts kept there. The treasure hold was situated behind the magnificence of the throne room in a nondescript cell near the center of a descending corridor. It was a place where the king spent a considerable amount of time in contemplation.

There were nearly forty items in the small room that appeared to have been crafted by artisans of varying degrees of skill. The king's eyes passed over the collection, slowly taking in the details of each item in the impressive tableau. Some of the pieces were created simply for the sake of beauty, such as the jewel encrusted necklaces, bracelets, and rings that glistened brightly under the light of the wall sconce torches. They were most likely fashioned to appeal to the vanities of former royalty who had once inhabited the castle. Bardazel had limited regard for such things, but he recognized the appeal their beauty inspired in others as they once had for his own wife. His craftsmen had fashioned many fine pieces of such ornamentation for her to delight in when she had been alive, but those items were not kept in the treasure hold. The items stored specifically in the treasury were unique and ancient, and the details of when and why they had been placed there had been obscured over time. It seemed they had always been there.

Bardazel continued to scrutinize the prodigious collection, turning his attention to the articles whose designs were less apparent. Some of them were small enough to share space in the ornate chests that held the jewelry while other larger pieces had been situated in small alcoves designed into the walls of the cell. Then, there were objects that were larger still and had to be placed on the floor.

He took a moment to consider the similarities in the items that did not conform to typical conception as he had done many times before. Most of them, both small and large, had been fashioned from highly polished stone which appeared to be the same variety that the mountain palace was carved from. Three of the pieces, however, were created from another kind of stone that was completely foreign to himself or others who had studied them. Two of those were deeply etched, geometric shapes that were perfectly symmetrical in their design and small enough to hold in the palm of one's hand. The king marveled at how precisely they had been crafted. It was hard to imagine anyone could have the skill to produce something so flawless. He wondered about the odd etchings. There were no references or translations to be found in the archives regarding them, so their meaning remained a mystery. He began to feel strange as he pondered the origins of the two small objects, and an inexplicable sense of dread began to fill his mind. He forced himself to tear his eyes from the artifacts he held in his hands; he had not even realized he had picked them up. Somewhat shaken, he returned them to their proper place within one of the ornate chests.

It was not unusual to have a mild, mental reaction when viewing the small stone pieces; everyone who had studied them shared a similar experience. He reminded himself to anchor his mind as he turned his attention to the remaining object crafted from the foreign stone which was by far the most unusual item contained in the treasure hold. The artifact was a highly polished pillar that stood nearly as tall as the king. The luster of the column itself would have been capable of reflecting the torchlight as a mirror would, if not for the thousands of tiny figures clinging to it, covering its smooth, vertical surface from its base to its topmost edge. Closer inspection revealed the tiny figures were carved representations of human-like beings that were miraculously cast from the stone of the pillar itself, creating a singular work. The minute creatures resembled misshapen men with unusually long arms, and fingers tipped with fierce talons. Their short legs were supported by bestial feet that were also taloned, and their hairless bodies were roped with lean, sinuous muscles. Upon their heads were long pointed ears, and they wore wicked, curving grins. Bardazel marveled at the incredibly life-like details of the fantastically carved stone creatures spiraling upward. They were formed with such precision it appeared as though the pillar was actually being climbed by tiny creatures.

At the pinnacle of the column was a statue representing a beast spawned from nightmares. It was similar to those among the swarm of climbing miniatures, but it was much larger which made every detail easily discernable. It stood on powerful legs that seemed a bit too short for its body, and its heavily muscled arms were disproportionately long. The arms were stretched outward, angling downward slightly while the palms of its large, taloned hands were facing up, making it appear as though it were lifting an enormous, unseen weight. Unlike its meager counterparts, it possessed large wings that stretched out from its brawny shoulders, and its head was crowned with horns, two of which were larger, curling downward on either side of its face—a face radiating pure malevolence. Perched atop the pillar, the demonic entity was poised as though it might spring from the pillar and launch itself into flight at any moment.

Bardazel imagined he could feel the hatred emanating from the statue's lifeless eyes as he examined it, and almost without noticing, he began to perceive the statue was growing larger. His mind began to swim, and he felt as if he were being swept away, spiraling downward. As the image of the beast continued to grow before his eyes, the feeling of drowning began to overwhelm him, dragging him to the bottom of a gaping abyss. His subconscious mind screamed for him to climb from the swirling depths threatening to swallow him. Stumbling to his knees as he lost balance, the king's gaze broke from the statue, freeing him from its unholy influence.

Bardazel closed his eyes tightly, shielding himself from the statue's effect. He knew better than to observe it too closely; its influence was much more potent than that of the small, stone pieces. As he clutched his aching head in his hands, he could not help wondering what purpose the statue and the smaller pieces served. He found it perplexing that there were no references to the objects themselves or to the entities they represented in any writings contained in the archives. It was also odd that there were scant similarities between the unusual artifacts and the design of the castle itself or any of the structures in the ancient ruins of the city. *"They must be of a foreign origin."* Bardazel thought. *"Maybe the strange, old man can find relevance in their design. Perhaps there is an unknown connection to something beyond this kingdom that an outlander would be able to explain."*

The king had studied the items in the treasure room for many years, always hoping the army's expeditions would shed some light on their mysterious nature. He was not anxious to encounter creatures like the ones represented on the pillar statue; it was bad enough the Grohldym were a reality, however, the discovery of something undocumented would prove there was more to the world than what was known. None of his ancestors had accomplished such a thing; they had not even managed to find anyone living beyond the kingdom. Bardazel began to grow extremely excited at the prospect of being the first to make such a discovery.

The outlander was a new piece to an ancient puzzle, and he was fully prepared to negotiate with the riches in his treasury to find out what the old man knew of the outside world. He hoped there was something among the items that would provide the necessary incentive to loosen the outlander's tongue, but he would have his answers one way or another when Skealfa returned.

The king was confident his battle-lord would succeed, and he would not allow himself to believe otherwise. He wondered how the search was progressing, but his thoughts were interrupted by the sound of approaching footsteps. Turning from the treasury, Bardazel stepped into the hall and saw his son heading rapidly toward him though the corridor. The prince bore a troubled look on his face as he approached.

"Father, I need to speak with you about Glithnie." Nieloch's voice was filled with concern.

"What of her?" the king asked excitedly. "Has she spoken?!"

"She has not," the prince replied dejectedly. "In fact, she is growing weaker. She will not eat or drink. She is slipping further away, lost within her mind. The royal physicians do their best to keep her alive, but I am not sure she will last much longer, even with their aid. I sit with her for hours each day offering any comfort I can, but it is not enough. I am losing her!" The prince struggled to control his grief as tears began to well up in his eyes. He knew his father was uncomfortable with displays of emotion.

"Try to calm yourself Nieloch," the king consoled. "Every effort is being made to save her. She has endured a devastating ordeal, and she has seen things no one has ever lived to tell. It is only natural that she is in such a state. It will take time for her to recover, but she is in good hands. The royal physicians have been instructed to take whatever actions are required to keep her alive, and so they shall. We *must* have her account of what happened. Her experiences could provide valuable insights about our enemies and possibly shed light on the lands that surround us."

"To hell with her experiences!" the prince burst out, "I do not want to lose the woman I love!" Nieloch realized he was shouting and checked himself by drawing a deep breath to regain his composure; even though he was speaking with his father, he was still addressing the king. He continued in a more subdued manner. "Father, I understand your desire to unravel the mysteries of this kingdom and the surrounding lands. It has been your obsession for as long as I can remember, but Glithnie is not a mere vessel containing information. She is my heart and soul. She bore our child! I know the physicians are managing to keep her alive, and they may be able to continue to do so for a time, but her heart is broken. I cannot begin to imagine the horrors she has endured, but I believe it is the loss of our child that is causing her to lose herself to despair. The child must be found if she is to be saved. If she could just hold her baby in her arms, I know she would be able to escape the darkness that grips her!"

"The search for the child has already begun, as you are well aware," Bardazel replied calmly. "Skealfa and his men left days ago. If finding the child is possible, they will be the ones with the best chance to succeed. Try not to trouble yourself unduly."

"There is no question that Skealfa and his elites possess skill enough to succeed, but the forest and wasteland are vast. I fear they simply will not have enough time before the child succumbs to the elements." The prince looked desperately into his father's eyes. "The child must be returned to Glithnie soon if she is to have any chance of survival. Please father, I implore you! Let me gather more men and assist in the search."

"That issue has already been settled," the king stated firmly. "You know I will not allow it. You have never even set foot in the forest. What makes you think you can endure its effects, not to mention the Grohldym? Only the most skilled warriors have a chance to survive an encounter with them. Just look at how many have recently fallen. Besides, there is no guarantee the child is even alive, and without Glithnie to enlighten us, it is doubtful she will ever be reunited with her child."

"How can you be so callous?" Nieloch cried. "The child is your own blood!"

"Begotten in secret by a peasant girl, outside the requirements of the royal standard for wedlock. The child should have never been! If it is claimed by the forest, then that is the will of the heavens, and the shame of the entire affair will never be exposed. Regardless of the outcome, I will not allow my only heir to throw his life away searching for one who could never assume the mantle of rule. I will not change my mind about this!" Bardazel had lost patience with his son on the matter but had not intended to be so harsh. Nieloch had always been overly emotional in his opinion, often following his feelings without thought of the consequences, and the king could see that he was distraught. He had to find a way to pacify him before he did something foolish.

"You must stay in the palace until Lord Skealfa returns. It is possible he is on his way back with the child as we speak," the king said persuasively. "Surely you can see that rushing out before learning how he has fared would be folly. You would be needlessly risking your life *and* the lives of others. For now, stay with Glithnie and see to her care. Your very presence may help her escape the darkness that has overcome her mind."

Nieloch could see that his father would not be moved. He knew it would be counter-productive to push him further, and he did not want to risk being placed under guard while the matter resolved of its own volition. "I will do as you command, father," he said contritely. "I will stay with Glithnie and do all I can to restore her, and I will pray to the heavens that

Skealfa returns in time." The prince could see relief in the king's eyes as he appeared to be the obedient son, but the thoughts racing through his mind were of a different sort entirely.

CHAPTER 10

Czarstostryx hardly noticed the landscape as he traveled toward his home. The events of the last few days had taken him to the outer reaches of sanity. His body and mind had been pushed to their limits, and he felt as if he were walking in his sleep— his mind lingering in a dream. A cold shiver ran through him as he recalled his recent discoveries. He had been shaken to his core by what he had encountered in the now distant tower, but he was familiar with the risks associated with attaining higher levels of the mystic arts that he pursued; there were always inherent dangers tied to them. His resolve had been tested countless times throughout the long years he spent developing his craft, but what he encountered in the tower made all past experiences pale in comparison. Again, he tried to shake off the cold, creeping feeling in the pit of his stomach.

Something caught Czarstostryx attention. Abruptly, his focus shifted to the horizon. He had entered the wasteland during the night and traveled a fair distance before the early morning sun began to shed its light on his surroundings. Now, in the distance, he could see that the typical dead calm of the wasteland had been disrupted. The shadow of a sandstorm loomed large along the skyline in the direction he was heading. Someone had intruded upon his sanctuary. He quickened his pace.

The fail-safe he had placed when he set out was designed to trigger a storm if an intruder entered its proximity, remaining unabated until it was dismissed. The violent winds would create a shroud of dust and sand intended to conceal his home, making its discovery virtually impossible. It was intended to activate in the presence of a legitimate threat, not by a disturbance from a mere scavenging beast of which there were few in the wasteland.

The last thing Czarstostryx needed was a confrontation in his diminished state; he was exhausted and in desperate need of rest, but even though the ward had served its purpose, he was not content to rely on its effectiveness alone. Clearing his thoughts, he prepared his mind to unleash a particularly devastating spell that would sunder the flesh of any unfortunate soul he directed it at. Driven by sheer force of will, he drew closer to the sands of the swirling storm, considering what might have caused the disturbance.

It was conceivable that soldiers had inadvertently stumbled across his abode, though it seemed unlikely. The usual deployments never brought troops too near his dwelling; it was one of the aspects of living in that particular location which had always been beneficial, but in light of recent events, anything was possible. He would know soon enough; he had reached the edge of the storm.

Czarstostryx strained his eyes, trying to distinguish any details within the swirling sands that might give him an advantage before quieting the winds. He knew there was a threat concealed within the tempest, something lying in wait perhaps, but he could see nothing through the storm. Unfortunately, there was no time to delay. He had to resolve the situation before he collapsed from fatigue.

His hands deftly traced the appropriate designs in the air, causing the howling winds to diminish. As sand and debris began to settle to the ground, he could begin to make out his surroundings more clearly. A lingering fog of dust still obscured his visual clarity, but he could see well enough to locate what had triggered the storm.

A glint of sunlight caught his eye, reflecting from a form lying not too far off in the distance. Even from where he stood, Czarstostryx recognized the shape as that of a man. The driving wind had mounded sand around the figure, grossly exaggerating the size of the individual, but as he drew closer, he realized the proportions were not as altered as he had thought. The man was enormous, larger than any other residing in the city. Czarstostryx had seen him from a distance on various occasions and recognized him as the fierce warrior who led the soldiers. He was extremely powerful and dangerous, and now he was lying motionless, alarmingly close to his home.

Czarstostryx knew the man was alive; the storm would have dissipated of its own accord otherwise. Stopping at a safe distance, he wondered if the huge soldier was injured since there were no signs of movement. As the dust continued to settle, much was still hidden from sight. Sand covered a good portion of the fallen intruder, but there were traces of highly polished armor glistening in the sunlight. He could see nothing of the soldier's face since the man wore a helmet, and he was lying face down with his arms cradling his head in an apparent attempt to shield himself from the driving sands of the storm. Still maintaining his distance, Czarstostryx called out to the half-buried man. "You are trespassing on forbidden land. Identify yourself or be destroyed!"

The figure on the ground shifted slightly to one side. Mounded sand slid from his armor as the giant man lifted his head slightly and turned toward Czarstostryx. His grim countenance was unsettling, half-hidden within an unusual helmet. Czarstostryx tensed in anticipation, preparing to release a spell that would tear the huge soldier apart.

"I mean you no harm," Skealfa replied dryly. "I was sent by my king to find you."

"Who is your king, and how does he know of me?"

Skealfa shifted again so he could see the old man better, and he began to sit up.

"Do not move!" Czarstostryx ordered harshly. "I prefer that you remain as you are until I have decided your fate."

Skealfa smiled to himself. The feeble, old man standing before him would not be the one to deliver his fate, but he knew that he must be tactful. He did not wish to use force unless it became absolutely necessary, so he remained still and continued with his explanation. "King Bardazel is my king; he rules the city to the north where I come from. He heard of you from his son, Prince Nieloch, who learned of your existence from a peasant girl he has had dealings with. She spoke of you to the prince in confidence, saying she had chanced upon you in the forest. It was only because of the dire nature of recent events that he chose to relate the possibility of your existence to the king." Skealfa would not reveal details about the improprieties of the relationship, even to an outsider.

Czarstostryx, still wary, maintained his readied stance. "You have explained how your king came to seek me out, now tell me why."

"He seeks freedom for his people." Skealfa told him. "You see, in all the recorded history of our city, no one has ever discovered a means of safe travel beyond our kingdom's borders. King Bardazel is determined to be the one to do it. He wishes to escape the oppression of the Grohldym who have attacked our city and slaughtered our people since time immemorial. We have tried to cross the wasteland seeking escape, failing countless times. Our ancestors fared no better in conquering the cruel expanse, leaving us to wonder if it is even possible. There has never been evidence of someone living beyond our kingdom, so when King Bardazel heard that it might be a possibility, he was resolute about finding you. He wishes to learn who you are and to see if there is anything you might know that could help his people. The king understands that you have chosen to live beyond the city for your own reasons and that you may have no desire to enter our kingdom, but he would like you to know that he has a small treasure trove of riches and unusual artifacts that he is willing to negotiate with, if you will meet with him."

Skealfa had delivered the king's message to the outlander as commanded, and he had answered the old fool's questions, but he was growing tired of being restrained under his scrutiny. His elite soldiers had disappeared in the sandstorm, and he was anxious to find them, if they could be found. He needed to get the outlander back to the city quickly, and he did not have the luxury of time to put the stranger's mind at ease. He would take him by force if he must.

Skealfa's muscles tensed, preparing to render the old man unconscious if he continued to press him, but to his surprise, the old man dropped his arms and calmly smiled at him. "I will return with you and meet your king."

CHAPTER 11

The sun was hanging low in the horizon as Skealfa scanned the barren sands. He had parted ways with the old hermit in the early morning shortly after their meeting. Since that time, he had been scouring the wastelands in search of his missing comrades. The outlander explained the nature of the tempest before Skealfa set out, imparting to him that the storm had risen as a defensive measure to prevent the discovery of his home and that someone in Skealfa's search party had gotten close enough to trigger it. The information was useful in helping Skealfa formulate a strategy to search for his men.

He recalled the position of the storm when it appeared suddenly on the previous day; it was spotted near the end of the search line, furthest into the wasteland. The signal horns were relayed, drawing those furthest away closer to investigate. One by one, they had all been engulfed by the fury of the storm and were confounded by it, becoming totally cut off from one another.

Skealfa had done his best to find his men in the blinding sandstorm but was unsuccessful, so he had decided it would be best to remain close to their last known position and wait for the storm to pass before continuing his search, but he did not realize the sinister nature of the storm. The magic that spawned it was designed to surround and follow the threat until it was neutralized. Czarstostryx had terminated the winds that engulfed Skealfa saving him alone, but the others remained within the grasp of their own storms, until they too could be released.

Skealfa had been able to find Toric, Varthaal, Brilldagh, and Crel with relative ease when he began his search anew. The storms were easy to spot as they rose high into the sky, and he had been fortunate that his men had not strayed too far before implementing a strategy of waiting. He was able to locate most of them without difficulty, but Hreydol was still missing.

The outlander had refused to accompany Skealfa in the search, and he had also not allowed Skealfa to see where his home was or how close he had been to discovering it. He had merely given Skealfa a talisman that would quiet the storms at his approach, then the battle-lord was on his own. Skealfa would have insisted they not part company, but he did not get the chance to protest. Somehow, he lost focus during the interaction and the old man vanished from sight. He remembered feeling as if he were daydreaming, and when he regained his senses, the outlander was gone. It was at that moment when Skealfa started to realize the strange, old man was more than he seemed. He possessed the power to control storms, and he was somehow able to disappear before his eyes. It was hard to know what else he might be capable of. Skealfa had never been one to back down from an adversary, but he found himself grudgingly considering the possibility that it might have been fortunate the outlander had agreed to see the king, before he made a move against him.

As Skealfa stood staring into the distance, his anger began to rise. He wished he had more time to search for Hreydol, but he knew his chances of finding him were slim. In the time he had been allowed to search, he was able to find four of his men with relative ease by rapidly closing the distance on all the storms that were visible. Unfortunately, there was no sign of the final storm encircling Hreydol which either meant he had traveled blindly in a direction that had taken him from view, or he had perished.

Skealfa was aware of the risks involved when he undertook the mission. Journeys beyond the city held many dangers, and casualties or death were a matter of course. It never sat well with the battle-lord to lose a soldier under any circumstance, but having lost a man as a result of the outlander's actions infuriated him, and he hated the idea of leaving a Hreydol behind without at least discovering his fate. He had done his best to locate him while the light of day made search possible, but the sun had dipped below the horizon. Now, he stood waiting at the time and location designated by the outlander.

Skealfa reminded himself that bringing the old hermit to the king was his priority, so persisting in the search was no longer an option; it would be futile in the dark at any rate, but as he continued to wait on the arrival of the outlander, his frustration and anger were incessant. The stars were getting brighter, and there was no sign of the outlander. Skealfa's blood began to boil. He resolved that if he had been deceived, he would scour the land until he found the old man and use whatever force necessary to bring him back!

From out of nowhere, the old man materialized not far off in the distance. Skealfa was disturbed he had gotten so close undetected, causing his feelings of rage to be replaced by suspicion. It was apparent the man had the skill to remain hidden if he chose to, so why did he reveal himself when he found him in the storm? Why was he willing to cooperate and enter a place he had always avoided? He doubted the old man had sympathy for the plight of the kingdom or for the hopes of the king. Perhaps he was intrigued by the promise of treasure, or maybe there was another reason entirely. He would know soon enough; the outlander was upon them.

"I was growing concerned you would not find us, or that you had changed your mind about meeting the king," Skealfa said flatly.

"I have arrived at the designated time and place as I said I would. You need not have worried." Czarstostryx glanced at the battle-lord's companions. "I see you were able to recover your men."

"Not all were found." Skealfa made no attempt to disguise his displeasure. "One remains yet undiscovered."

"Perhaps you will be able to resume your search once you have delivered me safely to your king."

Skealfa noticed the mocking undertone in the old man's voice but held his anger back. "King Bardazel impressed upon me his urgency to meet with you. I would have delivered you sooner had the choice not been taken from me."

"You will have to pardon my departure earlier. I needed some time to prepare myself for this unexpected venture into your city, and it gave you some time to locate your comrades, did it not?"

"Let us hasten," Skealfa replied brusquely. "Nightfall is upon us. I would have preferred us beyond the marsh road before being overwhelmed by darkness."

"Night's embrace shall not hinder us." Striking his staff to the ground, Czarstostryx invoked illumination. "The phantom flame will provide ample light as we travel."

Skealfa once again made a mental note of the old man's talents, grudgingly acknowledging the usefulness of the peculiar light. The moon would not rise before they reached the main gate of the city, and their remaining torches were almost used up. "I would have your strange light replaced with our own torches as we near the city," the battle-lord instructed. "The guards will be on edge after recent events, and the sight of an unusual light hovering in the darkness might unhinge them. The task to find you was covert, and only a few of my ranking officers were made aware of our departure. It would be unfortunate if our return in the night were to cause alarm among the watchmen. We do not want anyone to get struck with an errant arrow."

"I will discard the light when you deem it necessary," the outlander replied amiably. "We certainly do not want to invite avoidable danger upon ourselves, and it sounds as though your city has already encountered trouble of some kind. What are the recent events you spoke of earlier that have caused such unrest among your people?"

"Our city was recently attacked by the foul beasts that dwell in the forest—the Grohldym," Skealfa stated grimly. "Many of our people were slain. Some were taken for an unknown purpose. I assumed you knew of the Grohldym? They reside in the woods where you were said to have been seen by the woman from our city."

"Indeed, I do know of the Grohldym," Czarstostryx replied pointedly. "They are dangerous and highly intelligent, so I avoid them." He continued casually. "Since I rarely venture into regions near your city, it seems I am unfamiliar with current events, though admittedly there have been times in the past when I deemed it necessary to enter areas of the forest in closer proximity to your walls. It was during one such occasion that I *did* happen upon a young woman as you suggested. I must confess, I was concerned for her safety amidst the potential dangers of the forest. Tell me, how has she fared during these recent events?"

"She is alive," Skealfa replied plainly. "She is also largely responsible for inspiring the king to seek you out with such urgency."

"How so?"

Skealfa preferred not to divulge too much information until Bardazel had spoken with the outlander, but he felt an unusually strong compulsion to explain the matter further. "Throughout our kingdom's tragic history, the Grohldym have attacked many times, and the result of these attacks has always been the same: our people are either butchered or taken, never to be seen again, until now."

"Go on," Czarstostryx urged.

"The young woman you were concerned for was taken, along with some others. Several days later, she returned alone. When she was discovered, she seemed to be no more than a walking corpse. She appeared to be uninjured, but whatever horrors she endured stole her reason. When King Bardazel learned of her return, he was ecstatic, wondering what it might mean since it had never happened before. He hoped he would be able to learn more about the world surrounding us by speaking to the woman, and at the very least, confirm what had befallen the others who were taken. He thought it might have even been possible she was taken somewhere beyond the forest. Unfortunately, his efforts to learn anything from the woman were fruitless. Unable or unwilling to speak, she remains lost in her mind."

"If the woman has lost her reason, how is it she spoke of me?" Czarstostryx seemed intrigued.

"By a twist of fate, it seems; the king's son is acquainted with the woman and has been for some time. He cares about her, and he hopes to have her mind restored. It was she who spoke to him of your strange power, something I myself have witnessed. I believe the prince hoped you would be able to help her when he spoke to his father. Perhaps the king believes you can help her as well, but I would not presume to speak for him. He will make his intentions clear to you soon enough." Skealfa was surprised at himself for revealing so much to the outlander, but he had managed not to disclose the details of the woman's pregnancy and subsequent loss of the child.

Czarstostryx knew Skealfa had chosen not to discuss the pregnancy deliberately. Enough time had passed since he had last seen the woman that the child she carried would surely have been born. He found it interesting that the battle-lord had remained silent on the matter and wondered if the king would be willing to disclose more to him.

The torches along the city walls could be seen flickering in the distance. The group would reach the gate within the hour, and soon thereafter, Czarstostryx would have his first meeting with the ruler of the city he had observed from afar for so many years.

"It is time to be rid of your phantom flame," Skealfa directed. "We can cover the remaining distance with the torch remnants."

"Very well." Czarstostryx extinguished the light with a subtle movement of his staff.

The soldiers set about lighting their torches as Skealfa shared his expectations of how they would be received. "The guards standing watch will have been informed that we were sent on a mission beyond the city and to keep watch for our return. They know we could return at any time, so it should not be a surprise for them to see our torches. We should not encounter any conflict, but they will still be cautious at our approach until they know nothing is amiss. Leave it to me to put their minds at ease." Skealfa's men gave acknowledgement to his words, then the party set off to cover the remaining distance.

As soon as they were within a stone's throw of the main gate, a voice called down from the battlements. "Who approaches?"

Skealfa stopped the group and called back. "It is Lord Skealfa and his party."

The voice called back excitedly. "Lord Skealfa, you have returned!"

As the battle-lord and the rest of the men stepped into the full light of the torches mounted at the gate, the archers atop the wall relaxed their bow strings. Excited murmurs began to pass between the watchmen.

"Keep your voices down!" Skealfa hissed at the guards. "Open the gate." Immediately, the massive gate was swinging open, and Skealfa hurried to confer with the gate keeper. "I do not want our return to become common knowledge at this time. Send a runner to inform the king of my arrival."

Within a matter of moments, a lone runner was racing through the sleeping streets of the city as fast as his legs would carry him to the palace of King Bardazel.

CHAPTER 12

"Remarkable!" Bardazel exclaimed under his breath as Skealfa, and his party entered the throne room. He took a moment to scrutinize the old man as the group moved closer. The king was intrigued by the brilliant, white hair cascading down the stranger's shoulders which was accompanied by a long beard of matching luster that flowed over his chest, and he was astonished by the unusual, shimmering robe that the man wore which confused the king's perception of him as he moved. What really struck him though were the stranger's eyes. They were bright green and piercing, even from a distance. Skealfa and his men remained close to the stranger's side, watching <u>him</u> intently as they approached the king.

"Incredible!" The word escaped the king's lips as the men stopped at the foot of the steps leading up to his throne.

Bardazel noticed the way Skealfa, and the elite soldiers warily regarded the old man; they appeared ready to pounce on the outlander if given any provocation, but he also noticed there were no bindings on him, so it did not appear he had been taken by force.

The king had made it clear to Skealfa before his departure that if he was able to locate the outlander, he was to present him immediately upon his return. He would get a detailed account from Skealfa in due course, but after a lifetime spent seeking enlightenment with limited success, he had grown impatient to learn something new regarding his kingdom's troubled existence, and he was eager to discover what marvelous possibilities the stranger standing before him might have the keys to unlock.

The king's heart raced in anticipation. "Welcome to my kingdom," he began. "Words cannot describe the enormity of this moment. In our entire history, there has never been an account of anyone living outside of our city. When I heard it rumored there might be someone living beyond our borders, I had to find out if there was any truth to the claim, so I sent Lord Skealfa to seek you out, and to my amazement, here you now stand. I am King Bardazel, ruler of this city. I am eager to find out who you are and where you come from."

"My name is Czarstostryx," the stranger replied pleasantly. "I have come to you from the wasteland, where I encountered your Lord Skealfa attempting to locate me. I have spent my life living beyond your borders of my own choosing, but when I was told of your desire to consult with me, I believed it would be mutually beneficial, so I have come."

"Splendid! I am most eager to hear of your existence beyond our city. We will speak in private. Please join me in my council chamber." As the king stood, he addressed the battle-lord. "Lord Skealfa, you will accompany us. Have your men take their leave."

Skealfa nodded to his soldiers, signaling them to return to the barracks.

After descending the steps of the throne, Bardazel motioned for Czarstostryx to follow him as he strode toward a large corridor at the back of the great hall. Czarstostryx fell in step with the king while Skealfa remained close at heel. "Bring us food and drink!" Bardazel shouted to his courtiers.

Leaving the throne room, the king guided his guest through a wide corridor leading to an enormous door that was guarded by four soldiers. As they approached, one of the guards opened the door, allowing the three men to enter. Inside was a large rectangular table hewn from the stone of the room itself, melding with the floor as an eternal fixture. There were nine ornate chairs carved into the room in the same manner, surrounding the massive table: one at the far end and four on each side. The near end of the table had been left, oddly, without one. The chamber was much smaller than the throne room, but its highly vaulted ceilings and abundance of wall sconce torches gave it an atmosphere of comfortable spaciousness.

Bardazel sat down at the far end of the table and invited Czarstostryx to sit in one of the nearby chairs. Skealfa took a seat directly across from the outlander. As soon as they were settled, several servants entered the chamber and placed trays of steaming food in front of the men as well as a large pitcher of water, several drinking vessels, and a bottle of spirits. The servants took a moment to fill two of the goblets with the sparkling wine then quickly departed. The heavy door was shut behind them, leaving the three men in the privacy of the council chamber.

SERVANTS OF THE END

"Please, help yourself to food and drink," The king offered. "Lord Skealfa, you have been in the wilds for some time. You should replenish yourself as well."

Skealfa did not wish to appear diminished in the company of the old man, but he had not eaten in well over a day, and his stomach growled loudly as the smell of roasted fish and freshly baked rice cakes filled his nostrils. He hated to acknowledge it, but the king was right; he was famished, and sitting across from him was a strange outlander with considerable abilities and unknown motives. It was important that he restored his strength quickly should the need to protect the king arise. "Thank you, highness." Skealfa said, as he quickly piled a large portion of fish onto his plate. He devoured it ravenously, pausing only to fill a tankard with water which he swallowed down in mighty gulps to speed the process.

"Please, have something to eat," Bardazel again offered Czarstostryx. "Your journey must have been taxing."

"Thank you for the gracious offer, but I was able to prepare myself before setting out for your city, so I am quite comfortable." Skealfa noticed the quick, condescending glance the outlander shot at him and felt his anger rising in response to the old man's disposition. The outlander took one of the goblets. "I will have some of your wine though—a rare luxury."

"Is wine uncommon in the lands that you have traveled?" Bardazel asked eagerly.

"Indeed, it is, but do not misunderstand. I have not received offerings of wine in my travels, but I *have* found the means to craft my own from resources discovered in various regions." Czarstostryx raised the goblet to his nose, inhaled its aroma, then took a drink. "This is quite good."

"Please tell me more of the lands that you have traveled," Bardazel persisted. "Have you encountered other people beyond our borders—other civilizations perhaps?"

"I have traveled far and wide across the vast landscape surrounding your kingdom, but the only people I have seen were of this city. I occasionally observed their failed attempts to cross the wasteland throughout the years—not to belittle their efforts," the outlander said innocuously. "I have also plumbed the depths of the seemingly endless sands beyond your city and have fared no better."

"But you are not of this city. You must have come from somewhere beyond this realm—somewhere inhabited, surely." The king continued to press. "Where did you reside before you came to settle in the wasteland?"

"I would like to tell you what you are hoping to hear—that I hail from a grand kingdom beyond the sands of the wasteland, but I cannot claim it is so." Czarstostryx casually replied. "I also cannot tell you that it is not possible."

"Speak plainly man!" Skealfa interrupted angrily.

"Try to remain calm, Lord Skealfa. This man is my guest, and I would hear all that he has to share."

"My apologies, highness," Skealfa replied, regaining his composure.

"Please tell me what you mean," urged the king.

Czarstostryx continued with little regard to Skealfa's interruption. "I am not entirely sure how I came to find my home in the wasteland. I have no recollection of my childhood or anything before my existence in the wasteland. My first memory is of a time when I awoke to find myself on the floor of a ravine. I was a young man with barely the shadow of a beard upon my face. I had no idea where I was or how I had gotten there, but I noticed I was near the entrance of the ravine, and I could see that beyond, lay the scorched sands of the wasteland. I was hesitant to step into the burning sunlight, so instead, I cautiously ventured deeper into the ravine. It was actually a dwelling of sorts with scant furnishings and a small store of food and water. There was also a collection of books and scrolls I discovered tucked away, and to my surprise, I was able to read many of the words that were written in them although I could not fully decipher their meaning.

"It occurred to me that I must be in someone's home, and I began to grow worried that whoever lived there might return at any moment. I had no idea how they would react when I was discovered, especially since I would not be able to explain my presence, so I went back to the entrance of the ravine to explore my surroundings further.

"The ravine began to slope sharply upward, and I soon emerged from its cool shadows into the vast harshness of the wasteland. I had no idea what I should do. In all directions, I could see nothing that seemed promising. I doubted I would find answers by venturing blindly into the wasteland with no idea of where I was or what I might encounter, so I decided to wait and take my chances dealing with whoever occupied the strange dwelling instead.

"Days passed, then weeks, and still nobody came. I spent my days reading the books I had found and slowly began to grasp their meaning. In the cool of dusk and in the early hours of dawn's light, I would cautiously venture into the wasteland, taking care to keep thorough documentation of my exploits so I could always find my way back to the hidden sanctuary. Over time, I began to run low on food and water and realized I would have to replenish my supplies. My expeditions into the barren wastes had been fruitless in that regard, so I knew I would have to go further if I was going to find the means to survive, but I was not going to set out blindly and bring about my own demise. I decided to consult the books before my departure. Something I had seen within their pages seemed familiar somehow, and it did not take long for me to find what I was looking for.

"Some of the books contained unusual drawings with similarities I recognized as depictions of the landscape I had explored. I began to understand that the seemingly random drawings scattered throughout the books were mappings of the land around me. I still had no idea where I was or how I had come to be there, but I could see there were regions beyond the ravine where I might find the answers, at least according to the books. I studied the pages, carefully examining the most relevant references I could find. There were indications of a forest that looked to be half of a day's journey away, and there were details of a hidden glade within the forest where a water source existed. I gathered my last bit of food and water and prepared to set out, unsure if I would find anything or if I would simply die wandering."

"Was the map accurate?" Bardazel asked eagerly.

"It was indeed, although it took me most of a day to find the forest. I was unfamiliar with the additional charts and layouts of the mapping, but I was able to make out the general correlational of the sun's position at dawn, so I knew which direction to follow. It took a bit longer than necessary to find my way, and I was fortunate that I had been able to make the correct translations. When I arrived, I looked more closely at a map in one of the books I had brought with me. Its meaning made more sense when I was able to see the various aspects of the landscape in relation to where I stood."

"What did it show you?" Bardazel leaned forward.

"It showed me a depiction of the vast forest of trees that I saw stretching out in both directions. It also referenced the towering cliffs beyond the forest. According to the map, there were twin lakes somewhere to the west of where I stood. I was not exactly sure where my precise starting point had been, but I had documented my movement, so I had a general idea of my position. I had done my best to negotiate a true course to the forest, but I had surely strayed along the way. I knew the glade was hidden somewhere among the trees between the cliffs and the wasteland, so I plunged into the forest, hoping to gauge its position well enough to locate it." Czarstostryx paused. "I could go on for hours about my exploits. Suffice it to say that I did locate the glade and manage to replenish my supplies.

"Throughout the years that followed, I continued to explore my surroundings extensively. The various books and maps that I had found improved my progress immensely. I located your city in due course, but I was never eager to enter these walls without knowledge of who I was and where I had come from. The possibility that I was an outcast or a fugitive of this city was a concern. Perhaps I would be able to find the answers to my being in your city, or maybe I would find my demise. I decided to seek the answers on my own and avoid the risk, but it seems those questions have finally been answered, since by your own accounts, I am not of this city."

"Then you still have no knowledge of your origins, even after all your years searching? I find that hard to believe." Skealfa voiced his skepticism candidly.

"There are many things I have discovered over the years that are hard to believe. That does not make them any less true," Czarstostryx replied coldly.

"Skealfa, please. Let us not be harsh with our guest," Bardazel intervened. "Regardless of his past, it seems Czarstostryx has knowledge of the world around us. These maps you spoke of, do they show any regions that you have not yet explored?"

"I have studied the books extensively for many years and have yet to uncover all of the mysteries within their pages. Some of the book's entries took years to fully interpret. Many of my discoveries have provided opportunities to harness unique abilities and the means to improve upon them. These skills have afforded me a better understanding of what is hidden in the pages, and I have deciphered that there are indeed regions and landscapes I have not yet discovered."

"Then such places *could* exist!" Bardazel exclaimed, "places where we could escape the oppression of the Grohldym!"

"It certainly appears to be a possibility," Czarstostryx concurred. "The writings in the books have proven to be accurate in every instance where I have been able to meet the requirements to validate them. I think verifying the existence of unknown lands might be realized if the necessary components to unlock them have been obtained. I believe there is a good chance that certain keys to unlocking these realms may be within the walls of this palace. Your man, Skealfa, said you possess unusual artifacts that may be of interest. I would like to see if you have anything that might lend to both our causes."

"I do indeed have a small collection of various, rare and wonderful objects, some of which have never been definitively identified," Bardazel said enthusiastically. "I am eager to have you look at them and hear your thoughts on their purpose. If you can affirm something useful, then I would consider negotiating further."

"King Bardazel," Skealfa interrupted. "I will need a word with you in private before we proceed."

Bardazel heard the warning in Skealfa's voice, and it took him a moment to recognize that he had become somewhat giddy as he had been speaking to the old man. The promise of new discoveries and the impact they could have on his kingdom were exhilarating, but his usual, cautious objectivity seemed somehow compromised in the moment. He was grateful for Skealfa's intervention, as it gave him an opportunity to steel his resolve before continuing the negotiations. "Of course, Lord Skealfa. I should hear your accounts of the mission first.

"Please excuse us for a moment Czarstostryx," the king said congenially. "I was anxious to meet you without delay upon your arrival, but I do need to hear Skealfa's report before we can proceed. Feel free to make yourself comfortable here while I am briefed. We will return shortly."

"By all means," Czarstostryx replied calmly. "I am happy to indulge myself with more of your fine wine while I wait."

King Bardazel and Skealfa rose from the table, and the battle-lord moved to the entrance and pulled a small lever, signaling to the guards outside. The mighty door immediately began to swing open.

As the two passed through the door, Bardazel spoke softly to the guards. "See that our guest remains here and that he is comfortable until we return." The guards nodded as they resumed their station near the open door of the council chamber, keeping a close eye on the strange guest.

"Let us speak in the treasure hold," Bardazel said quietly to Skealfa.

The battle-lord remained close to the king as they made their way along the corridor leading to the small chamber. When they arrived, Skealfa instructed the guards on duty to remain alert before stepping inside and securing the door so his words would be heard by the king alone.

"Highness, I must advise you to use caution when dealing with the outlander. He is dangerous, and I seriously doubt he can be trusted. I lost Hreydol in the wasteland because of a bizarre sandstorm conjured by the old man, and the rest of us would have shared the same fate had the outlander chosen not to intervene. It is likely, he did so simply because he believed it would somehow serve his purpose."

"Tell me what happened." Bardazel was intrigued.

"After we left the city and passed beyond the marsh road, we utilized an efficient search pattern of my design. The technique kept us spread apart but always within sight of one another. We searched like this until the time to return to the city to resupply ourselves drew near, but before we were able to regroup, a violent sandstorm arose out of nowhere. Our party was divided, and we were unable to find one another. Since sandstorms in the wasteland are uncommon and typically short-lived, I expected the skies would clear before too long and I would be able to locate my men easily enough, but the skies did not clear. The blinding storm was relentless, and I knew it would be impossible to find anyone until it ceased, but I had no way of knowing that it never would.

"It was hard to tell day from night as the storm raged on, but I surmised at least one day passed as I waited, shielding myself. My food and water were depleted, and I knew my only chance of survival was to either set out blindly or die where I lay, so I committed myself to a course of action. Before I could make a move, the howling winds fell silent. As suddenly as it had begun, the storm ended.

"I felt a moment of relief, then I heard a voice calling out for me to identify myself or be destroyed. When I shifted to see who approached, I beheld the strange, old man who now sits in the council chamber. He appeared to be frail and weary, but I could sense power within him. As I began to pull myself from the sand that had nearly buried me, he commanded me to hold my position. My first instinct was to overpower and subdue him, but I knew I should try a tactful approach first as you had directed, so I submitted to his will and answered his questions."

"What did he ask?"

"He asked how I had learned of his existence."

"What did you tell him?"

"I told him that you had heard of him from a young woman who lived in the city. I also explained of your desire to find passage through the wasteland. He seemed interested in hearing me out, but he remained poised to attack until I mentioned the artifacts. After I told him of your willingness to negotiate a trade, he was instantly amenable to meeting with you."

"Did you speak to him of the missing child?"

"I did not. It seemed prudent to disclose only what was necessary to entice him to return with me. I thought it would be best to let you decide what details you would share, but I believe he knows more than he reveals." Skealfa looked pointedly at the king. "It is important that you are aware of this man's strange abilities. He admitted to me that the storms were of his design, and I witnessed his control over them. Upon questioning me, he threatened my destruction if he deemed it necessary, and he seemed entirely convinced that he would have no trouble dispatching me. He also conjured some kind of phantom flame to guide us through the marsh road, which seemed a trivial thing to him. These are only the things that I myself have witnessed and from what the prince has described of Glithnie's encounters, she too recognized the strange power possessed by the outlander."

"So, the old man has strange powers," Bardazel replied glibly. "He is an outlander who we know nothing about; he may well be dangerous, but he also has knowledge of the outside world that we do not." The king clapped Skealfa's shoulder. "You have faced many dangers and have never fallen. I have every confidence that you will be able to ensure the safety of the city as I negotiate with Czarstostryx."

"I will," Skealfa replied stoically.

"I need to find out what he knows," Bardazel went on enthusiastically. "Perhaps he will share more of what he has discovered in the books he acquired. He appears to be willing to help with our cause."

"That is what concerns me," Skealfa stated grimly. "He has known of our existence for many years, yet he has never come here or aided us in any way. In fact, he has gone to great lengths to avoid detection. We still have not located his home, and he seems determined to destroy anyone who tries." Skealfa paused, considering the treasures filling the small chamber. "It was only when he learned of the artifacts in this room that his disposition was radically altered. "There is something in here he wants. How can we be sure that once he obtains it, he will not just disappear into the wasteland? Who knows what power these relics hold— powers he might unleash for his own ends, perhaps at the peril of our city?" The battle-lord looked hard at the king, making his final point. "Hreydol was lost in the wasteland—a casualty of the outlander's self-serving motives. I have concerns that he will not be the last."

Bardazel regarded Skealfa silently for a moment. The giant soldier standing before him was a fearless warrior. No one in the kingdom could match his strength or courage. He was also an extremely intelligent tactician who had loyally served the kingdom his entire life, and his opinion was a highly valued commodity. "I have heard you Lord Skealfa," Bardazel said after some thought. "Your accounts are a cause for concern, but I must learn more of what the outlander knows. I will negotiate with him and allow him to choose one item to take as a token of good will, with one condition: You will accompany him when he leaves to ensure that his discoveries will benefit our kingdom's future and not just his own ambition."

"What if he refuses your terms?"

"Then he will not acquire what he came here for, and he will remain within our walls until we have persuaded him to join our cause," the king replied coldly. "Instruct the guards to be prepared for the call should it become necessary, then return to the council chamber. I will rejoin our guest and put his mind at ease until you arrive; we will see then if he is going to cooperate or if he will need further convincing.

CHAPTER 13

The blood pounded loudly in Prince Nieloch's temples as he lay with his ear pressed to the floor. The long-abandoned chamber above the treasure hold was one of many secret places he had discovered in the palace during his childhood. As a boy, he spent most of his time alone, rarely finding the opportunity to enjoy the companionship of other children since his position as the king's son left him isolated from those who were considered beneath his station. Occasionally, he would happen upon other youths in the palace who had managed to escape their parents' notice, and he would engage them in games of exploration or hide and seek adventures in the less traveled areas of the palace. There were many unused chambers above the main levels of the palace for their games, some of which had fallen into disrepair from neglect.

It had been during his numerous visits to the upper areas that he had found several locations where the rock of the mountain palace had been cracked as a result of structural damage sustained during some cataclysmic event predating the city's historical records.

By chance, he discovered the narrow fissures allowed sound to travel from several of the rooms below. Upon this revelation, he stopped inviting others into the forgotten chambers and kept knowledge of their hidden features to himself.

The prince overheard many private discussions between his father and the important men who met with him over the years, and his father was never-the-wiser to his eavesdropping. Most of what he heard were boring accounts of the city's management or conversations with the scholars about the lore of the kingdom or details of battles with the Grohldym. There had never been anything he had overheard before that was truly secretive or confidential, until now; what he had just heard was both. His heart continued to pound loudly in his ears as he rose from his spot on the floor.

Nieloch knew that Lord Skealfa had returned when the king cleared the throne room shortly after a breathless courier appeared in the night. None but the king's personal guards had been allowed to remain, so the prince had been forced to listen from the shadows of a nearby hallway. When he heard there would be a private meeting, the prince immediately ran to his secret listening post with hopes of hearing news that his child had been discovered.

But his child had *not* been found. No real attempt had even been made, and his father made no mention of it to the outlander. It was clear that he never had any intention of helping at all! Nieloch's fists clenched in anger as his mind raged. He realized that if he were going to find his lost child, it would be up to him to do so.

As soon as Skealfa and King Bardazel left the treasure hold, Nieloch hurried to return to the room where he had begun his eavesdropping. From the alternate site he would be able to continue listening in on the conversation taking place in the council chamber. He had to find out if the outlander would agree to the king's terms, and if so, he would need to find a way to speak to the old man in private before he left the palace.

Nieloch positioned himself in an alcove of the room he had just entered. There was a deep crack running through the wall and into the floor where he crouched, listening intently. After a few moments, he heard the voice of his father.

"Forgive my absence, Czarstostryx. Protocol demands that I am debriefed by all parties returning from forays beyond our walls as soon as possible."

"I understand completely," Czarstostryx replied nonchalantly. "Now that you have received Skealfa's account, how shall we proceed?"

"I believe we are each in a position that could benefit the other," Bardazel began agreeably. "Your knowledge of the lands surrounding my kingdom seems to be broader than the information I have obtained from the resources within these walls. I think that some of the things I have learned, and some of your discoveries, might be connected. Perhaps the books and documents you discovered are linked to those in the palace archives. Maybe, the knowledge contained within their pages has been separated over time, making it more difficult to unlock the mysteries of these lands.

"I am inclined to agree with you." Czarstostryx seemed to consider the possibility. "It does appear there might be elements of my research that could have eluded me. Perhaps they are within these walls among the artifacts that have been mentioned. I am anxious to see if it is so."

The conversation halted abruptly. Nieloch heard the operation of the massive door as Skealfa returned to the council chamber below him.

"Ah, Lord Skealfa, thank you for joining us. I have decided to offer a proposal to Czarstostryx with the hope that we can work together to achieve both our goals." The king turned his attention to the outlander. "Let me start by saying that the artifacts contained within these walls are ancient; most of them have been kept here for as long as our history has been recorded. They are as much a part of this palace as its walls which were cast from the mountains themselves, and they belong here. That is how it has always been." Bardazel paused. "Perhaps that is why there has never been salvation for the citizens of this kingdom; no one ever realized what we now know. There are critical resources that have been divided throughout time, and they are linked somehow. If we can make the right connections between them, who knows what might be accomplished?" A serious look crossed the king's face. "Inspect the artifacts in my treasure hold. If you find something that will enable you to access unexplored regions and further your own pursuits, I will allow you to take that item, with one condition. Since my own ambition lies in finding lands beyond my kingdom, I will require that an agent representing my interests accompanies you. Lord Skealfa will travel with you so he can report back to me on your discoveries. If unforeseen events prevent you from returning to our city, I will still be able to benefit from what is learned through his accounts." The king looked expectantly at the outlander. "Will you agree to these terms?"

Czarstostryx regarded the battle-lord for a moment before he replied. "I was not expecting a traveling companion; you see, the regions I have traveled are filled with dangers few could overcome. It might be possible for Skealfa to endure the hardships of the places I am familiar with, but I cannot guarantee his survival venturing into the unknown."

"I require no assurances from you," Skealfa cut in angrily.

Bardazel intervened quickly. "I am quite confident Lord Skealfa will prevail against anything he may encounter. He has proven himself countless times against remarkable odds. You need not worry on his behalf. So, will you agree to the terms?"

"Let me make sure I am clear on your proposal," Czarstostryx replied. "If I find a suitable item in your treasury, then it is mine to keep?"

"It is," the king gave his assurance with a nod.

"Then I agree." The outlander smiled as he stood and clasped his hands together. "Now, let us see if these negotiations were in vain or if you truly possess something that will help fulfill both our desires."

Nieloch was overcome with anger and disappointment upon hearing the door engage as the negotiations ended and the three men left for the treasure hold. He had been hopeful that his father would have discussed Glithnie with the outlander, but it was obvious he had no intention of revealing the existence of his child. Frustrated, the prince departed and hurried back to the room above the treasury.

As soon as he arrived, Nieloch settled into position and pressed his ear once again to the floor, listening closely. He could not afford to miss anything that was said if he wanted to have any chance of finding his opportunity.

"Here they are." Nieloch could hear his father's voice clearly. "These are all of the ancient artifacts and significant treasures within the palace. I have been here many times to study them, hoping to learn something that might help my people. Some seem to be designed simply for their beauty, and the various gems and stones are intriguing because of their unknown origins, but the sculptures of strange objects and creatures are a mystery. Their depictions are completely foreign to anything that has been encountered before. Since you have a unique perspective of the outside world and may have resources we do not, perhaps you can find meaning in something here."

"This is indeed a marvelous collection," Czarstostryx said as he moved slowly around the room looking closely at the artifacts. "The jewelry and gemstones do not appear to have any immediate relevance to my current studies, but this sculpture is incredible. The craftsmanship and detail are extraordinary."

"Does it have any relevance to your studies?" Bardazel asked hopefully.

"There are references in some of my books regarding a powerful deity who has dominion over armies of twisted creatures. His domain is said to be hidden, and his purpose is unclear, but I believe there may be a way to locate his realm. By deciphering arcane evidence and obtaining certain keys of power, it should be possible."

"So, finding this deity and his hidden domain would allow access beyond our borders," Bardazel stated excitedly.

"Indeed, it would. I have discovered a hidden path that will take me to his realm, but the way has been barred. It seems I am missing a vital piece in order to proceed—this piece." Czarstostryx picked up a small stone artifact; it was one of the carved, geometric pieces heavily etched with strange markings. "This is the item I will be taking."

"As you will," Bardazel replied. "If you believe it will help you unlock a path beyond our borders, then take it with my blessing."

Czarstostryx slid the artifact into a secret pocket within his robes while the king continued. "I know we are all anxious to begin the task at hand, but the hour is growing late, and I would like to invite you to stay for the remainder of the evening." Bardazel did not wait for a response. "My guards will escort you to your chamber. Please take what rest you can and make any necessary preparations. In the morning, I will have you summoned and escorted to the throne room before your departure. The corridors and hallways are vast and can be quite confusing to those who are not familiar with the layout of the palace," the king added frankly.

"As you say, good king," Czarstostryx agreed without hesitation. "I would not want to cause any unnecessary delays by losing my bearings within these walls. I will be ready and waiting for your summons in the morning."

"Very well then." Bardazel was clearly satisfied with the outcome of the negotiations. "Guards!" he called out to the sentries at the door. "Escort our guest to one of the vacant councilors' quarters for the evening and see to it that he is not disturbed until he is called upon in the morning."

"Yes highness," both men replied in unison. One of the guards motioned to the outlander. "Please, follow me."

Czarstostryx gave a cordial nod to the king before being led away from the treasure hold.

Nieloch heard what he needed to; he would have the opportunity he had hoped for. Most of the councilors' quarters stood empty, but Nieloch knew he would have no trouble locating where the outlander would be, however, meeting him secretly would prove difficult if there were to be guards at the door throughout the night. He knew he must find a way; Glithnie's life, and the life of their child was at stake. He could not miss the chance to save them. The prince waited a few moments longer to hear the final words of the king and Lord Skealfa before they departed as well.

"That went surprisingly well." Skealfa seemed skeptical as he addressed the king. "I was certain he would be opposed to being accompanied on this quest. He clearly strives to follow his pursuits in solitude."

"I made the terms as unrestrictive as possible to improve the chances that he would cooperate. He clearly required the artifact that he selected, and I suspect he would have agreed to most anything to possess it considering his reaction when he saw it. He did his best to conceal his excitement, but I detected a gleam in his eyes as he beheld it."

"Indeed." Skealfa snorted. "I was half expecting him to snatch up an armful of treasure and vanish into thin air!"

"I do not believe he told us much of what he truly knows about these items," Bardazel said thoughtfully. "He recognized what he was looking for within moments of entering the room. He may have also identified other items from his research. If so, he might try to acquire them for his own purpose as well.

Have the men guarding him tonight notify you immediately if he tries to leave his chamber."

"I will stand watch over him myself to ensure nothing is amiss during the night," the battle-lord responded dutifully.

"No, Skealfa. I want you to take what rest you can find. You will need to be at your best come dawn. I do not believe Czarstostryx will give us any trouble tonight. Whatever his motives are, they seem to align with my own, at least for the time being. Take your leave, instruct your men, and rest well. I will see you at first light."

"As you command," Skealfa replied.

Prince Nieloch listened for a few moments more, but there was only silence. The meetings were finished, and he knew what must be done. Quickly making his way out of the abandoned upper levels of the palace, he headed directly to his own chamber, knowing that if he were going to have any chance of success, he would need to wait a while before setting his plan in motion. It would be necessary to give Skealfa time to instruct the guards outside Czarstostryx's chamber and allow things to settle down for the evening.

Once he reached his quarters, the prince lit one of the notched candles on his desk that he found useful for gaging the passage of time. He decided to wait for an hour before setting out to see the old man. The guards were going to be a problem, but he was the king's son, a fact he hoped he could use to his advantage. He began to grow apprehensive over the magnitude of what he was planning. Musings of failure began to creep into his head, but he quickly struck the unwelcome thoughts from his mind. He would not allow himself to fail Glithnie and their child!

He began to gather the items he believed would be necessary for what would surely be a dangerous and difficult journey, doing his best to keep himself busy as the candle slowly burned. His thoughts drifted to Glithnie as he made his preparations.

The first time he had seen her was on the shore of the eastern lake. He recalled how her long, golden curls caught the light of the late, afternoon sun as she mended a large net near the water's edge. He was returning to the palace after a foray into the areas surrounding the city walls and was amazed to discover a young woman of such delicate form and exquisite beauty. He had done his best not to stare as he passed by, but she had noticed his lingering gaze, and he detected a small smile on her lips as she blushed and pretended to carefully inspect her work. Nieloch considered approaching her, but it occurred to him that perhaps the blush he perceived was merely the result of the harsh sun upon her face after a long day near the water. He chuckled to himself, remembering the butterflies he had felt in his stomach that prompted him to find an excuse to hurry home instead.

The image of the young woman remained fixed in his mind as days passed and he would frequently abscond from the confines of the palace to spend time revisiting the areas around the lake in hopes of seeing her again. He resolved that when next he saw her, he would introduce himself regardless of any enfeebling influence his stomach might have. It was weeks before he finally got his chance.

He was traveling along the banks of the eastern lake near the Forest of the Grohldym and was elated when he saw her emerge from the shadowed canopy stepping lightly with delicate grace. She had already recognized him as the prince of the kingdom but was unimpressed by his station as he introduced himself. During his stammering about the randomness of their meeting, she smiled broadly and lightly touched his cheek. Later, she would tell him how she had been able to feel the depth of his caring and capacity for love— things that were as much a part of him as his charming, good looks and uncompromising optimism. She recognized things that he himself did not realize at the time just by looking deeply into his eyes. Since that encounter, he had always held in awe the way she could sense the true nature of others with such clarity. Nieloch's eyes glistened with tears as he reminisced about the woman he loved, barely aware of the bags he was preparing for the journey.

By the time the prince had gathered and packed all the necessary items, he realized there was no way he would be able to carry it all. Having spent most of his life shielded within the walls of the palace, he had never journeyed into the wilds beyond the city. Mostly, he had observed Skealfa and his soldiers setting out and returning from their ventures, but he really had no idea what items were essential on such expeditions. It was not that he was oblivious to military matters; he had received a remedial education regarding some of the skills required by the soldiers he would someday rule, but he never fully applied himself to such pursuits.

Nieloch looked at the three large packs lying on his bed. They were mostly filled with clothes, blankets, and various implements from his room, and he still had not packed any food. It was obvious he needed to rethink his strategy. As he started to consider what he should leave behind, he noticed the candle; it had already burned down to the one-hour mark. It was time to go. He would resolve the packing dilemma later, but it would not even be necessary if the first part of his plan failed. *"No! I cannot think like that,"* he told himself. *"The outlander will help."*

Nieloch took a moment to steady his breathing. He had never done anything like this before, and the enormity of it was starting to make his head spin again. He thought about Glithnie, isolated in the cell where the king's scholars had tried without success to revive her. He remembered how happy they had once been, sharing stolen moments of precious time in their secret affair. He thought about their child and how happy they could all be together. "It *will* be so," he said aloud with firm resolve.

Setting his mind to succeed, Nieloch strode confidently down the hall toward the councilors' quarters.

CHAPTER 14

The four soldiers keeping watch over Czarstostryx saw the prince approaching from the far end of the corridor. "Good evening to you!" Nieloch called out cheerfully as he neared their position. The guards exchanged puzzled looks as the prince came to stand before them. "I need to speak with Czarstostryx for a moment." The guards continued to look at one another with uncertainty. "The man who is within this chamber," Nieloch clarified. "My father sent me to speak with him briefly on his behalf."

"Lord Skealfa will need to be informed," the ranking soldier replied. He gave a quick nod to one of the other sentries who began to depart.

"No need for that," Nieloch hastily intervened, keeping the sentry from leaving. "I do not wish to have Lord Skealfa disturbed before his vital mission."

"Our orders were to notify Lord Skealfa if the king's guest left his chamber."

"Well, since that is not the case, there is really no reason to disturb his rest, is there?" the prince rationalized.

"Lord Skealfa made it clear that our duty here is of the utmost importance and that he should be informed if anything is amiss," the guard insisted.

"And well he should," Nieloch agreed, "but it must be obvious to you that I am involved with the king's plans since I have knowledge of the man within this chamber and the details pertaining to him."

The ranking sentry regarded the prince skeptically.

"I assure you; nothing is amiss." Nieloch said innocently. He continued in a commanding tone. "Inform Lord Skealfa in the morning if you must, but I will not have him bothered with this now. I was sent here by order of the king, and I will see the man as I was instructed to. Now, stand aside!"

"Of course, highness," the sentry quickly replied. "As you say." The guards stepped aside and let the prince pass.

Nieloch entered the chamber and quickly shut the door behind him. He stood for a moment facing the door with his hands pressed firmly against it, breathing a small sigh of relief. He had managed to pacify the guards with his show of authority, at least for the moment. Now, to see if he could be as persuasive with the outlander. He turned from the door and was startled to discover the strange, old man standing in the center of the room staring at him intently. Czarstostryx's brilliant green eyes were unsettling, causing the prince to take an involuntary step backward. Nieloch found himself with his back pressed firmly against the door.

"So, you are the one who was listening in on secret meetings this night." There was a hint of amusement in the outlander's voice as he observed Nieloch's discomfort.

"Uh, yes. I am Nieloch," the prince stammered. "I am the son and heir to King Bardazel." He shifted uneasily under the penetrating scrutiny of the outlander. "Forgive my intrusion," he continued, as he stepped away from the door to regain his composure. "I have been anxiously awaiting Lord Skealfa's return with hopes that he would find you. There is a matter of dire importance I must impart to you, and I feared this would be my only chance to do so."

"It must be a matter of great concern indeed to take such measures to secure this meeting. How is it that you believe I might help you?"

"I heard about you from a woman that you met in the Forest of the Grohldym," Nieloch began. "She is a commoner from a fishing camp. Her name is Glithnie. You do know her, do you not?"

"Indeed, I do. She is a very special young woman."

"She is the love of my life!" Nieloch replied passionately.

"Well, love is a precious thing," the outlander stated with reverence. "I surmised that a woman like her would have someone special, but I am afraid she did not share many details of her personal life. Our rare encounters were usually quite brief, you see, but I would be most interested in hearing about the relationship you had with her if you are so inclined."

The prince brightened at the prospect of speaking about the woman he loved. "I met her less than a year ago while exploring the outlying villages of the kingdom. My father prefers that I remain within the safety of the city or inside the palace altogether, especially when the cycle of the Grohldym draws near, but many citizens live outside the city's walls. I was curious what their lives were like, and though my father is quite protective of me, I knew it was important to him that I have a better understanding of the people I might someday rule.

"From the first moment I saw her, I was captivated. Her beauty was beyond that of anyone I had ever encountered, and there was something in her eyes that drew me in helplessly. I knew from the start that my father would never allow me to pursue a relationship with a commoner, but she would not leave my thoughts, and so, I started to see her in secret every chance I could.

"Our love grew, and soon she was with child. We did not know what we were going to do. We wanted to have a family, but I knew she would never be accepted into the royal house. Our only desire was to be together, and I would have gladly relinquished my future role as king and run away with her to some foreign land, but there was nowhere to run. There is only death beyond the confines of this kingdom. That was when she told me about you. She said she had met a strange, old man in the forest who was not of our city. This was unheard of, and it opened new possibilities. She believed if a place beyond our kingdom truly existed, maybe we could find happiness there.

"My first impulse was to tell my father since his life's ambition is to free our people from the tyranny of the Grohldym. I thought if I told him of Glithnie's discovery, he might regard her as an asset to the royal family and consider my relationship with her, but she begged me not to tell him. From what I had told her of my father, she did not think he would let us be together under any circumstance. I knew she was right, of course. My father would only use the information for his own glory. His only concern for me has always been that I fulfill my role as heir. He has never shown any real concern for my happiness—a fact that he has proven yet again on this very evening!" The prince's voice had risen to a fevered pitch, and his fists were clenched in rage.

Czarstostryx spoke soothingly to Nieloch. "Your father seems to be a man driven by purpose, but his motives stem from desires that would serve the citizens of this kingdom well if he is successful in finding what he seeks. How have his actions this night disappointed you so badly?"

"Because Glithnie is the very reason my father knew to seek you out, yet her interests were not even discussed."

"What do you mean?"

"She hoped to beseech you on her own, so she started spending more time in the forest, expecting to increase her chances of encountering you. I was sick with worry over the risk she was taking as an attack by the Grohldym was imminent, but she assured me that she would be fine. She had a way of avoiding the Grohldym I never understood. Even as the birth of our child grew closer, she told me the risk would be worth it. She believed you were a learned man and that you might help us leave the kingdom if she could speak with you about the matter, but she never got the chance.

"When the Grohldym attacked, I was within the palace. There was no way for me to help her, and I was terrified that she would be killed, but I could not go to her until the Grohldym were gone. After the attack, I raced to her homestead as quickly as I could, discovering that her mother and father had been slaughtered. There was no sign of Glithnie, and I feared the worst—that she had been taken. I hoped that she had been in the forest during the attack and maybe managed to avoid them, but as days passed with no sign of her, I began to despair over the loss of my love and unborn child. I was heartsick with the knowledge that they were gone forever. Then, she miraculously appeared! It was the first time anyone had ever returned from the clutches of the Grohldym! She was whole and appeared to be unharmed, but our child was not with her. Clearly, she had given birth, but whatever horrors she had endured, robbed her of her reason and she was not able to speak a word of what had happened.

"The king's physicians and scholars have interrogated her extensively without success, and I have spent countless hours with her as well, hoping to reach her, hoping to learn of our child's fate, but I have fared no better. Knowing she would not last long in her condition, I became desperate to save her. That is why I told my father about you. I hoped if you were found, you might possess the skill to unlock her mind. Perhaps you could even find our child, but my father never even spoke to you about her or our missing baby! He assured me that Lord Skealfa would be dispatched to look for the child as he sought you out, but there was no mention that it had even been attempted! Now you are being sent out secretly at first light. Therefore, I had to speak with you tonight!" Nieloch compulsively grasped the outlander' arm. "I beg you, please see Glithnie and try to help her before you leave. If you could just get her to speak—if she could tell us what has become of our child, then I could reunite them, and she would surely be saved! We could still be a family!" Tears glistened in Nieloch's eyes as his appeal reached its crescendo.

"Well, I can certainly understand your need to seek me out," Czarstostryx said, soothingly as he gently removed the prince's hand. "Your father clearly does not share your concern for Glithnie's well-being or for the life of your child having made no mention to me in either regard. Skealfa, on the other hand, did tell me about Glithnie when we met in the wasteland. He told me of her capture and subsequent return. He also referred to her fragile mental state. There was no mention of the child though, a fact of which I am sure he was aware, but I expect he was leaving it up to the king to decide what should be disclosed." The outlander paused. "It has been quite some time since I have seen Glithnie. Evidently, the last time I saw her was *before* she decided to solicit my aid. I knew she was with child at our last encounter, and I showed concern for her, but she remained silent on the matter. She also seemed a little sad. Now I see why she was troubled." Czarstostryx appeared thoughtful. "Glithnie is quite remarkable. I have enjoyed our interactions over the years, and I am sorry to hear of her recent misfortune. I would like to help her if I can, but our time grows short. We must move quickly if I am going to see her."

Nieloch could not believe his luck! He had actually managed to meet with the outlander, *and* the man was willing to help. He half-believed that he would not get as far as he had, but now that the first part of his plan had been achieved, he had no idea how he was going to get the outlander past the guards outside and into the part of the palace where Glithnie was being kept. "Thank you, good sir!" Nieloch reached for the man's arm in his exuberance but refrained. "I cannot begin to tell you how much this means to me, but I must admit that in my excitement to beseech you, I did not pause to consider how I would go about getting you to Glithnie's quarters."

"What is the complication?"

"You see, after you were escorted from the council chamber, I lingered for a bit to see if my father had any intention of lending to my cause."

"And did he?"

"He did not," Nieloch replied bitterly, "I also overheard that you were to be carefully guarded throughout the night. The guards outside your room have been instructed to inform Lord Skealfa if you try to leave your chamber or if they discover anything amiss during the evening. I was barely able to gain access without them immediately informing him, but they will surely report my visit in the morning. It is possible they have already notified him while we have been speaking. There is simply no way for us to leave without Lord Skealfa learning of your absence."

"Leave that to me," Czarstostryx calmly replied. "Come, let us hasten to Glithnie."

Nieloch had no idea what to expect when the old man opened the chamber door to confront the guards and he did not much care. He was so close to finally helping Glithnie that he was willing to do almost anything. As he followed Czarstostryx through the doorway, he thought it odd that the guards were not questioning the outlander. Emerging from the room, he was stunned to see all of them standing motionless as if they had become living statues. Their eyes stared blankly ahead, and they did not appear to be breathing. Since Nieloch was behind Czarstostryx as they entered the hall, he had no idea what the old man had done to achieve the resulting effect, but he was not overly concerned at the moment. Czarstostryx motioned for the prince to take the lead as they quickly moved on.

"This way." Nieloch spoke with urgency and kept his volume low as he guided the outlander down the hallway. "We will take the service corridors to avoid notice. Glithnie is on the other end of the palace keep. We should not encounter any guards, and if there are servants about, they will keep to their tasks." Nieloch glanced back at Czarstostryx. "How did you manage to get us past the guards?"

"It was a matter of time manipulation, something quite useful I have learned over the years."

"So, they're not—"

"Dead?" Czarstostryx seemed amused at the idea. "Not at all. They are merely suspended within the moment I captured them in, just before I opened the door. They will remain as such until I release them, unaware that any time has passed or that we ever left the room."

"What if someone finds them like that?" Nieloch asked anxiously.

"The spell I used has a ranged effect that will capture anyone who is not shielded as you were. If someone draws near, they will also be held until I release them. The spell does have limitations though. It would be best if we hasten in our task to avoid less manageable complications."

Nieloch quickened his pace to a slow jog, uncertain if the old man would be able to keep pace with him. Looking over his shoulder after a few moments, he saw that Czarstostryx was right on his heels and appeared to be using little effort to keep up, so he increased his pace. Excitement filled him as they ran along the dimly lit corridors. They would reach Glithnie, soon!

The pair made their way down several long hallways and winding corridors into a somewhat neglected part of the palace. The torches that were lit were few and far between, but the prince had no difficulty navigating. He had grown up in the palace after all, and recently, he had been spending most of his time with Glithnie, so the route leading to where she was being kept had become ingrained in his mind. As the entrance to her chamber appeared in the closing distance, his heart leapt at the thought that she would finally be set free from the curse that held her mind captive.

Nieloch's hand trembled as he opened the door, fearing he was already too late. Glithnie had wasted away so badly, and he knew time was running out. She was sitting in a high-back chair in the center of the room when they entered. There was a bed in the corner that appeared as though it had not been slept in. Nieloch explained that before losing her strength, Glithnie had constantly paced the room with a vacant look in her eyes. She was unable to sleep and there had been no way to soothe her. Eventually, hunger, dehydration, and exhaustion took their toll, and she collapsed in the chair, continuing to stare blankly at the invisible horrors in her mind.

Czarstostryx moved past Nieloch to kneel before Glithnie. He studied her closely for several moments, saying nothing. Nieloch's breath slowed to a halt as he watched. Czarstostryx reached out slowly and gently cradled her face in his hands, looking intently into her eyes. Then, he spoke her name.

To the prince, the outlander's voice was quiet, but to Glithnie's perception, it was something different altogether. From out of nowhere she heard her name booming like thunder, overwhelming her mind, shocking her senses as if she had been plunged into ice-cold water. The sound of her name continued to resonate like the rumbling of a passing storm. Her eyes began to draw focus on a distant point of light in the darkness of her mind. The light grew brighter and larger, calling to her, welcoming her. She felt as if she were weightless, drifting toward the growing brilliance of the beautiful light. As she drew nearer, the light began to coalesce into something familiar—something she recognized...someone...

"Czarstostryx?" Glithnie's voice was a barely audible croak even in the stark silence of the room.

Nieloch could not believe it. Glithnie had spoken!

"Is it you?" Her eyes slowly began to focus on the face of the old man kneeling in front of her.

"Yes, Glithnie. It is I."

"Are we in the forest?" Glithnie's voice was weak, and she seemed dazed. "I do not remember how I got here, but I have found you at last!"

"I'm here too, my love!" Nieloch moved to step from behind Czarstostryx, but the old man held up his hand to stop him.

"Yes, you have found me," Czarstostryx replied gently. "Why have you been looking for me?"

"Time is running out. I had to find you. We need your help...I cannot remember..." Glithnie's voice began to trail off. It seemed the effort of speaking was almost too much for her.

Czarstostryx continued to hold her face firmly yet gently as he moved closer, keeping his eyes intently focused on hers. "What is the last thing you *do* remember?"

"Where is our child Glithnie?!" Nieloch pleaded.

Czarstostryx again shot his hand up to silence the interruption.

Nieloch clenched his teeth in frustration and held his tongue. He could see that the old man held Glithnie in some kind of trance in order to communicate with her, but for a split second he thought he could see a flash of recognition when she heard his voice. He was having a difficult time restraining himself.

"Waiting—I have been waiting for you in the glade. I must find out where you came from. Nieloch—"

"Yes, my love!" the prince responded hopefully, but Glithnie continued, unphased.

"Nieloch and I need to leave the kingdom. We want to start a life of our own for our family…our family—" Her hands involuntarily moved to cover her stomach. "My child!"

"What happened to your child?" Czarstostryx pressed.

Glithnie's breath came faster, and her eyes grew wide.

"The Grohldym have found me—nowhere to hide—surrounding me! Black eyes all around me— silent purpose—clutching at me! Taking me deep into the forest…beyond…"

"Where did they take you Glithnie?"

"Towering canyons—darkness—madness! I am in a nightmare! Strange, green sky—foul air choking me. The smell of decay—overwhelming!"

"What of your child?" Czarstostryx urged.

"My child is coming! The pain is unbearable! I cannot move. I am being held down—controlled. Screaming—my child is screaming! I see him—my baby boy! He has him! He is taking him away!" Glithnie screamed. "My baby is gone! He is gone…He is gone…He is gone…" Glithnie's voice grew weak, and her eyes once again became vacant and glossy.

Czarstostryx called out to Glithnie as he shook her face, but she did not respond. Her head slowly dropped forward, and her breathing grew quiet, and then she breathed no more.

"No! No! No!" Nieloch cried as he pushed past Czarstostryx and swept Glithnie up in his arms. "I am here my love! I am here. Please come back to me!" Nieloch held Glithnie's motionless body closely to his chest, sobbing as he slowly rocked back and forth. "I will find our son. I will bring him back. We can still be a family. Please, Glithnie. Please!" Nieloch turned to Czarstostryx. "Please, wake her!" he begged. "Surely you have the power to bring her back!"

Czarstostryx placed his hand lightly on Nieloch's shoulder, offering comfort to the grief-stricken prince. "It is beyond my skill to help her now. I am afraid that reliving the events she shielded her mind from was too much for her to endure. It is remarkable that she held on as long as she did. She was incredibly strong, and her strength allowed her to reveal much that was unknown. All is not lost. You have a son somewhere beyond the walls of this palace. The birthplace Glithnie described sounds very much like the realm I have been searching for. It is a place I can now unlock with the artifact I have acquired from your father's treasury."

Nieloch grew still and silent for several moments before speaking. "So, there is still hope that our son can be found." He looked sadly upon Glithnie's lifeless face. "Someone took him from her. Who took our son?"

"I cannot say for certain, but my research indicates the possibility of a population existing beyond our realm. Glithnie may have been taken there, though I could not guess what motives would drive those who reside there."

"Our son is out there, somewhere." Nieloch spoke fervently, looking into Glithnie's vacant eyes. "I swear to you my love, I will find our son and take him beyond this kingdom to a place where we can have the life we always dreamed of no matter the cost!" As he finished speaking, he lifted his hand to her face and gently closed her eyes. Then, he clutched her tightly to his chest and began weeping uncontrollably.

Czarstostryx stood silently while the prince grieved. After several moments Czarstostryx spoke. "I must return to my chamber and release the guards from the spell that holds them. Tonight's events will also require that I remove your visit from their minds in order to avoid any meddlesome inquiries. It is within my power to do so, but you will need to move forward under the same pretense. Stay with Glithnie and see to her final rest. I will have no trouble finding the way back. At dawn, I will set out with Skealfa in search of the foreign realm. If your son is there, I will find him and return him to you, but you must leave it to me. The road ahead will be treacherous and filled with danger. It would not serve your son's interests if you were to die attempting to find him yourself. Be here for him when I return." Czarstostryx gripped Nieloch's shoulder re-reassuringly then left the room, leaving the grief-stricken prince sobbing in the chamber.

CHAPTER 15

Skealfa strode purposefully to Czarstostryx's chamber. He had met with King Bardazel moments earlier to discuss a last-minute amendment the king believed would ensure the success of the mission. Skealfa wondered how the outlander would react to the sudden change of plans. He would know soon enough. The sentries outside the chamber saluted Skealfa as he approached.

"How did the night pass?" Skealfa asked.

"It was uneventful," the ranking sentry reported.

"Very good." Skealfa moved to pass by the guard so he could rouse the outlander, but the door to the chamber opened before he could reach it. Czarstostryx stood in the doorway briefly then strode past the sentries to join Skealfa in the hall.

Skealfa did his best to hide his agitation at the outlander's brashness. "The king awaits to confirm all is in order upon our departure," he said gruffly, "let us not delay."

"Of course," Czarstostryx replied smugly. "Lead on."

The two men spoke no words as they made their way to the great hall, but Skealfa did not have to endure the uncomfortable silence for long. Soon, they had reached the throne room. When they entered, Varthaal, Toric, Brilldagh, and Crel stood in the chamber with the king.

Bardazel greeted the outlander with enthusiasm. "Welcome, Czarstostryx. Please join us. I hope you were able to find some rest before the critical journey ahead."

"I am well prepared and admittedly anxious to begin." The outlander said before making a slight gesture with his hand toward the soldiers. "I see our numbers have grown."

"Yes, I have made a small adjustment that should further improve the chances that my interests in this campaign are fulfilled." The king continued, frankly. "Your success on this mission is critical. The addition of these few elite soldiers will certainly be beneficial, considering the opposition you will likely face. These are Lord Skealfa's most capable warriors. Their steel and courage will lend greatly to his own."

"I am sure they will be a great asset to Skealfa, as they were in the wasteland," Czarstostryx replied, with a mocking undertone.

"I hope you will forgive me for altering the arrangement we discussed last night, but I must do what I believe will best serve my people in a matter of this significance."

The outlander nodded his head slightly. "I am quite confident in my ability to achieve the goal before us on my own, but it seems our fates are tethered in this endeavor. I will not oppose your wish to include these men on the path ahead if they are necessary to bolster Skealfa's confidence."

The veins in Skealfa's neck bulged as he restrained himself from reacting to the outlander's obvious provocation. Bardazel quickly intervened to move the matter forward. "Very well then. I know you are all clear to your purpose and anxious to be underway, so hasten on your journey and remember: The future of our kingdom may well be in your hands."

"Yes, highness!" Skealfa and his men replied in unison.

The soldiers bowed before taking their leave, then Skealfa led the group from the throne room. As they moved through the hallways, the elite soldiers fell to the rear while Skealfa and Czarstostryx continued in the lead discussing the course of travel they would use to reach their objective.

"We need to set out in the eastern forest after leaving the city," Czarstostryx instructed. "If there is a route exiting the city that can take us there directly, we should use it."

"There is a seldom used access gate at the far end of the eastern wall near the base of the cliffs. It leads directly into that part of forest," Skealfa replied. "There is also a lookout tower there that will give us a clear vantage point to see if the Grohldym are present before we enter."

"We enter the forest regardless. That is the path we must follow."

"My men and I will follow where you direct, but in matters of military strategy, I will keep my own council," Skealfa replied coldly. "It would be ill-advised to be reckless when dealing with the Grohldym, and I will use any advantage available to thwart them."

"And well you should. They appear to be agitated and restless after the recent attack which is uncharacteristic."

"You have seen them since the attack?" It concerned Skealfa that Czarstostryx had not been forthcoming with this information.

"I have indeed. Before I found you in the wasteland I had need to travel through the forest. Avoiding conflict with them was unusually tedious. They seemed to be actively searching for something."

"That *is* odd." Skealfa considered the outlander's words. "I have scouted the forest many times in the past and they are rarely present after an attack. They seem to do their best to remain hidden."

"It does make one wonder what would cause them to behave in such a way," Czarstostryx replied coyly. "Perhaps it has something to do with the woman's liberation."

Skealfa had not missed the tone in Czarstostryx voice. "Possibly," he replied blandly. "Her return has sparked events unheard of, but who can say what twisted inspirations motivate the Grohldym?" He was certain the outlander was aware of more than he or the king had divulged, and he wondered how it might affect their mission.

The group moved quickly through the streets of the city without incident in the early hour, and it was not long before they reached a remote and somewhat desolate part of the city. The streets were poorly lit, remaining in the perpetual shadow of the towering cliffs. Most of the structures in the area consisted of ancient ruins that melded with the cliffs, making it difficult to discern where nature ended, and man's influence began.

Scholars sometimes visited the ruins to study the structures and conduct research, but it was a part of the city that was mostly uninhabited. Those who did reside there were the unfortunate few who had entered the Forest of the Grohldym and succumbed to its mind-twisting effects. They now roamed the shadowed streets and alleys in squalor, trying to cope with the influence corrupting their thoughts. They could be violent if provoked, but they did not present a real threat to Skealfa and his party. The only reason the king allowed the outcasts to remain among the ruins rather than imprisoning them was because they never ventured from the shadows of the cliffs to cause trouble. It seemed that whatever madness had entered their minds was not willing to release its grip, keeping them close to the ancient ruins.

The watchtower had come into view. Skealfa instructed Toric to hasten to the lookout and see if the Grohldym were stirring. Afterward, he was to rejoin them at the access gate to give an account of what he had seen. As Toric raced from sight, the rest of the party continued down the street toward the rarely used gate. Skealfa was hopeful they would be able to enter the forest with an advantage.

Varthaal moved close to Skealfa. "There is a strange feeling in the air," he whispered. Skealfa had felt it too. The air hung still and silent as if something were watching—waiting.

"Steel yourself," Skealfa said encouragingly to Varthaal as he gave his shoulder a good-natured smack. Then he addressed the rest of his men.

"We have been through trying times in recent days, and it seems that lately there have been strange and powerful forces at work. Whatever lies beyond the wall, we will overcome it, but for the moment, stay focused on the enemy we do know—the Grohldym. We will be entering the woods presently and if they are about, they will suffer our wrath. Be prepared to take your revenge upon them if the opportunity presents itself."

The group approached the gate just as Toric was returning from the watchtower. "What did you see?" Skealfa inquired.

"I saw nothing stirring. The forest is eerily still and silent, but as I peered into the canopy from above, I started to feel—" Toric cut his explanation short. "It was nothing."

"Tell me," Skealfa ordered. "There is too much at stake to leave out any details."

"Of course, Lord Skealfa." Toric continued with some reluctance. "As I scanned the woods from above, the stillness of the forest seemed to grow loud in my mind. The silence was ominous, and I began to feel dizzy and off balance. It felt as if I were being drawn in by an unseen force. I barely caught myself as I somehow began to topple from the tower." Toric noticed the worried look Varthaal shot at Skealfa and the others. "I am fine," he said quickly. "My mind is intact, I assure you. I have experienced the effects of the forest before, but I have never felt its influence so quickly without even being among the trees!"

"Something has changed," Czarstostryx said, causing the party to shift its attention to him as he spoke. "The forest's power has grown."

Skealfa looked at the old man intently. "You have been in the forest recently. What should we expect?"

"You should expect the unexpected. Many things have changed beyond these walls. You have all felt it. I imagine the extent of these changes is far-reaching, affecting things that were once familiar as well as things undiscovered. The time is upon us to see for ourselves. Open the gate."

Skealfa retrieved the key from his belt and inserted it into the lock. He turned it firmly, expecting some resistance from disuse, but it turned easily. He was mildly surprised but said nothing as he pushed the gate open to allow the party to pass through. Czarstostryx went first with the rest following closely. When the last of his men passed through, Skealfa closed the gate and locked it behind him, then he took a position beside the outlander and began scanning the forest. The outlander also scrutinized the mist-filled woods for several moments.

"Is something the matter?" Czarstostryx inquired of the battle-lord, noticing his troubled look.

"Nothing you need to concern yourself with," Skealfa replied roughly. "Lead on."

"As you say." The outlander responded noncommittally, but Skealfa noticed the brief, self-satisfied look that crossed the man's face as they continued in silence, making their way deeper into the forest.

CHAPTER 16

The boy stood frozen with his chest pressed tightly against the trunk of the large, twisted tree. His arms were outstretched in a clinging embrace, his hands gripping the bark tightly. Slowly, he shifted sideways, peering cautiously from his hiding place. The man he had been watching since sunrise was still there, crouching in the shadows of a thicket near the gate from which he had emerged a short time earlier. The boy had only been in this part of the forest on a few other occasions. He typically kept his distance from the large wall that surrounded the city of men, but the Grohldym had been pursuing him relentlessly of late, and he had noticed they seemed to avoid the wall as well which was why on this particular morning, he had chosen to linger near it.

He had been shocked to witness the young man emerge from the small gate and creep into the nearby bushes. The only other person he had ever seen in the forest was the strange, old man he had encountered in the glade. The boy recalled the noticeable, ambient energy that surrounded the old man. He sensed something distinguishable about the young man who was hiding in the bushes as well, but it was not the same; it was not as easy to define. He felt a strong connection to him, like something from a dream. He could not take his eyes off him, and he could not help wondering who he was and what he was doing.

His speculation was cut short by the sound of a sharp click followed by a shrill squeal. The gate the young man had come from was once again being opened. The boy's focus shifted as he adjusted his position to ensure that he was still well hidden. He was astonished that the gate was being opened a second time, and he could not imagine why anyone from the city would have a reason to enter the forest.

His breath caught in his throat. The old man he had seen in the glade was now leading a small group of strangely clad men through the open gate. One of the men was enormous, standing head and shoulders above the rest. He wore a frightening mask that hid half of his face, augmenting his grim countenance. The others appeared formidable in their own right as they moved stealthily in line. All of them except the old man were covered with what appeared to be shiny scales, similar to that of the frightening beasts in the forest, and they all held dangerous looking implements in their hands.

The giant man looked around warily in the manner of a hunting beast. To the boy, he appeared to be akin to the monsters that stalked him daily. As the giant man surveyed the trees, his fierce gaze rested for a moment where he hid. The boy's heart froze in his chest, fearing he had been spotted. After several tense moments, the giant's scrutiny moved past him as he continued to scan the surrounding area.

The boy breathed a cautious sigh of relief having escaped the giant's notice, but his blood turned to ice as he realized the old man was staring right at him! An intrinsic surge of energy flooded his being as he made himself unseen. The instinctive technique had saved him from discovery countless times in the past, occurring during moments of extreme duress. He knew the old man could no longer see him even though he continued to stare fixedly where he hid. He saw the giant exchange words with the old man, but he could not discern what had been said. The old man then motioned to the others and the group began to move cautiously past his position.

After the group departed, the boy turned his attention back to the person hiding in the thicket and discovered that he had crept from his hiding spot; he was now following the group of men into the woods as quietly as he could manage.

The boy's curiosity was piqued, and questions filled his mind. *"Who are these men? What are they doing in the forest? Why is one secretly following the rest?"* He was compelled to find the answers, and since it seemed he had managed to elude the beasts in the woods for the time being, he decided to follow the unusual party deeper into the forest.

The boy kept a fair distance from the young man who trailed the others, but he had no trouble tracking his movement. Even though he was not able to see him most of the time through the thick tangle of trees, he was able to feel his presence. Again, he wondered why the young man should have such an effect on him. He also wondered where all of them were going. It did not appear they were trying to move beyond the forest, but rather pushed deeper into it as they made their way along the cliffs.

They had only traveled a short distance when the boy began to hear voices not far off in the distance. He had lost sight of the young man but knew he was nearby. The voices grew louder as he cautiously approached their source, spotting the group in a small clearing. The young man had been surrounded by the others. The giant seemed angry as he confronted him. The boy crept closer so he could try to understand what was happening.

"It is madness!" Skealfa restrained himself from shouting at Prince Nieloch. "You should have never set foot in this accursed forest. Its influence will surely drive you mad, and if it does not, the perils of our mission will undoubtedly be your end. You are a liability we cannot afford."

It had not taken Skealfa and his men long to realize they were being followed. Since Nieloch had no skill as a soldier, he had quickly been discovered and subdued.

"I will not return to the palace without my son," Nieloch replied firmly. "I would have followed you on your first mission had my father not deceived me and led me to believe that you would find him. Now that I know it was never his intention, I have no choice but to find him myself. I know that my son lives and that he is most likely being held captive in the realm you seek." Nieloch looked at Czarstostryx. "I am sorry. I know you said you would find him, but in a matter this close to my heart, I could not stand idly by!"

Skealfa turned to confront Czarstostryx. "So, you knew of the prince's mad notion to find his missing child?"

"I am as surprised to see the prince here as you are," Czarstostryx replied innocently.

"Wait." Skealfa puzzled for a moment. "King Bardazel chose not to disclose the details of the child at our meetings, and you have never met the prince, so how is it that you came to learn any of this?"

"I knew Glithnie was with child when I saw her last, but I had no idea who the father was at the time or that the child had been born during her capture until this very morning," Czarstostryx replied calmly. "I found it interesting that your king was not willing to share any information on the matter."

"You were under guard last night and never left your chamber. There was no opportunity for you to discover any of this; so, how did you?" Skealfa was losing his patience with the outlander.

"It does not matter, Lord Skealfa!" Nieloch interrupted. "I have learned the truth about my son's disappearance, and I know that the path you travel will lead me to him. I am coming with you to find him no matter the cost!"

"The cost will very likely be your life," Skealfa replied harshly, "but I cannot allow you to meet your demise under my watch, so I will be returning you to the city where you are to wait. You will leave this matter to those who are capable."

"I will not return to the city!" Nieloch shouted.

"Keep your voice down!" Skealfa hissed. "We are in hostile territory."

Czarstostryx cut short the debate. "The time for turning back is gone."

The boy noticed a growing sense of dread as he listened to the men argue. It was a feeling he knew well. The Grohldym were near.

CHAPTER 17

S kealfa's sword moved like a whirlwind amid his enemies. The black blood of the Grohldym sprayed as mist from a crashing wave, covering him from head to toe, running in rivulets down his armor. The elite soldiers fought with equal ferocity as they attempted to repel the advancing hoard which had sprung from the forest without warning. The group barely had time to react as the Grohldym hit them with the force of a landslide, slamming into them headlong. The soldiers fought with their backs to one another, forming a tight circle of flashing steel the Grohldym could not penetrate. Within the protective circle, Nieloch cowered in terror, his faculties overwhelmed by the sudden and violent attack. Czarstostryx stood next to him, creating a barrier spell that would envelope them all as it grew in size and power.

Toric's arm hung limply at his side as he continued to fight; it had almost been completely severed by the slashing claws of the first Grohldym that had crashed through the trees. Everyone had managed to survive the first surge of the attack, but the situation was deteriorating rapidly. The sheer numbers of the

Grohldym would certainly overwhelm them before long.

Czarstostryx continued to focus on the barrier he was creating, and its effects were becoming noticeable to Skealfa and his men. The Grohldym's attacks were falling short. Their slashing claws were no longer reaching them, and the soldiers were finding it necessary to lunge out with their weapons in order to inflict damage upon the creatures. Even as he concentrated, Czarstostryx realized not all the Grohldym seemed interested in pressing the attack. A larger number continued rushing past them into the trees the party had just emerged from—the same trees where he thought he had caught a glimpse of the forest child moments earlier. He had also spotted him hiding near the access gate as they left the city. He was sure it was the same child he had seen in the glade, but the boy looked as if he had aged by several years. It was a matter for future consideration. Now, it was critical that he maintain focus on the barrier spell in order to keep the Grohldym from overwhelming them.

"Stay within the barrier I have created!" Czarstostryx shouted. "The Grohldym cannot penetrate it! Stay close, and no harm will befall you! I will take us safely through the forest!"

"I need no protection from you, outlander!" Toric bellowed in a frenzy. "I will have their blood!" Leaping from the protection of the barrier and into the fray of rushing Grohldym, he was immediately engulfed and lost from sight.

"Protect the prince!" Skealfa shouted, as he too sprang from the circle. Moving like a man possessed, he smashed and carved his way through the swarm, imbued with unusually potent battle frenzy. He reached Toric in a matter of seconds but was too late to save him. Snatching his mangled body from the ground, Skealfa pulled him quickly back into the circle and dropped him within its protective shield. "Get up, Nieloch!" Skealfa roared, roughly pulling the cowering prince to his feet. Once Nieloch had regained his stance, Skealfa lifted Toric's body from the ground with his free hand and turned to Czarstostryx. "Keep moving old man; we are with you!"

"Quickly then, follow me. We still have a great distance to travel before we will reach the passage that I seek."

The group remained in a tight, circular formation as they hurried through the forest along the towering cliffs. The last of the Grohldym crashed against the barrier briefly before falling away and continuing in the direction they had been heading before colliding with the party.

Czarstostryx led the group rapidly through the woods, quickly putting distance between themselves and the Grohldym. When he was sure the danger had passed, he stopped to address the group. "I am going to release the barrier. Prepare yourselves." Skealfa and his men remained much as they had before the barrier had been created; its absence would have little impact on their readiness. Prince Nieloch, however, grew pale as the barrier was dispelled, desperately clutching the ornate dagger he had brought in a white-knuckled grip.

Skealfa regarded the prince with exasperation then turned to Czarstostryx. "What happened back there? Why did the Grohldym relent as we moved on?"

"Let us consider the matter once we have departed from the forest. We dare not allow ourselves to be taken unaware again because of distraction. We are close to reaching our first destination where we can discuss it further in relative safety."

Skealfa agreed, then instructed his men. "Keep the prince close and bring Toric with us. I will not leave him behind for the Grohldym to desecrate." Crel and Brilldagh took Toric's lifeless corpse from Skealfa, sharing the burden between them. "Lead on, Czarstostryx," the battle-lord said.

The group moved swiftly and silently through the forest, their weapons at the ready. Czarstostryx was also poised to react as he led the party through the snarled trees. Nieloch regained some of his composure as they traveled, staying close behind Czarstostryx, grim determination showing on his face. They covered the remaining distance without incident, and after traveling for most of the day, Czarstostryx slowed his pace and raised his hand. "The canyon path lies just ahead."

The others looked uncertainly at the cliffs, unable to see any indication of a path, until Czarstostryx turned abruptly and appeared to walk through the solid wall of stone. As the rest of them drew closer, they could see a narrow split in the cliff, cleaving its sheer face with razor precision. One by one they stepped into the elusive gap, taking a moment to adjust their eyes to the phantom flame Czarstostryx had produced upon entering. Once inside, they could see that the small fissure they had passed through opened above them, creating a canyon that grew wider as they moved further in. The outlander's dull, yellow light cast towering shadows on the walls as they continued on in single file.

It was almost beyond comprehension for Skealfa and his men to be in such a completely foreign place. They had scoured the forest, marshes, and wasteland extensively over the years, confident they had a keen understanding of the world around them. It was strange to find themselves in such surreal surroundings where menacing shadows and towering walls crowded around them. It troubled Skealfa that he had not been able to locate the canyon path himself. It was true the entrance was practically invisible, but he had been very thorough and systematic throughout the years in his exploration, and it seemed to him that he should have been able to find it.

As they moved through the canyons, Skealfa could not help marveling. In all his years he had never seen anything that compared. The sheer magnitude of the towering cliffs was considerably more impressive, due to the narrowness of the ravines they traveled through. Perhaps it was why he noticed a creeping sensation of being suffocated as he continued along. Looking upward, he spotted a crack of light impossibly high overhead that resembled a streak of lightning frozen in a pitch-black sky. It was merely the distant, late-afternoon sun, but its light would not help them navigate within the imposing darkness of the canyon floor; it was also impotent against the bone-chilling cold radiating from all sides. Skealfa and his men were hardened against the elements, so the physical aspects of their surroundings would have a limited effect on them, but he doubted the prince would fare as well.

Again, Skealfa noticed a sense of dread lingering in his mind. It was much like the sensation he had felt before entering the forest. The growing feeling was getting harder to ignore. He turned his attention to the eerie, yellow light radiating from Czarstostryx's walking stick. It appeared to be expanding somehow. He wondered if the old man was creating the effect, then he realized the canyon walls were widening, causing the light to fill a larger space.

Skealfa felt his breathing come easier as the narrow confines of the walls continued to open, revealing a fork in the canyon and what appeared to be a central cavern between the two paths. Czarstostryx stopped at the entrance of the cave, motioning for the party to remain where they were, then he quickly ducked into the interior of the cavern. The group stood closely together in the darkness, straining to see by the small glow of light emanating from the interior of the cave. Within moments, the dim glow was replaced by the warm light of a burning torch as Czarstostryx emerged from the cave. "Let us gather inside," he said. "It is safe."

Nieloch followed Skealfa closely as they entered. Next, was Varthaal, followed by Crel, and finally, Brilldagh who still carried Toric's corpse.

The interior was well-lit by several torches that Czarstostryx had ignited. The walls were unusually smooth as if they had been shaped by skilled hands, but it was hard to know for sure, considering the naturally flowing contours. The group was surprised at how large the cave's interior was. There was no evidence of a traditional ceiling; the walls simply went up and out of sight. The effect created a feeling of vast spaciousness as the darkness overhead consumed the oily smoke rising from the torches.

"Where are we?" Nieloch asked nervously. "Is this where we will find my son?"

"This is merely a staging point along the road we will travel," the outlander replied. "It is a place I have utilized many times in my pursuits."

"How is it that the canyon path which led us here has remained undiscovered?" Skealfa was clearly vexed. "I have entered the forest many times, thoroughly scouting the region where the entrance was located. I should have been able to find it long ago."

"Do not be disconcerted." Czarstostryx seemed amused. "It would have been remarkable for anyone to have ever found this place. The entrance is virtually undetectable even if one *did* know where to look, but that is not the extent of its disguise. The entrance is only present for a brief period during a span of decades, coinciding with the attacks on your city. I learned of it long ago and I have returned at every opportunity to further my understanding of this place."

"So, it is connected to the cycle of the Grohldym." Skealfa considered the explanation. "The complexities of the foul creatures continue to grow. Now, tell me what happened in the forest earlier. Why did they break from their attack and move on?"

"I do not believe the Grohldym were intent on our destruction. I think we were merely obstacles in their path. They are searching for something in the forest— something which has created a disturbance. It may be why their behavior has been so erratic since the recent attack."

"Glithnie!" Nieloch interjected. "Could they be trying to reclaim her?"

"She is not the one they seek," Czarstostryx replied. "The Grohldym are clever; they would know she is not in the forest. No, when they came upon us, they were in active pursuit of their true quarry."

"If you know something, then out with it!" Skealfa was growing impatient with the outlander's evasiveness.

Czarstostryx regarded the battle-lord's anger casually then appeared thoughtful for a moment before speaking. "I have seen a small child in the forest on several occasions since your city was attacked."

Nieloch's eyes grew wide. "My son!" He cried out hopefully. "Is it my son?"

"I cannot say for certain," the outlander mused. "I saw a child in the glade recently. I would have guessed his age to be around seven or eight years. I saw the same child in the forest today, but he appeared to be much older and yet I am sure it was the same child." The outlander looked directly at the prince. "I have considered when your son was born. Logically, he would still be an infant under normal circumstances, but I have also considered the nature of his birthplace. If it *is* your son, he seems to be living in the forest currently, but he may have been born somewhere beyond these canyons, maybe even living there for a time. It is impossible to know what kind of influence it has had on his development." He turned to the others. "You are all familiar with the mind-twisting effects of the forest. You all seem to have a resistance to it, but you would all ultimately be overcome by it if you attempted to linger there indefinitely. My guess is that the child has remained in the forest since finding his way there. It is hard to know if his mind is intact, but I have sensed great power flowing through him. It may be that the forest's effects are actually making him stronger and more capable of survival. Maybe, it is why he has been able to outmaneuver the Grohldym. The effects within these canyons are much more potent than those of the forest, as you will soon discover. Who knows what the realm beyond is like or what kind of effects it will have on us or one who was born there?"

"It must be my son!" Nieloch cried. "We have to find him!"

"I believe he will find us," Czarstostryx replied. "The first place I saw him was in the glade where Glithnie spent time. I only got a glimpse of him earlier when the Grohldym attacked, but I sensed his presence for some time before they struck. He may be trying to find some kind of connection to his being. I think he is curious about us since we are most likely the only ones of his kind he has ever encountered. We do not have much choice in the matter at any rate since the child appears to possess a remarkable ability to disappear at will. I witnessed him vanish when he was startled on both occasions. If the Grohldym have been unsuccessful in capturing him, I doubt we would fare any better even if we knew where to look."

"Our primary objective is to find the hidden realm in any case," Skealfa reminded the group. "We have to push forward and remain focused on the king's directive."

"I agree," said the outlander. "We must move forward and with haste. The effects of the canyons are at least twice as strong as the forest, so our time here must be limited." Czarstostryx turned to Nieloch. "Do not despair young prince. I believe the child will seek us out as we continue. I will make it known if I sense his presence as we move forward, but whether or not we will be able to engage him is another matter entirely."

"I will find a way," Nieloch said with conviction. "He is my son."

"What of Toric?" Varthaal asked Skealfa.

Skealfa regarded Toric's broken body thoughtfully. "We have spared him further desecration from the Grohldym, but we cannot harbor his memory without a pyre. From what I have seen of these canyons there is naught but stone in this region. We will have to leave him here until we return this way."

"There are means to complete your death rites in this very cavern," Czarstostryx offered. "The table of stone at the far end of the cave would serve your purpose."

Skealfa looked where Czarstostryx indicated and saw a section of the cavern wall jutting out from the sheer surface. He moved closer, and upon further inspection, noticed the rectangular section of stone was carved from the wall itself. It was nearly the same size as a typical dining table, except the surface was slightly hollowed out like that of a very shallow bowl. It was easily large enough for a person to lay in.

"It would be a convenient place to leave his body until our return," Skealfa acknowledged, "but without timbers to burn his flesh away, the rite cannot be done."

"Look closer," Czarstostryx said, as he approached with his torch. "See the light's reflection at the base of the table?"

Skealfa noticed the light was being cast back at ground level. Then he realized there was a trench carved into the stone floor encircling the base of the table; it was filled with strange black liquid that flowed slowly.

"What is it?" Skealfa asked, regarding the oozing substance suspiciously.

"It is something like sap from a tree," Czarstostryx explained. "I use it to soak the torches I have stored here. It allows them to burn in much the same manner as pitch-soaked torches would. I have also used it as a larger fire source when needed. The liquid burns hot and does not diminish easily or quickly. The table, filled with this liquid, could serve as a platform to release your fallen comrade from his mortal shell if you choose to use it."

Skealfa hesitated. He had seen many things that were hewn from the stone cliffs throughout the kingdom. The entire palace was woven into the cliffs in a similar fashion. The stone table in the cave was of a comparable design, but he had never seen anything exactly like it before, not even in the ancient ruins of the city. Perhaps it had been created for the exact purpose Czarstostryx had suggested. Maybe it was simply some sort of fire pit. In either case, he did not like the idea of leaving his fallen brother's body behind, potentially trapping the memory of him in a strange and unfamiliar place. Surely, it would be better to set him free while there was a chance to do so since the opportunity might not present itself again. "Bring Toric here," Skealfa said, having made his decision. "Let us see our fallen brother to the flames."

Crel grasped Toric's legs and helped Brilldagh position the body carefully on the stone table.

"I would participate in this honor as well," Varthaal offered.

"Then take the vessel by the wall and fill the tabletop with the liquid," Czarstostryx instructed.

Locating the large bowl against the wall near the base of the table, Varthaal began scooping up the oozing black liquid, transferring it into the recessed area where Toric's body had been placed. Sooner than expected, the hollow was filled.

"You can use this torch to ignite the pyre."

Varthaal took the torch Czarstostryx offered and touched it to the liquid surrounding Toric. Roaring flames shot up instantly, engulfing Toric's body. The group stepped back from the heat of the quickly rising flames that lit up the cavernous walls of the chamber.

Black smoke billowed from the table, roiling into the yawning blackness above which remained strangely unaffected by the brilliant illumination of the flames.

"The fire will burn for hours achieving the end that you require for your death rite, but we cannot linger," Czarstostryx stated. "We still have far to go before we reach the gateway. We must move quickly lest the influence of madness corrupts another's thoughts."

"You think Toric was taken by the madness of the forest?" Skealfa asked incredulously. "He undertook many excursions into the forest over the years and withstood its curse as well as any of my elite soldiers."

"Perhaps in times past, but things are much changed in recent days. Your man did make mention of unusually strong influences affecting his mind as we set out from the city. His frenzied engagement of the Grohldym seemed unusually reckless for a seasoned soldier, would you not agree?"

Skealfa *had* noticed Toric's rapid decline of rationality during the skirmish but there had not been much time to consider it before. He grudgingly admitted to himself that the outlander was probably right, and if Toric had succumbed so quickly, then the same thing might happen to any of the others. "The outlander is right," Skealfa agreed. "We must not tarry." He was amazed that the prince still seemed to have his wits about him. Nieloch had never been exposed to the forest, so there was no way to know what kind of influence it would have on him, but it seemed he was resistant to it, at least for the time being.

"What can you tell us of the dangers that await in the canyons?" Skealfa asked the outlander.

"Not as much as you would hope to hear, but I will tell you what I know." Czarstostryx took a moment to inform the party. "There are Watchers in the canyons. The nature of their being remains a mystery to me, so I cannot say for certain if they are dangerous. Throughout my time exploring the canyons they have never molested me or revealed any hostile intent. I have never gotten a clear look at them since they dwell high above the canyon floor nestled in the walls of the canyon's sheer surface somehow. There also seems to be a distant, violent storm high above this realm that is active at times. I have often heard the crashing of thunder throughout the canyons as I have explored, but the source has never manifested near enough to threaten or be identified. The real danger in these canyons is the possibility of getting lost within the labyrinth's twisting turns and deceptive paths. Navigating the maze of pathways has been a painstaking process. It has taken me years to find the gateway that is hidden within these towering corridors. I have carefully mapped the course we must travel, and it has become etched in my mind. You need not fear losing your way if you stay with me, but we must hurry."

Skealfa turned to the prince. "Stay close and do not fall behind. We must not fail in this endeavor."

"I am here for my son, and I will not fail him," Nieloch said resolutely. "Lead on, Czarstostryx."

The group moved from the cavern as the raging fire continued to consume Toric's body. Emerging from the cave, they were cast once again into the frigid darkness. Czarstostryx produced his phantom flame, bathing the party in its eerie glow. "This way, quickly!" he directed, as he began jogging up one of the corridors near the cave's entrance. Prince Nieloch was close at heel, followed by Crel, Brilldagh, Varthaal, and Skealfa.

Czarstostryx moved deftly though the canyon labyrinth with unfaltering precision. Since discovering the tower, the route leading there was now seared into his mind, never to be forgotten. The group maintained the brisk pace the old man set, being sure to stay within close proximity of his guiding light. Nieloch felt a mixture of fear and excitement coursing through him as he strained to see beyond the light of the phantom flame, hoping he would see his son, hoping they would reach their destination without encountering the mysterious Watchers, hoping none of them would lose their mind.

Suddenly, a thunderous booming began to resonate loudly throughout the walls of the canyons, startling Nieloch and causing Skealfa and his men to pause momentarily. It was impossible to tell which direction the sound had come from as it echoed all around them. They quickly doubled their pace and closed the distance to Czarstostryx.

"So, this is the storm you spoke of?" Skealfa asked.

"It is," the outlander replied.

"If there is a storm brewing overhead, I would imagine these narrow canyons would be prone to flash floods. That could be a problem for us. Has there ever been rain when the thunder comes?"

"I have never witnessed such a thing. It seems the impact of the elements high above does not influence these lower regions. Notice the stagnation of the path we travel. There is no evidence of wind or rain within the depths of these corridors. Everything here is still and unchanging. I am not sure what causes the thunder, only that it occurs sometimes."

"Strange," Varthaal muttered.

The group continued without incident for several hours. Occasionally, the thunderous crashing interrupted the sound of their heavy breathing as they ran through the canyons.

"The thunder grows louder as we travel," Skealfa observed, raising his voice to be heard. "It sounds as if it is coming from just around the next corner."

"It is much louder than I have heard it before." Czarstostryx stated, as a matter of fact. "Perhaps we will discover its source on this journey, but now, we have almost reached our destination. At the end of this corridor the tower awaits!"

BOOM! BOOM! BOOM!

The sound was deafening. Everyone froze in their tracks.

"What *is* that!" Nieloch cried out, holding his hands tightly over his ears.

"It sounds as if the storm is upon us, but I see nothing!" Crel exclaimed.

Czarstostryx peered upward. Skealfa's eyes followed the old man's gaze. He could barely make out a strange outcropping on the sheer face of the canyon wall a stone's throw from the canyon floor. Czarstostryx raised his walking stick high overhead, tracing a pattern in the air. The phantom flame began to grow brighter, illuminating more as its light crept further up the walls. Skealfa could see that there were more protrusions above them as the light continued to penetrate the darkness. The shadows cast by the climbing light gave the impression that the outcroppings were moving. Skealfa quickly realized it was not just the shadows that moved.

"Run!" Czarstostryx shouted. "The Watchers are upon us!"

CHAPTER 18

The booming, crashing strikes shook the canyon walls all around the group. Czarstostryx quickly cast his barrier spell and began running at full speed down the corridor with Nieloch on his heels.

"Be ready!" Skealfa yelled to his men. "They attack from above!"

The movement of the Watchers was almost too rapid to follow as they descended in a blur of speed. The creatures ricocheted between the walls, closing the distance in scant moments. Skealfa barely had time to raise his sword to block the hulking figure that hit him at full force. The power of the impact sent him reeling, slamming him against the opposite wall, knocking the wind out of him as he crumpled in a heap.

Varthaal dove across the narrow pathway, barely avoiding the crushing impact of another. Brilldagh reacted without hesitation to his attacker as well, but the unnatural speed of the creature prevailed over the seasoned warrior's guard. Crel rushed to aid Brilldagh but was struck from behind and driven to the ground.

Skealfa could not see the attack on his men clearly as he sprang back to his feet, sword in hand. It looked to him as though Brilldagh had been run through with a spear of some kind as the creature propelled itself between the walls. As Crel moved to intervene, he too was struck by one of the fast-moving creatures. Skealfa only had a moment to catch a glimpse of the beast from behind as it engaged Brilldagh. It seemed to have impaled and pinned him against the wall. His blood sprayed everywhere as the beast paused momentarily, holding him fast. Crel had managed to get back to his feet and rushed to attack the beast that held Brilldagh, but in the next instant, the Watcher sprang from the canyon floor and launched itself back to the wall it had come from, still grasping Brilldagh's body. Then, it leapt back to the opposite wall, higher than before. Again and again, it repeated the process. The shock of the impact echoed loudly as it climbed.

Skealfa quickly returned his attention to his own assailant, slashing at it viciously with his sword, but the creature sprang back too quickly for his blade to reach. The Watcher braced itself against the far wall, resembling a pile of broken tree branches that had been carelessly thrown into a corner, but as the creature prepared for another attack, Skealfa could see it clearly. It was massive, easily as large as one of the Grohldym, but it had the characteristics of a spider. He could see that it crouched on unusually long, heavily muscled legs that had spear-like tips. He counted at least six limbs, but it was hard to know for sure. Amid the tangle of legs, he saw the head of the beast which seemed to be tightly connected to its torso. Its multiple eyes glistened menacingly in the fading light. There appeared to be a pair of small arms below the row of eyes; it was possible they were some sort of mandibles like those of the Grohldym, but they were much larger.

Skealfa only had a moment to register what he was seeing before the creature launched itself over his head, crashing into the wall behind him. Sparks of light flashed from the spear-tipped legs as they were driven like javelins into the solid rock, attaching the Watcher firmly. As soon as it hit the wall, it sprang back to the other side, higher still. Over and over, it bounded between the walls until it was out of sight far overhead.

Skealfa scanned the dimly lit corridor as the Watchers withdrew, trying to locate his men. He had seen Brilldagh slain, but he had lost track of Crel when forced to confront his own assailant. There was no sign of either of them, but the amount of blood dripping from the canyon walls bespoke of violent ends for both. He raced to where Varthaal crouched and snatched him up by the arm, pulling him along and continuing at a dead sprint. Varthaal quickly regained his footing and fell into stride with Skealfa, and the two rapidly closed the distance on Czarstostryx and the prince.

As they sprinted down the corridor, they heard the thunderous clatter begin anew, hailing the descent of the Watchers. The speed at which the creatures dropped from the heights was practically a free fall as they gained momentum, springing back and forth between the canyon walls. They would be upon them again at any moment.

"Keep moving!" Skealfa shouted to Varthaal as he skidded to a halt and turned back. "I will do what I can to slow them!"

Varthaal stopped and took a position beside Skealfa. "I will stand with you!" he protested. "We will have a better chance if we work together!"

"No! I will face them alone. If I fall, you must continue on your own and complete the mission. Do not falter. You must accompany the outlander. Stay with him and keep the prince safe. Now, hurry!" Skealfa roared.

Varthaal had no desire to leave his commander's side, but he obeyed Skealfa's order nonetheless. Turning, he continued racing toward the light of Czarstostryx's phantom flame without looking back. As he fled, he could feel the impact of the Watchers as they hit the ground just behind him. He was barely ahead of their attacks but managed to make it safely to the protective barrier, joining Czarstostryx and the prince.

"Just around this bend and we will be there!" Czarstostryx shouted above the earth-shaking noise as he ran.

Varthaal risked a quick glance over his shoulder hoping to find Skealfa, but there was no sign of him.

The three continued to race around the final curve of the corridor which began to widen, opening into a huge canyon. By the light of Czarstostryx's phantom flame they could see a towering structure looming before them. As they drew closer, the sounds of pursuit began to diminish. Nieloch and Varthaal looked up in awe as they beheld the massive tower rising before them, obscured by darkness.

Czarstostryx slowed his pace as they reached the tower. "The Watchers should not be able to follow us here, and it sounds as though they are withdrawing into the canyons."

"Where is Skealfa?" Nieloch asked, clearly alarmed by his absence.

"He fell back to slow the Watchers so we could escape," Varthaal explained as he searched the darkness concealing the receding enemy, hating that he had left Skealfa behind. He knew he had done his duty as ordered, but he could not help the feeling of shame growing inside him.

"Should we go back?" Nieloch seemed hesitant about revisiting the narrow canyon.

"No." Varthaal replied bitterly. "We cannot prevail against them. "Skealfa's final command was that I escape, see to your safety, and complete the mission. His sacrifice will not be in vain. We must keep going." Varthaal regarded the tower warily before addressing Czarstostryx. "What is this structure?"

"This is the tower I have recently discovered. It is where we must go in order to reach the unknown realm."

"Lead on then," Varthaal directed, noticing Nieloch's look of apprehension as he did. He understood how the prince felt but kept his concern masked with confident resolve.

Czarstostryx continued guiding them around the base of the massive tower. The narrow canyon they had fled was quickly lost to sight, and the sound of the Watchers grew faint. Once they were halfway around the structure, Czarstostryx slowed his pace, approached the tower, and stood directly in front of it. Nieloch and Varthaal could not see what Czarstostryx did next, but suddenly, a large doorway materialized in the tower wall, gaping darkly before them.

"The gateway to the hidden realm lies within," the outlander stated. "This is where we will enter, but you must remain here for a moment." Czarstostryx entered the darkness of the tower and raised his staff high overhead. He spoke several words in an unknown language and began to trace a pattern in the air with his phantom flame. The yellow glow of the flame began to shimmer, then it changed into a radiant blue color. The vibrant light began to grow brighter, permeating the walls around him until they began to radiate with their own azure illumination. After finishing the incantation, Czarstostryx turned and invited the others to enter with a sweeping motion of his arm.

Prince Nieloch regarded the glowing interior with uncertainty as he stepped across the threshold. Varthaal entered behind him, keeping a watchful eye on their strange new surroundings.

Once they were all inside, Czarstostryx moved back to the doorway and uttered more peculiar words. He then extinguished the phantom flame and addressed the pair. "It seems the mystery of the ever-present storms and the nature of the Watchers has been revealed at last, exposing the two as one. It is most unfortunate that this revelation has come at the loss of three valiant warriors, but their sacrifice was not in vain. Indeed, it was because of their fearlessness that we three were able to reach this place."

"Lord Skealfa was the greatest warrior our kingdom has ever known." Varthaal seemed shaken as he spoke. "I cannot believe he has fallen. Do we even have a chance of succeeding without him?"

"The path that lies ahead is unknown to me," Czarstostryx replied. "When I spoke to your king, I gave no assurances that any of you would survive if you accompanied me. It is a fact that is now painfully obvious. I am confident that my own skills will allow me to endure until the end of this journey, but if either of you hope to live through this, you must heed my words." He looked sternly at Nieloch as he finished speaking.

"I will do as you say," Nieloch replied, abashed. "It was reckless of me to attach myself to this party with no regard to how my actions would affect its other members. I am truly sorry, Varthaal, for my part in the loss of your fallen comrades."

"It is a soldier's duty to protect the kingdom and the royal house whether it is serving the king's interests or fighting to save a life in the wilds. We all knew the risks and gladly accepted them. Do not trouble yourself overmuch, highness. They met their end in glorious battle. It is all a soldier can hope for."

Nieloch nodded solemnly then took a moment to take in the surroundings. "What is this place?"

"It is what I have sought for most of my life," Czarstostryx answered. "I was aware long ago that there was something powerful hidden within these canyons. It was this tower I sensed. It is a gateway to a hidden realm. I have carried the key to unlock the tower for many years, unsure of its purpose until recently. It is what guided me here and allowed me to open the door to gain access just days ago, but I was only able to scratch the surface of what lies within these walls. I learned that a second key would be required in order to go deeper inside. I now possess that key, and I believe it will unlock a clear path to a hidden realm where a source of power beyond anything I have encountered awaits. It is a power I mean to control." He looked intently at Nieloch. "I also believe the path leads to the location that Glithnie spoke of where your son was born and subsequently abducted; if it does, it will prove that a link between the two realms exists." Czarstostryx then directed his words to Varthaal. "The possibility certainly serves the king's desires. This could be a passage beyond your kingdom that does not require traveling through the wasteland—something that has proven to be an impossible feat. It is the mission that was given to Skealfa—a mission you can still complete."

"What must be done to reach this place?" Varthaal asked eagerly.

"When last I was here, I gained knowledge that the key I recently acquired from the king's treasury would allow passage beyond what has been discovered so far." Czarstostryx continued in grave tones. "I am not clear on what to expect once the second door is unlocked. For your own safety, I advise both of you to remain here while I go into the next chamber and unlock it. If it seems reasonably safe to proceed, I will return, and we will move forward together."

"If I am to complete my mission, it is imperative that I remain with you at all times," Varthaal responded emphatically. "Should some unexpected tragedy befall you, I must be present to be able to give an account and continue on. Lord Skealfa was very clear on that point. We were all willing to lay down our lives to succeed in this endeavor, and as you have witnessed, my brothers made that sacrifice. I will not fail them."

"So be it. You have chosen to follow me into the perilous unknown, and I will respect your decision to do so. Perhaps your sword will prove to be a valuable commodity in what lies ahead." The outlander turned to the prince. "Nieloch, you will remain here for the time being until we know the way is clear. I will have no argument on the matter. You ignored my instruction to remain in the palace, believing your oath to Glithnie would somehow protect you through the perils we have faced, but the truth of the matter is that I have ensured your survival with my skill. Heed me now and stay where you are. I will need all of my focus when opening the next door. I will not be able to make considerations for anything beyond that critical moment. If you truly wish to see your son, then you must do as I say this time."

"I promise, I will do as you ask," the prince replied sincerely. "I was overcome with emotion when I set out to join you, and I have seen the consequences of my actions. My eyes have been opened to the perils of this journey, and I understand now that my best chance of seeing my son will be realized through your guidance. I will not act against your wishes again."

"Let us hope for your own sake that you do not," Czarstostryx said firmly. "Come, Varthaal. Remain close to me as I unlock the next barrier." Czarstostryx and Varthaal passed through a large archway near the entrance that led to the central portion of the massive tower. The area inside was a vast courtyard filled with eerie, blue light. Czarstostryx strode with purpose toward the center of the huge expanse. Varthaal looked around as he closely followed the outlander, feeling exposed in the open courtyard.

When Czarstostryx reached the center of the expanse, he stopped and knelt on the floor. Reaching into his robes, he withdrew the artifact he had brought from the treasure hold. He took a moment to position it carefully in his hand. Then, he held it out and violently slammed it into a barely visible opening in the floor. Varthaal noticed there was blood on the old man's hand, and on the floor, afterward. He surmised the force of impact and the sharp edges of the artifact had caused the injury. Czarstostryx said nothing as he stared intently at the spot where he had driven the key. A low, rumbling sound began to grow from deep beneath them, and the floor directly behind the bloody handprint began to drop away, one section at a time. The progression continued deeper into the floor becoming a stairwell that plunged into unknown depths. Czarstostryx quickly got to his feet and began his descent, followed closely by Varthaal.

Nieloch strained his eyes when the two men were lost from sight, trying to see what had become of them from the alcove near the entrance where he had been instructed to remain. It was as if they had simply melted into the floor and vanished. His first impulse was to race after them to see what had happened, but he forced himself to calm down and resist the reckless impulse, knowing that if he were to have any chance of finding his son, he must do as Czarstostryx had commanded. Maintaining his position, he continued to stare intently at the spot where the two had disappeared.

CHAPTER 19

Czarstostryx's heart raced as he descended the stairwell. After so many years of studying, searching, and preparing, he was finally within reach of a source of power worthy of his ambition. Upon his first visit, he heard the voice of the tower's master describe the details of the intricate rituals that would have to be completed in order to unlock the path ahead. The voice promised that if he succeeded, there would be power bestowed upon him, so vast in its magnificence, it would rival that of a god. The voice had been somewhat vague about the exact nature of the promised power, but it assured Czarstostryx that all would be made clear once the rituals had been successfully completed and all the doors had been unlocked.

The nature of the rituals to be performed were extreme, but Czarstostryx's hunger for knowledge and power was all consuming, fueling his desire to achieve the status of a god, and he was more than willing to do whatever was required to achieve that end. The time had come at last to prove his commitment to the unseen voice that guided him.

Having reached the bottom of the stairs, Czarstostryx stepped to one side, allowing Varthaal to join him at the bottom level. They stood in a small chamber that was illuminated by the same blue light filling the tower above. The room was at least five times wider than the narrow stairs leading to it and only spanned a dozen or so paces to the far wall. It was empty except for a slightly hollowed out, rectangular table carved from the stone of the wall itself.

"The stone table is the same," Varthaal stated with a hint of curiosity in his voice. "It is the same as the one in the cave that we used for Toric's pyre."

"It is similar, but its design is for a different method of sacrifice," Czarstostryx replied, as he quietly positioned himself directly behind Varthaal.

The menacing tone of the outlander's voice instantly filled Varthaal with a sense of impending peril, and he knew something was amiss. He instinctively unsheathed his sword and spun around to confront the old man but was instantly seized by an unseen force that stopped his movement and held him fast. Czarstostryx's spell was cast at the same moment Varthaal sensed danger and quickly immobilized him; he now stood as a statue with his sword at the ready, unable to move.

Varthaal's feeling of dread coalesced into cold fear as the outlander stepped nearer with a twisted grin on his lips and removed the sword from his frozen grip. Without a word or hesitation, Czarstostryx swung the sword with as much force as he could muster, cleaving Varthaal's sword arm at the shoulder. Varthaal watched in horror as his arm fell to the ground. The pain of the blow was undiminished, but secondary to the shock of the moment. Frozen where he stood, he was unable to defend himself from the unexpected attack.

The outlander raised the sword and swung it again, removing the other arm cleanly at the shoulder. Blood jetted across the chamber in opposite directions, saturating the walls. Varthaal was compelled to cry out in agony, but no sound would escape his lips. It seemed all of his faculties were locked, except for his perception. Somehow, he was able to follow the grizzly scene with focused clarity. Czarstostryx reaffirmed his grip on the sword and raised it over his head. Using all his might, he brought the sword down in a vicious arc. The precision of his swing resulted in the swift removal of Varthaal's left leg at the hip.

Varthaal toppled to the floor, landing heavily on his side. He lay helpless, looking directly at the feet of the old man. He watched Czarstostryx side-step, then he felt the excruciating pain of another well-aimed strike as it dismembered his other leg. At that moment, he felt the invisible bonds release him. He was able to move again, but with no arms or legs it was as if he were still being held captive. Aghast, he considered the deranged mechanics of his demise.

Varthaal had experienced vicious battles in his life. The carnage he had witnessed and dealt were familiar aspects to a soldier, but he was bewildered by the violent and unexpected turn of events. Fear began to take hold of him. He felt powerless and alone. The unusual surge of emotion conflicted with a lifetime of strict discipline and conditioning. In anger, he pushed the weakness from his thoughts. Struggling to maintain consciousness despite massive blood loss, he focused on the outlander standing above him holding his blood-drenched sword. A sickening realization assaulted his mind; he would not receive a warrior's death. Instead, he would die at the hands of a vile betrayer! Filled with rage, he used his last breath to shout in defiance of a bitter fate as the final fall of his sword removed his head from his body. The room spun before his eyes momentarily, then darkness took him at last.

Czarstostryx placed the sword on the floor and methodically moved forward with the ritual. Lifting the bloody torso, he placed it upon the stone table, positioning it lying chest down with the shoulders facing the stairwell behind him. He continued the grizzly process by collecting the arms and legs and arranging them precisely with the torso. Lastly, he collected Varthaal's head and placed it atop the carefully organized pile. He moved quickly to allow as much blood as possible to collect in the table while he stabilized the pieces of the body in the manner that had been described to him. When he was sure everything was properly organized, he retrieved the sword from where it lay and stood before the altar. Raising the sword high above his head with the blade pointing downward, he drove it forcefully through the severed head and torso. The sound of steel striking the stone table should have been greatly muffled by the blood and flesh mounded upon it, yet its impact rang out as clearly and loudly as the tolling of a massive bell. The ritual was complete.

Once again, a low rumbling came from deep within the bowels of the tower, loudly resonating all around him. Czarstostryx could barely contain his excitement as he waited with great anticipation, unsure of what to expect. The voice had only told him that once the ritual was completed, the path would be revealed.

Suddenly, the table shifted and began to sink slowly into the floor. When it reached ground level, it began to tilt backward into the wall which opened to receive it. The wall behind both sides of the table shifted as well, revealing two panels that mirrored the size and shape of the table. The two panels began to rotate in the opposite direction—out of the wall. Czarstostryx's eyes remained transfixed on the shifting components. As the table tilted past the halfway point, Varthaal's body slid from the table and seemed to be consumed by the gaping recess. As the other panels continued their progression, Czarstostryx recognized what he was seeing. The center altar was being replaced by two others.

Once the final positioning of the two new altar tables had been achieved, he noticed something in the wall where the center table had retracted. His heart sank when he saw a small hole cut with precision in a shape he recognized. It was another keyhole that was akin to the ones he had used to unlock the tower and open the stairwell, but the key to unlock it was not in his possession; it was in King Bardazel's treasure hold.

Czarstostryx continued to wait as silence fell on the chamber. His frustration grew with each passing moment. He had expected an open door or passage of some kind, not another lock! He had been promised that he would be shown the way to a source of unlimited power! His rage began to boil as he continued to wait in the silent room, hopeful that the way might still be revealed, but all remained still and silent. The way forward, it seemed, would require the acquisition of yet another key and further sacrifice, but why had he not been told of the need for the additional key? He had seen it in the king's treasury and could have employed his abilities to simply take it at that time.

Czarstostryx began to shake with fury. He had come so far, doing all that was required; when would he finally be able to claim what he had been promised? He forced himself to calm down so he could think clearly and consider what it all meant. As his breathing slowed, he began to work it out in his mind.

If he had known of the need for the additional key, he could have taken it by force, but that would have meant escaping the castle and leaving on his own. It had been necessary for the soldiers to accompany him so he could make the required sacrifices. As it turned out, it appeared he would need two more. He considered where he would find them. Nieloch alone was with him in the tower, so he would have to acquire another. He surmised that it could not be a random victim. The voice had been very specific about the requirements so far. Varthaal had been chosen because he burned Toric's body, which was the first sacrifice. The kill was made by the Grohldym, so the true nature of sacrifice had been disguised to the others. If Skealfa had known what was really going on, he would have been a problem; in fact, if Skealfa had made it to the tower, he would have been an obstacle, but the Watchers had taken care of the issue.

It seemed the entity behind the unseen voice was playing an active role in events. Czarstostryx reasoned that it must have dominion over the Watchers and the Grohldym, guiding their actions for his own purpose. He had always sensed the impressive nature of the power he was pursuing, but as he began to unravel the machinations of recent events, he began to truly realize the magnitude of that power and the strength of the one who wielded it. Who, or whatever was behind the voice, commanded a vast source of power. It certainly possessed the ability to deliver what it offered.

CHAPTER 20

Nieloch was terrified when he saw Czarstostryx rising from the center of the courtyard like a fiend from the abyss. His robes were covered in blood, and the heavily soaked garments left a trail as he walked across the courtyard toward him. The prince knew something was wrong when he noticed Varthaal was not with the outlander, and he began to panic. Czarstostryx held up his hands in a gesture of reassurance as he drew near.

"What happened?" Nieloch gasped.

"Do not be alarmed," Czarstostryx said calmly. "You are not in peril. There was a devious mechanism in the chamber we entered—a hidden trap placed by the keeper of this tower. The entity who resides within these walls does not welcome armed men into the inner sanctum it seems. Apparently, Varthaal was perceived as a threat. I was unable to save him."

"Did you not know of the danger?" Nieloch asked, clearly shaken.

"I was aware of the risk as was Varthaal, but he was unwilling to heed my warning. You saw how he refused to let me enter the chamber without him. I was uncertain what we might encounter, and I did what I could to protect him from harm, unfortunately the ingenuity of the trap was beyond my skill to overcome. It is a tragedy to have lost another valued member of our party—a tragedy indeed, to have lost all of the valiant soldiers whose sacrifices made it possible for us to get where we are."

"And where is that?" a note of hysteria crept into Nieloch's voice as he looked around frantically. "We are far from home in a hostile land, and my father's most valuable and skilled warriors have perished. How can we hope to find my son now? Surely, we cannot proceed without their help."

"I am inclined to agree with you. Moving forward into the unknown without additional forces could prove disastrous. I think it would be wise to return to your city and beseech your father for further aid before we venture ahead."

"But what of my son? If we are close to finding him, can we afford to lose time gathering reinforcements?"

"I do not believe has moved beyond this tower. The gateway beneath the courtyard was still sealed when Varthaal and I entered. Unless he gained passage some other way, which is unlikely, he is probably still in the forest. In fact, there is a good chance we will cross his path upon our return to the city, and if we do, I will make sure he does not elude us again. I promise, we will find your son."

"Thank the heavens! That is all I have been hoping for throughout this entire ordeal." Nieloch's voice was filled with relief. "Do you think we can make it back to the city unharmed without Skealfa and his men?"

"I will be able to keep us safe," Czarstostryx assured him. "Since it will just be the two of us, I can utilize a smaller protective barrier that will require much less effort to maintain. We will also attract less notice than before. Do not worry overmuch. We will manage, but we do need to hurry back. The effects of the canyon and the forest will continue to grow more oppressive the longer we remain under their influence, and we still have a great distance to travel before we are free of it. I must admit, I am amazed at your resistance so far."

"It has not been easy," Nieloch confessed. "Keeping the terror in my mind at bay is a constant struggle, and I have not been entirely successful as you have witnessed. The overshadowing dread invading my thoughts continues to grow. I am anxious to be gone from this place, but I am resolved to find my son, and I will not succumb to fear."

Czarstostryx gave a nod of approval. "Let us get moving then. Stay close and stay silent. I will let you know if I sense your son as we travel. I may need your help to engage him, so be prepared."

As the two men exited the tower, the illumination within faded into darkness. Czarstostryx brought forth his newly altered phantom flame and took a moment to scan the perimeter of the tower by the light of its cold, azure radiance. All was quiet.

"We need to move quickly," Czarstostryx said softly.

The two set out at a brisk pace around the massive tower toward the mouth of the canyon labyrinth. Once they returned to the winding path, they traveled without pause along the canyon floor, listening intently for sounds of false thunder. To their relief, the only sounds they heard were those of their own footfalls and labored breathing.

The old man deftly navigated through the seemingly endless network of twisting turns and forks in the path until they reached the large cave where Toric's body had been burned. They began to breathe easier as they slowed their pace, relieved they had made it so far without incident.

"Let us take a moment to recover our strength within the cave and consider the path that still lies ahead," Czarstostryx suggested.

"Yes, please!" Nieloch gasped. "I could use a moment."

As they entered the cavern, their eyes were drawn to the back of the cave where Toric had been consumed by the fire.

"How can this be?" Nieloch asked in disbelief. "There is no sign of Toric's body being burned. It appears exactly as it did when we first arrived. Should there not be some sign of the fire or Toric's ashes?"

"I would have expected as much, but things within these canyons are far from typical."

"Maybe it did not happen at all. Maybe this is all some kind of bizarre dream." Nieloch slumped against the wall, clutching his head. "I feel like I am losing my mind!"

Exhaustion and prolonged exposure to the forest and canyons were taking their toll. Czarstostryx knew he had to keep Nieloch from unraveling if his plan was going to have any chance of success; never mind the fact they still had to make their way through the forest.

"The events of the last few days have been more than enough to make any man question his reason, but you have persevered," Czarstostryx said reassuringly. "You have shown incredible strength for the sake of your son. You will need to rely on that strength as we continue, but now you must rest, briefly." The old man guided Nieloch away from the altar table and helped him to the floor. As the prince sat leaning against the wall, his head began to droop heavily to his chest. "Do not fear for your safety while we are here," the outlander told him. "I will put a protective barrier on the entrance of the cave so nothing can harm us. Take what rest you can."

Nieloch had already begun to draw long, deep breaths as fatigue and mental exhaustion overwhelmed him. Within moments, he was fast asleep...

When Nieloch woke, he looked around bleary-eyed and bewildered. Scanning the dimly lit cavern, he realized he had no idea where he was. His heart began to race as he tried to make sense of his surroundings. He noticed an old man standing near the far wall with his back to him. The old man heard his movements and turned to face him. He immediately recognized the face of Czarstostryx, and all memory of recent events came crashing back into sharp focus.

"I am glad to see you were able to find some rest," Czarstostryx said comfortingly. "You will need your strength as we move through the forest."

"I feel well enough," the prince said, rubbing his eyes. "How long was I asleep?"

"Long enough for me to plot a reasonable course of action to locate your son and implore your father for aid. Let us first discuss how best to find your son. We have found ourselves, for the moment, free from the entanglement of the king's objectives. With no soldiers dogging our moves, we have the opportunity to seek the child in earnest. I think our chances of finding him in the glade are good enough to warrant a visit before leaving the forest, but if we are unable to locate him, we will have to continue on to the city to gather the soldiers. I am fully committed to finding your child as I promised, so once we have the additional forces, we would of course remain vigilant looking for signs of him as we travel back to the tower, but I think it is important that we take full advantage of this chance to seek him out while it is just the two of us."

"I agree wholeheartedly!" Nieloch's enthusiasm was revitalized. "Let us not delay."

Emerging from the cave, Nieloch felt truly optimistic for the first time since embarking on the increasingly perilous undertaking. Locating his son had finally become a priority. He was sure to find him now that the outlander would be able to focus all his attention and skill to that end. He hoped Czarstostryx really would take all the time necessary before returning to his father.

"The outlander has more compassion for my son than his own grandfather," the prince thought bitterly. *"For all his talk about the importance of our bloodline, it clearly only matters when it suits his own purpose!"* Nieloch decided to let his anger fuel his resolve, knowing that he must succeed as this would surely be his last chance to find his son.

Upon reaching the forest, the pair continued to move cautiously, pausing occasionally to allow Czarstostryx opportunities to scan the forest and search for signs of the boy's presence. Nieloch had no idea where the glade was located, but he did not concern himself over it while he remained attentively at the old man's side, searching for signs of his son as well. There was no trace of the Grohldym as they traveled, but the air still hung heavy. Nieloch felt chills run through his body as he observed the eerie stillness of the woods, and he was unable to shake the feeling that they were being watched.

Suddenly, Czarstostryx froze in his tracks, signaling Nieloch to do the same. The old man drew near to the prince and whispered quietly. "The child is close. I can sense his presence near the glade just ahead. See the clearing beyond those trees?"

The prince focused his attention on the area Czarstostryx had indicated—then he saw it. Just beyond the dense canopy of trees where they stood was the cherished glade of his beloved. He marveled at the small clearing that was so out of place in the gloomy woods; it was filled with lush ferns and dazzling sunlight. He also noticed there was a sparkling stream running through it that fed a small pool. Straining his eyes, he tried to spot his son. "I do not see him," Nieloch whispered.

"Nor do I. He may be aware of our presence and could be hiding, but he is near. I want you to go ahead, alone. I think he is curious about you. He may approach if he does not feel threatened. Go to the stream and drink. Relax on the bank and be at ease. I will be watching closely, keeping you under my protection should the Grohldym appear." The prince nodded and began to move forward. Czarstostryx quickly grabbed Nieloch's arm and stopped him. "Do not be alarmed if your son appears to be much older than you expect. Remember, he has developed outside the laws of nature under the influence of the forest and the unknown realm as well. It may seem impossible that it could be your son, but I assure you, it is. I recognize the presence I am sensing as that of the child I have perceived from the beginning." Nieloch again gave a quick nod, then Czarstostryx released his arm, and the prince continued moving forward alone.

When Nieloch stepped onto the tender, green grass of the glade and left the dark canopy of trees behind him, he had to shield his eyes from the brilliance of the shining sun. A warm breeze drifted through the glade, carrying with it the tranquil melody of the quietly flowing stream. As his eyes adjusted to the abrupt brightness, he took a moment to take in the serene beauty of the place. He became overwhelmed with emotion, finding himself within the sanctuary Glithnie had so often spoken of, understanding at last why she had stolen away to be there. The sharp stabbing pain of her loss struck him, but it quickly gave way to a sense of closeness to her in the moment, filling his heart with love and joy.

In his mind, he spoke to his beloved. *"Our son is alive, my love. I will fulfill my vow to you. I will find him."*

CHAPTER 21

The boy's intrigue grew as he watched the young man enter the glade. He had been curious about him since the first time he saw him crouching in the bushes outside the city walls and had been following him ever since. The inexplicable connection he felt toward the man intensified as he observed him standing quietly in the clearing. Prismatic light danced around him as he stood studying his surroundings. The boy felt strong emotional surges emanating from the man that seemed to be creating the visual effect somehow. He had never seen anything like it, and he was captivated by its strange beauty.

After several moments, the man knelt by the creek and drank deeply before settling comfortably on the bank where he appeared content to rest by the serene pool. It was the first time the boy had seen the man alone since he first spied him hiding near the wall. He had considered approaching him then, but the appearance of the soldiers and the strange, old man had stopped him, and when the shimmering beasts attacked, he had to take action to avoid them as well. Fortunately, his ability to elude the creatures had left them bewildered, and he was able to return to his pursuit of the group.

He had followed the party cautiously through the forest and into the canyons, trailing them to a large cave where they left behind the fallen soldier. He noticed a large fire burning within the cavern when they departed but only had a moment to glance inside before continuing in his pursuit of the group. They moved quickly, and he was forced to do the same in order to avoid losing them in the confusing labyrinth. He also had to utilize extreme tactics in order to stay hidden from the old man, so he constantly kept himself shrouded. This had undoubtedly saved him when the rumbling creatures attacked the group from above. He witnessed the assault and watched as two of the soldiers and the giant man were taken into the shadowing heights, yet he continued to follow undaunted. He saw the survivors enter a massive tower where, yet another soldier was left behind. Only the old man and the one he had an interest in remained as they made their way back to the forest, so he continued to follow, hoping to satisfy his curiosity.

He was surprised when the pair separated, and the younger man entered the glade alone. He knew the strange, old man was nearby; he could feel his energy, but for the moment, the other was by himself. He could not understand why he was so compelled to find out who he was, but he had to know! Cautiously, he stepped from the shadows of the forest, slowly entering the glade in front of the man lounging by the creek. The man saw him immediately.

As Nieloch's eyes fell upon the boy, his face was a reflection of awe and deep admiration as he beheld his son for the first time.

The boy was overcome by an intense feeling of affection radiating from the man; it felt like home.

The man rose from the ground, tears of joy glistening in his eyes as he opened his arms in welcome.

The boy felt a sense of familiarity wash over him, putting him at ease as he continued to draw closer.

The boy froze in mid-stride and his eyes bulged in terror as he felt himself being restrained by invisible bonds holding him in an unbreakable grip. Panic filled him as the strange, old man emerged from the shadows of the forest with his hand pointed directly at him. The boy knew the inescapable force was being directed by the old man. Frantically, he tried to vanish, but he could not connect with the energy that had saved him so many times before. He was firmly ensnared as if he were wrapped in chains.

"No!" Nieloch screamed as he rushed toward Czarstostryx. "Do not hurt him! He was coming to me. He wants to know who I am. You need not restrain him. Let me speak to him, please!"

"I will not release him," Czarstostryx replied coldly as he moved closer to the boy. "Not until I know he will not flee. He has been far too elusive to allow him a chance to vanish again. This may be the only way we can ensure interaction with him."

"Perhaps, but if you hold him against his will, it will only frighten him, and he will mistrust us." Nieloch argued.

"Speak to him," Czarstostryx replied. "Convince him not to flee. I will continue to hold him until you succeed."

Nieloch could see the old man had made up his mind. Instead of wasting time arguing, he resolved to put his son's mind at ease. He began walking slowly toward the panicked boy with his hands raised in a non-threatening manner, attempting to calm him with gentle words. "You need not fear," He began soothingly. "We mean you no harm. I have been trying to find you. My name is Nieloch. I know your mother. She is very dear to my heart. I know you were taken from her when you were born. I promised her that I would find you."

The boy had heard the words of men spoken before from a distance, but he had not been able to make sense of anything they had said. Somehow, he was able to understand Nieloch as he slowly approached.

"Your mother's name is Glithnie. She often visited this glade before you were born. It is where she met the man that is with me now. His name is Czarstostryx. He has great and strange powers. He means you no harm. He is holding you so that you may hear my words. We have been trying to find you for days, and he does not want you to leave before I have spoken to you. He was a friend to your mother. He is the reason I was able to find you."

Nieloch was within arm's reach of the boy. His heart overflowed with joy. He had finally found his son! He reached out and gently placed his hand on the boy's shoulder. "The reason I have been trying so hard to find you is because you are my son." Tears began welling up in Nieloch's eyes as he spoke the words.

The boy was able to understand the words Nieloch spoke, but more importantly, he could feel the sincerity and emotion behind them. He knew the man was telling the truth and that his feelings were genuine. The boy understood at last why he had reacted so strongly to this person when he first discovered him. It was his father!

Nieloch saw the terror in the boy's eyes fade; it was replaced with a calm look of understanding. The prince raised his free hand towards Czarstostryx, motioning for him to release the boy.

"Are you certain he will not disappear?" The old man asked.

"He is my son," Nieloch replied harshly. "I will not have him restrained any longer. Release him at once!"

The boy sensed the loyalty and devotion his father felt for him, and he knew that he was not only someone he could trust, but someone who would protect him as well.

"As you say," Czarstostryx replied with reluctance.

With a subtle movement of his hand, the invisible bonds fell away. The boy stood silent for a moment regarding his father. Czarstostryx tensed, prepared to cast the holding spell again if necessary. Then, the boy embraced his father, hugging him tightly. Prince Nieloch returned his son's embrace, holding him closely as tears of joy streamed unchecked down his cheeks.

After several moments, Nieloch released his son and looked into his eyes. "I cannot believe it is you!" he exclaimed. "You have grown beyond belief! Less than one cycle of the moon has passed since you were born, yet here you stand as a fine young man." Nieloch continued to regard his son in wonder, noticing his countenance was more comparable to that of a young man than a boy. His hair was shaggy and unkempt. Grime and sweat covered his face and body. He was somewhat slight yet well-muscled. Despite his filthy appearance, the prince could see that he was quite handsome.

"*Where is my mother. Why was I taken from her?*" To Nieloch's amazement, he could hear the words of his son clearly, but the boy was not speaking aloud. The prince was already baffled by his son's accelerated growth, but he had accepted it in due course, knowing it to be a byproduct of surrounding influences. It appeared those influences had altered his mental capacity as well, increasing it in tandem with his physical development. Nieloch was not overly concerned about the rationale behind it. He was just content to be able to communicate with his son.

"I will tell you all about her and everything I know about what happened to you," the prince assured, "but it will have to wait until we are safely away from this place."

"I see there is an unspoken understanding between you and the boy," Czarstostryx said as he drew near.

"Yes, it is amazing! He understands my words, and he is able to communicate his thoughts directly to my mind."

"Perhaps he will understand my words as well." The boy regarded Czarstostryx warily. "My apologies for holding you against your will. It was extreme, but it seemed necessary at the time. Please know that I mean you no harm, and I will offer my protection as we pass through the forest."

The boy understood the words of the old man but was having a hard time interpreting his sentiment. It was as if his true feelings were obscured like the pebbles beneath the waters of the stream, but he could sense the old man was curious about him and that he was sincere about seeing them safely from the forest. The boy gave a quick nod, acknowledging the old man's intentions.

"Truly amazing." Czarstostryx seemed impressed by the boy's capabilities. "I am sure there are many questions to be answered, but I must insist that we keep moving until we have left the forest behind us."

"Yes, of course," Nieloch replied with enthusiasm. "I am anxious to return to the palace. My father will see that despite his best efforts to hinder my success, I was able to find my son, proving I am not as incapable as he believes."

"I do not think returning to the palace is our best course of action at the moment." Czarstostryx kept his voice low as he began to coax the pair back towards the edge of the forest. "Your father will have little interest in meeting his grandson, and I doubt he will applaud your success in finding him; quite the contrary. He will most likely place blame on you for compromising the mission. I am sure he will be most displeased when he learns of the loss of his soldiers and highly valued battle-lord. From what I have seen of the man, he is relentless in his pursuits, giving little regard to the concerns of others."

"I had hoped to alleviate my father's disapproval, but it seems I always manage to disappoint him, despite my best efforts," Nieloch replied despondently.

"I think we should consider your son for a moment. You have only just found him, which was no easy task. Imagine how the boy would react within the city walls surrounded by strangers. He would vanish in an instant! You may not be fortunate enough to find him a second time."

"True." Nieloch considered the old man's words thoughtfully. "What do you suggest?"

"We will go to my home in the wasteland where you can recover your strength. You will both be safe there, and it will give you and your son an opportunity to become further acquainted without interference. I will devise a plan while we are there that we can discuss further once we are safely beyond the forest. Agreed?"

Nieloch looked at his son, unwilling to risk losing what he had so desperately sought and finally achieved. "Agreed."

CHAPTER 22

Czarstostryx led Prince Nieloch and his son through the forest and into the wasteland without incident, and they arrived safely to his home. Once there, Czarstostryx stayed just long enough to show Nieloch and his son the general layout of his dwelling which was situated in a deep, seemingly narrow, ravine hidden beneath the burning sands of the wasteland. A deep split in the stone-like earth marked the entrance to his home and led down to several cavernous chambers that ran the length of the ravine. The shadowed alcoves were cool and spacious, despite the scorching heat overhead. From the surface, one's gaze would most likely pass without notice over the large, nondescript crack, and Nieloch was amazed the old man had been able to locate it in the featureless terrain. He had not even seen it, until the old man pointed it out when they were mere steps away from the entrance.

The brilliant light of the midday sun streamed through the length of the crack, keeping the majority of the caverns surprisingly well-lit. The outlander showed the prince and his son a place where they could get some much-needed rest, and he also indicated an area in the furthest depths of the ravine where he did his research. Czarstostryx asked that they refrain from going into that part of his home for their own safety. He then presented them with a basket of rice and mushrooms he had stored away and also made an offering of strange looking fish he had salted and hung to dry on lengths of twine. The outlander also pointed out several naturally formed basins that he kept filled with water; one was for drinking, and the other for washing. He invited the pair to eat, drink, and wash themselves.

Czarstostryx disappeared into the furthest caverns while Nieloch began washing away the blood of his fallen companions, and his son tentatively partook of the food that had been offered. After a bit, the outlander reappeared from the shadows in clean robes and joined them to wash the blood from his own face and hands. He told them he was formulating a plan on how they should proceed but that he would need to see how his meeting with the king went before he made a final decision on the best course of action. He informed them that they should expect his return at dawn, then he set out to meet with the king.

Nieloch's son had remained close at his side as they had traveled to the outlander's home. He was very uneasy around the old man, regarding him cautiously whenever he was near. Now that Czarstostryx was gone, the boy seemed much more relaxed. He joined his father who was continuing to wash away dried blood and grime. Nieloch invited him to also cleanse himself, showing him how to soak the cloth with water and ring it out. The prince demonstrated how the moistened cloth removed the dried blood and dirt from his face, offering to do the same for his son. The boy seemed a bit uncertain but allowed his father to wash his face as well.

As Nieloch began to remove the heavy layers of dirt and grime from the boy's face, he was amazed to discover that his son was much closer to manhood than he had first perceived. He began to see his son's features more clearly, noticing there were characteristics of his face that were passed on to him from Glithnie. He had recognized the shape of the boy's striking eyes when he first saw him, but now he detected the same jawline and tilted mouth as that of his lost love. His heart ached as he observed several of her unmistakable qualities reflected in the face of their son. As Nieloch continued to wash away the filth, he was struck by the realization that the boy's hair was not dark brown as it first appeared; it was a golden blond color like that of his mother's vibrant curls. Tears began to stream from Nieloch's eyes as he stopped to appraise his son.

"*What is wrong?*" The boy's thoughts were as clear as words.

"Nothing is wrong, my son. I am simply overcome with joy and awe. I cannot believe I have found you! Looking upon you as a young man makes me feel like I have lost so much time with you. You see, to my understanding, you have not even seen the full cycle of one moon. It is difficult for me to comprehend the nature of your being."

"*Why?*"

"Well," Nieloch began, "normally, the growth of a child takes many years. Looking upon you, one would guess that you have seen sixteen or seventeen winters, but your mother spoke of your birth happening not long ago. You have been in the world for such a short time, but it is obvious that your mind and reasoning have kept pace with your physical development. I wonder if you will continue to age in this way or if it is an effect that only exists in the realm in which you were born."

"*Please tell me of my mother. Where is she?*" The boy interrupted.

"Of course, I am sorry. There is so much to discuss. It is hard to know where to begin. It saddens me to tell you that your mother died recently." The boy seemed troubled to hear that his mother was gone but listened attentively as Nieloch continued. "She was a kind and gentle soul who saw the good in all things even when others could not. I loved her with all my heart. I love her still. She was a child of nature who cherished spending time in the glade where you and I met. It always seemed dangerous and somewhat foolish to me, but she would not be deprived of the time she chose to spend there. Somehow, she managed to avoid trouble in the forest and eventually met Czarstostryx which has ended up being a truly fortunate event since it was with his help that I was able to locate you." The prince paused in reflection. "When your mother and I found out that you were going to be born, we knew we would face challenges, but we were overjoyed at the thought of having a child. We spent hours dreaming of how things could be. Your mother even chose a name for you, confident that you were a boy. 'Mecursto.' It was the name of one of her family's forebearers; she had always been very fond of it. Now that I have found you, I was hoping to call you that, in memory of her."

"*I would like that very much!*"

"Very well then—Mecursto." Nieloch's face beamed with pride as he continued. "As the day of your birth drew near, we hoped to find a place of our own to start our family, and we began devising a way of making it come true, but before our plans could be put into action, the Grohldym attacked, and they took Glithnie."

"*The shimmering monsters in the forest,*" the boy stated flatly.

"Yes, they have long been a plague on our kingdom. When I found out she had been taken, I lost all hope of ever seeing her again. You see, none that are taken by the Grohldym ever return, but Glithnie did! When she came back, you were not with her, and she was not herself. She was unable to speak of what had happened, and her health began to deteriorate rapidly. It was not until the night before I left the city that I discovered you had been taken from her when you were born.

"I do not know exactly where she was taken or who stole you from her or how you ended up in the forest, but I was hopeful that Czarstostryx would be able to find the answers. That was why I secretly joined his party. Now, Czarstostryx seeks to find a way to enter the hidden realm where he believes you were born—the place your mother and I had hoped to find someday." Nieloch noticed a troubled look come over Mecursto's face. "What is it?" He asked.

"*Who is Czarstostryx? Tell me what you know of him.*"

"I really do not know much about him. He is an outlander who is not of my city. He lives here in the wasteland. Your mother was the only one who knew of his existence until recently. I know that he is a learned scholar who possesses vast knowledge and strange powers. Does he frighten you?"

"*I do not know. There is something familiar about him. I felt it the first time I saw him. I sensed energy flowing through him that I recognized but did not understand. I was not able to define what it was. When I saw you hiding in the bushes outside the walls of the city, I felt a similar sensation, but it was much stronger. I am still not certain what it all means. I am curious to find out more about him, but I am not sure if I should trust him. His thoughts are shielded from me. I cannot see his mind like I see yours, so it is hard to know his true intentions. I know he is powerful, and I know that I share something in common with him. I do not understand the nature of it, but I believe he does. I would like to learn more about it."*

"Perhaps he will be willing to enlighten you when he returns from the palace. I have many questions for him myself, but I expect we will not have time for lengthy conversations since we will surely be leaving for the tower soon after his arrival." The prince found himself trying to suppress a yawn. "We should try to get some rest while we can so we will have the strength to make the journey. Let us retire to the sleeping area he showed us."

The two found their way to the cool, shadowed alcove and chose a place to rest. The smooth, contoured stones were surprisingly comfortable, meshing with their bodies as they settled themselves. They were exhausted from the journey and were both on the verge of falling asleep, but they found themselves talking for several more hours before fatigue took its toll, and sleep finally claimed them.

CHAPTER 23

King Bardazel stood in the treasure hold staring blankly at the artifacts. Another restless night was passing slowly as he anxiously awaited Lord Skealfa's return. It had been days since the group departed, and there was still no sign of them. There was no sign of his son either. The prince had vanished that same morning—the morning Glithnie had been discovered dead in her quarters, finally expiring from the trauma she had endured. Bardazel doubted it was a coincidence that his son had not been seen since her death. It was likely he had foolishly set out to find his lost child, despite having been warned against it. He could only hope Nieloch had enough sense to try and join Skealfa's party rather than attempting it on his own, but he doubted that had been the case. Skealfa would have surely returned the prince to the city if he had discovered him.

The king was faced with the real possibility that his only son was either lost or dead. It was a troubling thought. Bardazel had always felt concern over his hold on the throne since he had only one heir, but now that Nieloch was missing, it was a legitimate, looming threat. Without an heir to ascend to the throne, the crown would pass to one of the other noble houses. The laws of succession were rigid and unsympathetic to tragedies that severed a royal line. If his son did not return, the rule of the kingdom would change families for the first time in centuries. He was so close to fulfilling his life's ambition, and now his throne was at stake!

Bardazel knew he had to keep Nieloch's disappearance from being discovered, at least until he could prove that he had found a way beyond the kingdom. Once he delivered the city from the Grohldym, everything would change, and nobody would dare challenge his right to continue his rule, heir, or no.

The king was confident that Czarstostryx and Skealfa would be able to reach the unknown realm, maybe they already had, but it was unfortunate he had not yet been able to confirm their success. Perhaps, they had decided to explore further before returning to receive additional instruction on how to proceed. As unanswered questions assailed his thoughts, the king regretted he had not gone with them, but he had learned long ago that the duties of the crown required him to forgo the impulse of participating in perilous endeavors—a lesson his son clearly did not understand!

Bardazel found himself shaking with rage as he thought of his son's foolhardy actions. Turning his back angrily on the treasure hold, he stormed back to the throne room, fuming.

The king's eyes fell on the throne as he entered the great hall. For generations, his forefathers had ruled upon it. Maybe, he would be the last. Bardazel forced himself to maintain some optimism. *"My most capable soldiers are seeing to the success of the mission. Soon, the path to a new realm will be standing open before me. I will lead my people into a future with unlimited possibilities. I will be hailed as the savior of the kingdom! Nieloch will find his way home and my bloodline's rule will remain unbroken. All will be as it should."* He said these things to himself with conviction, but it was getting more and more difficult to silence the doubt plaguing his mind, and it was more than just himself he needed to convince.

"Has there been any word?" Lord Mortram's voice carried loudly across the throne room as he entered from the opposite hall. The councilor of the city's palace district had been making inquiries over the absence of Skealfa and his elite soldiers for several days. The battle-lord had not been seen within the city walls for quite some time, and people were demanding proof that they were still under his protection. Rumors had begun to spread that he had fallen during a recent mission, and fear was growing among the people. Mortram had already suggested to King Bardazel that he present Skealfa to the citizens in order to show them that its revered battle-lord was still watching over them.

It had not been the king's intention to impart knowledge of the party's quest to anyone, even though he was obliged to inform the council heads of any mission that required the dispatch of soldiers beyond the walls of the city for more than a few days. He had little patience explaining himself to others, especially under the current circumstances where the plan had materialized so quickly and unexpectedly. He preferred to keep the operation covert until he had a definitive outcome of success to present to the councilors; when that occurred, he would disclose the details, but he saw no reason to raise hopes if it turned out his plan held no merit. Unfortunately, he had expected events to unfold more quickly, and he had not foreseen that his son would disappear and leave the city's governors wondering as to his whereabouts as well.

Since the absence of the prince and battle-lord could not be ignored, the king had told the councilors that Skealfa and a select few soldiers had been dispatched for reconnaissance in the forest. He offered several flimsy theories on his son's absence as well, suggesting that he might be spending time among the commoners to gain a better understanding of how they were managing after the recent attack, but as the days passed, the councilors began to grow impatient. They were no longer pacified by speculation; they were demanding answers.

Bardazel sensed that Mortram was skeptical about the theories he had offered on his son's whereabouts. Prince Nieloch was well known throughout the palace as being an overly emotional non-conformist who was also a bit of a daydreamer. He would be more inclined to indulge in poetry or music within the safety of the city walls than to pursue a greater understanding of the affairs of the kingdom. Suspicions over the matter would only grow, so the king knew he would have to act before the truth came to light.

Bardazel had little choice but to consider informing Mortram and the other council heads of Skealfa's mission. He had no intention of revealing that the prince might be dead unless there was conclusive evidence to confirm it, especially since Mortram represented the next bloodline of royal succession.

It was no secret that Mortram was anxious for his family's return to power. His lineage had ruled before Bardazel's for an even longer period, but its rule had ended centuries earlier by events that were shrouded under mysterious circumstances. Historical records were unclear on the details of what exactly had happened, and it was rumored that most of the documents on the subject had been destroyed long ago.

"No word yet, but I am certain Skealfa's party will return soon." Bardazel tried to sound convincing as he responded to Lord Mortram's inquiry. "There are sure to be unforeseen factors in a mission of this nature, but I have every confidence they will return to report before long."

"I am sure you are right, but something must be done to pacify the people," Mortram pressed. "Fear is beginning to spread, and it will not be long until a mob is gathering at the palace gate demanding answers. You must do something!"

"And so, I shall," Bardazel replied calmly. "I have an idea that I would like to submit for consideration, and I am prepared to discuss it with all of the council members. I am dispatching notification for a gathering in the council chamber at dawn. I will explain what I have in mind at the meeting."

"What are you planning?"

"You will be informed in the morning with the others, but for now, you must excuse me. There are still preparations I must make before I present my plan."

"In the morning then," Mortram said as he bowed. "Good evening to you, highness."

Bardazel watched with disdain as Mortram left the throne room. It rankled him that he must explain his actions to appease his subjects. He knew this undertaking would set them all free, yet they still needed constant reassurance regarding his leadership. Who were they to question his judgment? They would soon see that his ability as king would surpass all others before him.

Bardazel had hoped for more time before he had to intervene on the battle-lord's behalf. Based on the intelligence given by Czarstostryx and Skealfa regarding time frames for the mission, he had not expected their return until the following day or soon thereafter, but now that the council would learn of the mission, it was likely he would have to enact a strategy he had planned to reserve until circumstances gave him no other choice. The king had formulated the contingency procedure as soon as the party departed. There was too much at stake not to act if the first mission fell on misfortune or if the outlander betrayed them. His plan involved a large-scale, military maneuver that would leave the city virtually unprotected, and he had to make sure he could convince the councilors it would be necessary.

"Inform General Scorthis to meet me in the council chamber at once!" Bardazel barked at the guards nearest the throne. One of them bowed and quickly left to retrieve the general.

The king turned from the throne room and headed down the corridor that would take him directly to the meeting spot. It did not take him long to reach the nearby chamber, and General Scorthis was already waiting inside when he arrived.

Scorthis was second-in-command of King Bardazel's army and had served as such for many years, but in his younger days, he wore the mantle of battle-lord. Most of his long life had been spent in the king's service, and it showed on his hawkish face. The closely cropped hair that crowned his balding head was stark white, hinting at his advanced years, but he was still well muscled and possessed skill and power enough to rival most of the much younger men in the army by whom he was highly revered.

It was Scorthis who had trained Lord Skealfa, guiding him as he climbed the ranks to eventually replace him. He had not been angry when Skealfa defeated him in ritual combat to seize the mantle of honor and take his place at the head of the army. Scorthis had actually been quite proud of the young man's skill and battle prowess, and it brought a sense of fulfillment to him that as the razor sharpness of his own youth faded, he had been replaced by one so capable.

"How may I serve?" Scorthis said, bowing as the king entered.

"There has been a development regarding Skealfa's mission."

"Have you received word from him?"

"Not as yet but growing suspicion among the governors and unrest among the people have made it necessary for me to consider actions that I believe to be premature at this time. Regardless of how I choose to proceed, I need to know the current state of the army. Are my soldiers ready to march in force if called upon?"

"They are, highness. The number of able-bodied men was diminished after the attack, but a large majority of the army is intact."

"Good. I will meet with the councilors in the morning. I am hoping Lord Skealfa will return before then, but if he does not, I will be forced to disclose the details of his mission and convince the council to support dispatching additional troops in due course. I want you to be at the meeting so you can give assurances that sending a large force to follow up on Lord Skealfa's patrol will not put the city in danger."

Bardazel looked hard at the general. "The success of this endeavor is critical to the future of our kingdom and bold moves may be required to see it through. Even if the council does not agree, I need to know that my army will stand ready to do what is required of them for the good of all."

Scorthis was slightly taken aback by what the king was suggesting, but he did not let it show and responded without hesitation. "You have my assurance, highness. We are with you."

"That is good to hear. We shall see what the night brings and plan on meeting back here in the morning if nothing further develops. You may go." Scorthis bowed and left Bardazel to consider his options.

As the night slowly passed, the king decided to return to the treasure hold to ponder, as he often did...

The king found himself absently staring at the statue of the winged creature atop the pillar, carelessly losing himself in thought. Before he realized it, he was once again falling under its influence. He began to perceive that the demonic figure was growing in stature, rising up before him. Its cruel eyes began to draw him in, causing his head to swim.

A chill ran down the Bardazel's spine as he felt the presence of someone inside the chamber behind him. The sensation was impossible to ignore, and the disturbance compelled the king to break his gaze from the statue. He spun to confront the intruder and was startled to find the outlander standing there. Bardazel took an involuntary step backwards, stumbling on one of the chests. Czarstostryx quickly caught his arm, stabilizing him effortlessly, causing the king to take notice of the unusual strength the old man possessed.

"Do not be alarmed," the outlander whispered. "Nobody knows I have come here to meet with you."

"How did you get past the guards?" Bardazel whispered the question in kind.

"I have my ways, and I thought it best that you received this news without delay, in private."

"What news? What has happened? Where are Skealfa and his men?"

"Things did not go as expected I am afraid. The soldiers you sent to reinforce us have all perished."

"What of Lord Skealfa?"

"He yet lives."

The king breathed a sigh of relief. "Have you seen the prince? He disappeared on the morning of your departure."

"Indeed, I have. He attached himself to our numbers just outside the city walls. Events unfolded quickly, and we were forced to move deeper into the forest when the Grohldym attacked. We lost the opportunity to return him, so for his own safety, he stayed with us. He too, lives."

"Why are they not with you? Explain yourself!" Bardazel demanded.

Czarstostryx calmly began to give his account. "The mission started with unexpected challenges when the prince was discovered following our party. As we negotiated his return, we were set upon by a large number of Grohldym. We were driven deeper into the forest as we fought our way clear of them. One of the soldiers fell in the melee during the encounter. I concentrated my efforts on protecting the prince and managed to keep him safe through the ordeal. By the time the danger subsided we had nearly reached the entrance to the canyon's labyrinth. The time to return your son was behind us, and we had to keep pushing forward.

"In the canyons, we faced unexpected obstacles as well. The creatures that reside there revealed themselves and proved to be hostile and formidable. The other soldiers lost their lives there. Only Skealfa, the prince, and I made it to the tower.

"The tower was as I had left it, so we cautiously approached, and I utilized the artifact that I retrieved from this treasury. A hidden door was exposed, but as I prepared to open it, the ground on both sides of where I stood fell away. Skealfa and the prince dropped into the darkness below. Before I could make an attempt to rescue them, the openings they had fallen through snapped shut. In that same moment, the door in front of me swung open, revealing a long hallway. I entered the hallway hoping to find a clue within that would shed light on the whereabouts of Skealfa and your son."

"What did you find?" Bardazel asked anxiously.

"I found what you seek—a realm beyond this kingdom."

"Describe what you saw!" The king's excitement was growing as Czarstostryx's tale unfolded.

"The hallway seemed endless, and I noticed as I progressed that the tower walls began to transition into the stone of the canyons themselves. Eventually, the hallway became an ever-widening tunnel that led to a massive gate made from an unusual metal I have never seen before. Looking through the gate, I beheld an enormous cavern that opened to the skies of an unknown horizon, but I could go no further. The gate was locked. I placed my hands on what I perceived to be the lock. At that moment, a voice came to me from the cavern, revealing that I stood at the final barrier between our realms.

"I learned that another artifact would be required to gain access—an artifact held in this very treasury. I took note of it when I was here last time but did not know it would be necessary to unlock another barrier.

"The barriers have been a mystery in and of themselves, but I have discovered more about their nature. The barriers can only be opened if they are approached by a lone individual. That is why I was able to open the first one without incident, but when three of us approached the second barrier, two were removed. The final barrier will be the same. It must be approached by one man alone, or it will not open. I must take the artifact to the gate by myself in order to gain access to the other realm."

"The whole point of this quest was to gain passage for my entire kingdom!" Bardazel interrupted angrily. "Now you tell me that only one may enter?"

"I tell you that the barrier must be unlocked by a lone individual, but once it has been opened, others may follow as they will. That is what I was told."

"What of my son and Lord Skealfa?"

"They were not destroyed, only detained. Once the gate is unlocked, it is my understanding they will be released near the tower's entrance. After this information was given to me, I returned to you straight away to retrieve the final artifact required to gain passage. When I return to the tower, I will open the gate and meet Skealfa and your son at the tower's entrance to explain what has happened. Skealfa can then return with the prince, and you can assemble your soldiers to march on the tower and enter the unknown realm in force."

"What of you?" Bardazel asked with suspicion. "Your covert appearance this evening leads me to wonder that if I had not been in this treasury when you arrived, I would not have learned any of the information you carried. It seems you intended to claim the artifact, regardless of my approval."

"I assure you, that is not the case." Czarstostryx held up his hands innocently. "The methods I employed upon my return were aimed at seeking you out directly so I could disclose what I have learned. The prince and Skealfa are alive, and since our wills have been aligned to unlock the hidden realm, I thought you deserved the opportunity to see them returned unharmed.

"I must confess, however, that I am prepared to take any necessary actions to obtain the final artifact and return to the tower immediately. For you see, I have also learned that the barriers operate in sequence with one another, corresponding with the appearance of the entrance to the canyon labyrinth. Once the barriers begin to open, the final gate must be unlocked before the entrance to the canyon disappears again, which will happen much sooner than it has before. If the entrance disappears, all of our efforts will have been in vain. The tower will lock down, and it may not be accessible again in our lifetime."

"How long do we have?" Bardazel did his best to disguise the worry in his voice.

"Not much more than a day," Czarstostryx replied gravely. "If I leave immediately and do not encounter any unreasonable obstacles, it should be enough time. Traveling alone, I will be able to utilize my skills to focus on speedy passage instead of the protection of others.

"Now, I need to know." Czarstostryx paused and fixed the king in his piercing gaze. "Will you let me take the artifact and finish our quest?"

Bardazel paused to consider the outlander's words. "I suppose you could have used your talents to steal the artifact without my knowledge, yet you chose instead to seek me out and explain events, giving me hope that my son and Lord Skealfa can be saved." The king nodded with conviction. "Take the artifact and do what must be done. Send Lord Skealfa back to me with my son. I will organize my army and stand ready to depart upon their return, but know this: If they are not back within two days' time and I discover that you have betrayed me, I will set out with my army and find this tower by sheer force, and there shall be a reckoning. There will be no realm, hidden or otherwise, where you will escape my justice."

"Then let us hope your faith in Skealfa is well-founded and that he is able to return your son quickly and safely," Czarstostryx replied unfazed. "Now, I must make haste." Quickly stepping past the king, he snatched the artifact from its place on the table of stone.

"I assume you will be leaving the palace unseen to retain the integrity of this undertaking," Bardazel stated as the outlander was exiting the treasure hold.

"Of course, good king," Czarstostryx replied over his shoulder as he stepped into the hall. "The cause remains intact."

Bardazel was unsettled by the old man's final words. On impulse he moved to follow him, but when he stepped into the hall, the outlander was nowhere to be seen in either direction of the long corridor.

"*No matter,*" Bardazel thought. "*I will lead my army to the tower in two days' time regardless of any outcome that should arise. I will fulfill my destiny. Nothing and no one will stop me!*"

CHAPTER 24

"It is time to go." Prince Nieloch woke to find Czarstostryx standing over him, shaking him by the shoulder. Mecursto stood behind the outlander with an anxious look on his face. The prince had no idea how long he had been sleeping, but it felt as if he had just closed his eyes.

"How did you fare with my father?" Nieloch asked.

"I described a scenario that spoke to his ambition, and he is eager to assist in our endeavor. He is assembling his army to march on the tower as we speak. I retrieved the necessary artifact, so I will be able to unlock the final barrier. We must hasten to the tower to ensure the way is open upon their arrival. Gather your effects so we can be on our way.

"Should we not travel with the army for safety?" Nieloch's concern was obvious.

"We cannot delay if I am to unlock the final barrier in time. The tower's gateways will not remain open for long. You need not worry. I will be able to ensure our safety as we travel."

Nieloch rubbed his eyes, grabbed his dagger, and collected his freshly stocked pack. After a few moments, the three were on their way. Nieloch grasped his son's shoulder briefly as they emerged from the ravine, giving him a reassuring nod as they set off.

The air hung heavy as they made their way across the wasteland. The wind did not stir, and it was unusually quiet. Strangely, the unnerving calm did not abate as they traveled. Nieloch felt the urge to ask Czarstostryx if he could explain the strange phenomenon but refrained from breaking the palpable silence, concerned that doing so might set off a disastrous chain-reaction that would bring about their demise. He was not as worried about the risk of communicating with his son since speaking aloud was not necessary; it was for that reason they had been conveying their thoughts to one another since their departure from the outlander's dwelling.

Mecursto was uneasy about being led by the old man through unknown terrain. He knew there was no choice in the matter since neither he nor his father would be able to find their way through the featureless wastes, but the idea of relying on someone else to guide him was worrisome. He had always been alone, taking care of himself, free to go where he pleased. Now, finding himself in the company of his father and the outlander, he was beginning to feel like a captive of circumstance. He was torn by his urge to flee and his desire to stay with his father.

Mecursto knew he could trust his father, and he felt at ease around him, but he did not share those feelings toward the old man. It was only his desire to learn more about the power he had in common with the outlander that enticed him to remain in his company. He told Nieloch he could sense Czarstostryx was hiding something, but he could not say what it was. It was also difficult to know for certain if his suspicion was truly founded because the outlander's aura was almost unreadable. If he *were* hiding something from them, it would not be easily discovered.

Nieloch encouraged his son to stay the course. He was sure the risk and effort would be worth the reward. He and Glithnie had desperately hoped for such an opportunity for the sake of their family, and even though she was no longer with them, they might still be able to realize that dream.

The sun was climbing high overhead when the Forest of the Grohldym began to loom large in the distance. As the small party continued in silence, it became undeniable that there were powerful, unseen forces influencing their surroundings and its few inhabitants. Czarstostryx spotted a Pillar in the distance using the backdrop of the forest to mask its presence. He motioned to Nieloch and his son, alerting them of the danger. Nieloch looked where the old man indicated and was just able to make out the stark outline of the tall, motionless beast. He had heard of the creatures from Lord Skealfa and his soldiers when they spoke of their exploits into the wastelands.

The Pillars were sleek, towering creatures that were covered in pale, leathery skin that stretched tightly over their sinuous bodies. From a distance, they appeared to be nothing more than a rock formation that resembled a tall pillar, but when the creatures sensed the approach of any living being, they launched themselves straight into the sky like arrows shot from powerful bows. As they ascended, they opened their long, slender wings and surveyed their surroundings, gliding lightly upon the wasteland's hot, thermal currents. Upon locating the disturbance, they tucked their wings tightly to their sides and dove with blinding speed. Their prey was enveloped upon impact—wrapped in the creature's large, leathery wings which constricted tightly, making escape or rescue impossible.

Encounters with the creatures were extremely rare. Lord Skealfa was one of the few men alive who had experienced an assault from one of the beasts during his many years of campaigning into the wasteland when one of them attacked a soldier on an expedition he led. The battle-lord and his men had done what they could to intervene, attacking with swords and axes, but their weapons had proven useless against the creature. It was discovered that when attacked, a Pillar would only tighten its grip, becoming as stone while slowly consuming its prey. No Pillar had ever been slain, so much was still unknown about them. Several facts were consistent, however. They could not be approached unaware, and they always attacked when advanced upon.

Nieloch grew concerned when he realized Czarstostryx was not changing course to avoid getting any nearer to the Pillar. Unwavering, he continued to lead them in the same direction in which they had set out. The prince could see that the old man was poised to react as they drew ever closer to the beast, but the creature did not stir. By all accounts, it should have launched itself into the sky, but it remained motionless.

Mecursto had also sensed the danger as they approached, but he recognized something was holding time somehow. When the prince asked if it was the old man's doing, Mecursto told him it was not that simple. He explained that the outlander was expending energy that seemed to be intertwining with something all around them—something much more powerful.

As they continued to draw nearer to the forest, they could see the Pillar more clearly. Although they were still a fair distance from it, they were able to discern distinctive traits of the creature—things few had ever witnessed. The Pillar was nearly as tall as the walls surrounding the palace. It stood erect, but the prince could see that the creature's legs were folded in a crouched position much like those of the frogs he sometimes saw on the palace walls in the evenings. The wings of the beast contributed largely to its height as they were held over its head and pointed at the sky like twin spires of a tower. Its face could not be seen clearly being shrouded within the shadow cast from its poised wings, but Nieloch could feel its gaze upon him burning with malice as they made their way past its position. As they left the creature behind, it continued to stand unmoving and eventually dropped from sight as the three of them left the burning sands of the wasteland and entered the Forest of the Grohldym.

The sudden shift in their surroundings was stark. The thick canopy of trees blocked out the light of the sun, and the group was forced to pause momentarily in order to adjust their eyes to the gloom. The temperature had dropped drastically, but the palpable silence still hung heavy in the air. Nieloch had expected that upon entering the forest the oppressive stillness of the wasteland would dissipate, but it was not to be; if anything, it had grown more intense being surrounded by the twisted trees. Nieloch noticed his son breathe a sigh of relief as they stood in surroundings that were familiar to him, but he could tell that his mind was still troubled by the strange energy clinging to them.

To the prince, passage through the trees began to feel surreal, like floating weightless in a dream, and he could no longer hold his tongue on the matter. Edging up next to Czarstostryx, he leaned in close to whisper as they continued moving. "Do you have any idea what is happening? Why is everything so still?"

"I am not sure," Czarstostryx replied. "I have never experienced anything like it. The land is being held in thrall by a powerful force. It seems to be connected to everything surrounding us."

"Is that why the Pillar did not attack?" Nieloch asked incredulously.

"I must admit, I was surprised as well. I held a powerful defensive spell at the ready as we approached its position. At first, I thought the creature was wary of my power, but as we drew closer, I could see that was not the case. There are much larger forces at work."

"Do you think the rest of the creatures we encounter will be affected in the same way? Perhaps the Grohldym will not pose a threat as we pass through the forest."

"I would take nothing for granted in that regard," Czarstostryx warned. "We must continue to remain vigilant against attack. How is your son faring?"

"He is keenly aware of the forces you speak of, but he seems to be more at ease since we have returned to the forest." Nieloch had no intention of revealing his son's misgivings about the outlander, so he did his best to keep his answers somewhat vague in order to prevent Czarstostryx from reading into them while giving enough information to keep him from pressing further.

"Perhaps our journey will remain uneventful, and he will continue to feel the same." Czarstostryx studied the boy as he spoke. "Is he committed to our quest?"

"He is," Nieloch stated simply.

No further words were spoken as they continued through the forest, but Nieloch and his son remained deeply engaged in silent conversation.

The rest of the trek through the woods went without incident. The three moved swiftly, keeping ever vigilant against an ambush from the Grohldym, but there was no sign of them. As they entered the vicinity of the labyrinth's entrance, the sun was hanging low in the unseen horizon, and Czarstostryx was forced to employ the phantom flame in the gathering gloom. He would have preferred not to draw attention to their presence in the forest, but they were close to the hidden entrance, and it would be required upon entering the perpetual darkness of the canyons at any rate.

It was not long before the group stood in front of the narrow crack in the sheer cliff wall. Darkness seeped from within the depths of the fissure, causing Mecursto to freeze in his tracks. He stood, trembling, staring into the foreboding blackness. Czarstostryx noticed his reaction and paused, addressing Nieloch with concern in his voice. "Will he continue?"

Nieloch held up his hand to Czarstostryx then moved nearer to his son. Leaning in closely, he whispered. "What is the matter? Do you sense danger?"

Mecursto remained silent, continuing to stare into the darkness.

"This is the path we must travel to reach the unknown realm," Nieloch said encouragingly. "There is a new life waiting for us there."

"*Something is waiting—watching,*" Mecursto replied somberly.

"What is troubling the boy?" Czarstostryx inquired.

"I think he is afraid to enter. He is sensing something unsettling."

"You need not be afraid, child," Czarstostryx said reassuringly. "What you are sensing is foreign to you, but it is known to me. It will not harm us. In fact, it seems to be inviting us, removing obstacles that would have normally impeded our progress. I have traveled this path many times, and I know how to deal with any trouble that might arise, so you need not worry. We are nearing the end of the journey, just through this canyon. You and your father can be at my side to witness the first glimpse of the unknown realm. It is the chance of a lifetime!"

"It is what your mother wanted for us, son," Nieloch added. "Ahead, lies a place where we can make our own decisions and be who we want to be. It can be a new start for us. I believe we are meant for this. The way will be open for us as Czarstostryx has said. Are you willing to try?"

Czarstostryx and Nieloch looked at Mecursto intently to see what his answer would be, but the boy remained silent as he continued to stare into the crack. Nieloch began to grow concerned and gently touched his son's arm. "If you do not wish to continue, I will not ask it of you. We can return to my father's palace and let the army go before us. We could return another time."

Mecursto's eyes quickly shot to the outlander, and he seemed momentarily panicked. His thoughts quickly entered Nieloch's mind. *"I will go."*

"Are you certain?" Nieloch asked, concerned at his son's abrupt change in demeanor.

"Yes. I am ready. Let us continue."

"He says he will go," Nieloch said to Czarstostryx, "but something seems to have him quite shaken. Do you think it is wise to continue on our own? Perhaps we should wait for my father's army to join us."

"I am afraid we do not have time to wait," Czarstostryx reminded him. "I must unlock the final gate before the chance is gone for good. It is understandable that your son is afraid. There are powerful energies at work, and he is highly attuned to them, but he does not know how to interpret them like I do. Our best chance to succeed lies before us now."

"Very well then," Nieloch replied resolutely. "Lead on."

CHAPTER 25

After Czarstostryx left King Bardazel in the treasure hold, the king went to the council chamber to consider his strategy as the evening dwindled away. There was no longer a conflict in Bardazel's mind as to whether or not he should reveal his plan. Having finally received word of the mission's outcome, the time to inform the council members had arrived, and it was imperative that he organize the next move as quickly as possible.

Arriving just before daybreak, General Scorthis entered the council chamber and took a temporary position near the entrance as he waited with the king until the others arrived. As dawn's first light fell upon the palace, the councilors of the various regions began to assemble. Bardazel waited impatiently to address them until everyone was present. When the final councilor took his seat, the general ordered the guards outside the chamber to seal the door then sat himself next to the king in the chair typically designated for the battle-lord, drawing a few speculative glances.

"Welcome to you all," the king stated formally. "The matter which has brought us here at this early hour concerns the single most significant event in our history. It is with great satisfaction I am able to inform you that the future of our kingdom is no longer set in stone!" Puzzled looks passed between the councilors as Bardazel continued. "As you are all aware, it has been my sole ambition as ruler of this kingdom to find passage beyond the borders that have confined us and our forefathers before us. After the recent attack, an extraordinary chain of events was triggered that has been secretly unfolding, known only to myself and a select few. Those few, embarked on a perilous quest days ago, guided by a strange and powerful outlander who was discovered to be residing undetected in the wastelands for untold years." There were scattered gasps at the table. "Lord Skealfa was tasked with over-seeing my interests in this endeavor with the aid of his most trusted elite soldiers. I have just learned that unbeknown to me, Prince Nieloch managed to join them on their quest as well. Sadly, most of those who set out were slain. Besides the outlander, Lord Skealfa and my son are the only ones who managed to survive, but they have been taken captive and are being held against their will within a gateway to an unknown realm that we are about to unlock."

The looks that passed between the councilors sitting at the table turned from puzzlement to shocked concern and outrage.

"Why were we not informed of this?"

"Who is this outlander?"

"Where is this gateway?"

The questions rang out from the men as they sprang from their seats to confront the king, trying to grasp the unprecedented information he had just imparted.

"Calm yourselves!" Scorthis barked. "Regain the dignity that your stations demand, and let the king continue."

The councilors' mouths snapped shut at the command of the former battle-lord, and they were compelled to return to their seats with deference.

"I am glad to see your ability to command is undiminished General Scorthis," Bardazel stated with regard, "since you will be assuming the role of battle-lord and leading the campaign to free my son and Lord Skealfa."

"No! I will be the one to lead!" Shocked looks unified the faces of everyone in the room. None of them even noticed the door had opened during their outburst. Lord Skealfa stepped into the chamber, bloody and weary.

General Scorthis sprang to the battle-lord's side, lending him aid as he entered the room. With some assistance, Skealfa made his way to his seat and collapsed into the large, stone chair. Scorthis quickly looked him over to assess his condition. "You are gravely wounded!" the general exclaimed. "Send for the physician!" he barked to the guards at the door. One of them quickly sped away at his command.

The king was also on his feet the moment Skealfa entered and had moved to stand near him. "Lord Skealfa, praise the heavens you have escaped! Where is my son? Did you bring him back with you?"

"I do not know where the prince is, highness. He was alive when last I saw him in the canyons where we were attacked by the foul demons who dwell there. He was under the protection of the outlander when we were separated." Skealfa grimaced in pain which spoke to the severity of his wounds. It was clearly an effort for him to remain conscious.

"So, you were not captured." Bardazel seemed deeply concerned as he commented to himself, then he quickly directed his words to the sentries standing near the entrance. "Guards, help Lord Skealfa to the infirmary at once, there is no time to wait for the physician."

The council members' protests were silenced by the king before they could begin. "Lord Skealfa is severely injured. He needs immediate medical attention. I will accompany him to the infirmary and find out what has happened. It is critical that I get his account of events without delay so we can be well informed on the best course of action. You are all to remain within this chamber and await my return. No one outside this room shall be allowed to learn of this until we know for certain what is going on."

Two large guards entered the room and moved quickly to assist Skealfa.

"I will help," Scorthis insisted, dismissing one of the guards as he offered support to Skealfa. Considering Skealfa's enormous size and the fact that he was fully armored, it was no easy feat for the two men to get him up and moving. Fortunately, they did not have far to go. Soon after leaving the council chamber, the physician was upon them with litter bearers at his heel.

The old doctor's face was flushed, and he was breathing heavily. He had been rushed to the council chamber from his nearby station where he was still tending to the most severely wounded soldiers injured in the recent raid. The elderly physician had been mending the soldiers of the king's army for most of his life and despite his tendency to indulge in drink, he was quite adept at his trade.

The group quickly transferred Skealfa to the litter and continued conveying him to the infirmary. The physician looked Skealfa over as he was being transported, evaluating the extent of his injuries. When they reached the infirmary, he instructed the litter bearers to place Skealfa carefully on several cots that were moved together to support him, then he addressed the general. "Lord Skealfa has lost a great deal of blood. His armor must be removed so I can treat his injuries and stop the bleeding."

Scorthis acknowledged the physician's direction, and carefully set to work removing the heavy armor from Skealfa's battered body. Skealfa did his best to assist in the process, but his crushed armor made movement extremely difficult, especially in his weakened state. As soon as the battle-lord's cuirass was removed, the physician inspected the most obvious injury near his shoulder and began applying pressure to the large puncture wound to staunch the bleeding as he continued to look him over.

"Will he live?" Bardazel anxiously implored.

"The damage missed any vital areas, and there appears to be no major damage to the bone near the injury, but from the looks of his armor I would wager he also suffered several cracked ribs at the very least. I will bind them and dress his wounds. With rest, he should make a full recovery."

"Thank the heavens! "Bardazel's voice was filled with relief. "I will need a moment with Lord Skealfa in private before you finish mending him. Time is of the essence." The king made it clear that he would have no argument. "I will call for you shortly."

Considering the battle-lord's seriously battered state, it was obvious the physician was perturbed that he would have to delay his charge He acquiesced to the command nonetheless, but only after directing the king to continue applying pressure to the wound until his return. Bardazel quickly took the physician's place, tending to the injury.

"All of you, leave us!" the king said sternly to the remaining medical staff as he regarded them impatiently. He turned to General Scorthis. "Please return to the council chamber and see to it that everyone remains where they are until I return." The general seemed hesitant to leave the battle-lord's side but did as he was told and departed with a bow.

Once everyone cleared the area, Bardazel spoke to Skealfa with a keen sense of urgency. "It is fortunate you arrived when you did. It was not my intention to inform the council of your mission until learning the outcome of your undertaking, but recent events made it necessary to move forward with a contingency plan, and I was not expecting you to be able to join us. The council meeting was called so I could disclose the nature of your mission and alleviate unrest among the people and the governors. Now that you have returned, it changes matters greatly. I must hear your account before I can finish with the council. Tell me what transpired after you left the palace with the outlander."

Skealfa quickly recounted the events that led to the discovery of Nieloch and their subsequent flight from the forest. He described the journey through the canyons leading up to the point of the attack by the cliff dwellers and his separation from the group.

Bardazel listened intently as Skealfa described the deadly conflict in the canyons. "The outlander claimed he did not know the origin of the distant thunder echoing through the canyons, but his words have been woven with deceit since the first day I met him. When the creatures descended from the heights with a thunderous clamor, Czarstostryx appeared unsurprised, and he did not seem overly concerned with our well-being. He did manage to protect himself and the prince, but the barrier spell he wielded was useless to me and my men since it only encompassed the outlander and your son as they raced away from our position.

"Brilldagh was slain instantly, impaled by one of the creature's spear-like legs as it bounded between the walls of the canyons. Crel rushed to his aid and was lost from sight during the melee, but evidence of his demise was undeniable. Varthaal and I managed to withstand the unholy speed of the creatures as we closed the distance to the outlander and your son, but they were gaining on us, so I sent Varthaal ahead while I held my position to give them more time to escape.

"The light grew faint as the others moved further from me, making it impossible to see the next attack which hit me at full force, slamming me into the wall of the canyon. I felt an intense, stinging pain in my shoulder and realized I had been impaled by one of the beasts as Brilldagh had. I tried to roll away from my attacker, but I was pinned against the wall and unable to move. I looked for Varthaal and saw that he had managed to reach the outlander and your son. They were all shielded and unharmed as they continued their flight. Before they disappeared, I noticed a look in the old man's eyes reflecting grim satisfaction at what he clearly perceived to be my demise.

"Turning my attention back to my attacker, I gripped my sword tightly, preparing to thrust it into the eyes of the beast, but it immediately leapt to the opposite wall carrying me with it, hooked like a hapless fish. I was slammed into the rocks over and over as it ascended into the darkness. The last thing I saw before being knocked unconscious was Czarstostryx and Prince Nieloch fleeing far below me as Varthaal followed." Skealfa's brow furrowed. "I do not believe the outlander had any intention of letting me reach the tower. Perhaps, the beasts in the canyons do his bidding. If that is the case, then I am deeply concerned for the well-being of your son and Varthaal."

"That is a troubling account," Bardazel said with obvious concern. "Yet, as always, your might has proven to be an indomitable force. How under the heavens were you able to survive and find your way back?"

"I wish I could tell you it was because of my battle prowess and skill with a sword. However, that was not the case in this instance.

"When I regained consciousness, I thought my time was surely at an end. I was still being held firmly by the spear-like appendage of the creature as it continued to leap to and fro along the canyon walls. In utter darkness, I had no idea where I was or how long I had been unconscious. I realized my sword was missing, but I still had my dagger in my belt, so I gripped it hard and prepared for one final assault on the beast once its furious momentum ceased. I was savagely thrashed about as it propelled itself through the darkness, but the violent impact that had knocked me out was not repeated. I was being carried in a way that was meant to harm me no further, so I braced myself and waited for my moment.

"After some time, I began to perceive that the sound of impact against the walls had changed slightly, and I noticed a faint crack in the closing distance where the darkness was less complete. We hurled through the canyon towards it and began to descend from the heights as we approached until we came to a halt on the canyon floor. Finally, the journey had come to an end, and I realized I had been returned to the entrance of the labyrinth.

"The creature repositioned itself onto the ground while continuing to hold me firmly, turning its hideous gaze upon me. I steeled myself to lunge at any opening I could find, but it did not give me the chance. In one quick motion it withdrew its leg from the wall that it held me pinned to, and with a powerful flick of motion, I was flung free and thrown clear of the canyon onto the forest floor. I rolled on impact, still clutching my dagger as I found my footing then coiled myself to spring and spun back towards the canyon to engage the foul creature, but the beast launched itself back into the darkness with blinding speed before I could strike. The thunderous crashing of its retreat resounded from the walls, but I remained poised for attack until the clamorous booming diminished into silence.

"I knew the creature could have slain me, but it had chosen instead to banish me from the canyons. I considered my options as I peered into the gaping fissure. If I rushed blindly into the canyons, I would never be able to find your son or reach the tower, and even if I could manage to navigate through the maze-like corridors without light, the distance ahead was potentially greater than the distance back to the palace. Tactically, it made sense to return for supplies and gather reinforcements since returning through the canyons will require both."

"But how can you hope to enlist reinforcements?" Bardazel inquired thoughtfully. "Your most capable soldiers are no longer with you, and the vast majority of the army's soldiers are highly susceptible to the forest's influence. I imagine they would fare no better in the canyons."

"I was unsure how I would be able to bring our forces through those regions as well, but I noticed that the effects of the forest were much diminished as I stood among the trees, and the bestowments I typically experience had also faded. When we first set out, I thought my abilities were compromised because of the outlander's power, and perhaps they were, but now, there is a kind of stillness that has fallen over the land. It has remained the same since I left the canyons. I believe it may now be possible for the army's entire force to endure exposure and make it to the tower if we move with haste." Skealfa's head dropped back onto the cot, pain and exhaustion finally overwhelming on him.

"That is enough for now, Lord Skealfa. We will talk more after your wounds have been properly attended to and you have had some time to regain your strength. Speak of this to no one." Bardazel called for the physician who quickly returned to tend to the wounded battle-lord. "Let me know when he has been stabilized and returned to his quarters. There is more I must discuss with him."

"Yes highness," the physician replied as he resumed treatment of Skealfa's injuries.

The king took a moment to consider what he had heard before making his way back to the council chamber. When he arrived, everyone was waiting anxiously. "I apologize for the delay," Bardazel began. "The unexpected turn of events had to be addressed. Fortunately, it has clarified the current state of the mission I spoke of. Now, let me tell you what has transpired so you can fully understand the magnitude and urgency of this undertaking as well as the reason I chose to keep it temporarily guarded."

It was nearly midmorning by the time King Bardazel was able to satisfactorily explain the events that had led to the current state of affairs.

"So, you see," Bardazel concluded, "the mission was expected to be merely reconnaissance to discover if there was a genuine need to explore further. If the findings proved such, then all of you were to be informed and a royal announcement would have been issued. I chose to keep the matter quiet to avoid raising the hopes of the people until I was certain that passage beyond our borders existed. Now that those questions have been answered, it is time for the people to accept some very unsettling news; there will be a full-scale military campaign launched immediately. I will coordinate my strategy with Lord Skealfa and General Scorthis. What I will need from each of you is to keep panic from spreading through your districts while the army is gone. You will need to utilize your own agents to maintain order and keep watch along the city walls in our absence."

"Does this mean you will be leaving as well?" Lord Mortram inquired.

"It does," Bardazel said firmly. "This is to be a historic moment for the kingdom, and I will be the one to lead the army when we seize control of the foreign realm. I will be there when my son is rescued, and my family is restored, and you will play your parts by keeping order throughout the kingdom in our absence."

"What if the Grohldym attack while you are away? The city would surely fall without the army's protection." The governor of the western province voiced a concern shared by all.

"It is unlikely they would attack again so soon. It has never been known to happen," Bardazel replied confidently.

"Perhaps that is because the army has always stood ready to defend against them," Mortram contested. "Who is to say how that might change in their absence?"

"That is a risk that must be taken if we are to have our freedom," Bardazel stated with conviction. "Perhaps the army's presence in the forest would draw the Grohldym to us as we journey to the canyons. If we were to meet them with our full force when we are prepared, the outcome would surely be to our advantage. At the very least, we would be able to reduce their numbers."

"You mean to travel through the Forest of the Grohldym?" Mortram's tone was incredulous. "What of the madness? Surely, the army will suffer its effects. How do you plan to overcome its influence?"

"Lord Skealfa has informed me that a kind of stillness has recently diminished the effect. The army should be unaffected if we move swiftly."

The governors appeared skeptical. They were obviously troubled and doubtful of their king's optimism.

"Regardless of what might happen, you must all do your best to keep our people safe through this." The king spoke to his councilors firmly. "Bring all the citizens from the outskirts within the city walls while we are gone and keep them under your protection. I know this is not an ideal course, but I believe it is what must be done, and so, it shall be done." Bardazel looked at the men seated at the table. His level gaze shown with unbreakable conviction, compelling his appointed leaders to remember that it was his will guiding the fate of the kingdom, and his rule was absolute as long as he wore the crown.

CHAPTER 26

After the council meeting adjourned, the governors returned with haste to their prospective regions to prepare their deputies for the forthcoming decree. General Scorthis began to organize a strategy to move the army from the city and make other preparations for the campaign while Skealfa was being tended to. The king went to the throne room where he restlessly waited to receive word that Skealfa had been returned to his quarters. Bardazel knew it was imperative to speak with the battle-lord as soon as possible and expose the lies that Czarstostryx had spun, but he had known better than to assess the conflicting stories in front of the governors. Since Czarstostryx's deception had influenced his actions, it was critical to conceal the fact that he had been misled, lest his judgement be called into question when he delivered his decree.

After waiting for what seemed an eternity, the physician entered the throne room to inform Bardazel of Skealfa's stabilized condition, stating that he was out of immediate danger and had been returned to his quarters to rest. The king barely managed to refrain from running as he rushed to see him.

Bardazel entered Skealfa's chamber to find him sitting on the edge of his bed. The king motioned for him to remain seated as he entered, but the battle-lord continued to his feet and bowed before the king. "Please do not exert yourself," Bardazel said with concern as he crossed the room. "I was told you have sustained great injury,"

"I am sure the physician has overstated the severity of my wounds. I have survived far worse," Skealfa replied resolutely.

"True enough. I am relieved that you survived your ordeal. Had you not, it may well have led to the downfall of the entire kingdom."

"Surely not." Skealfa seemed skeptical at the king's appraisal. "As it stands, I failed my mission regardless of my survival. I did not discover the location of the tower, nor was I able to return your son. Had I fallen, these facts would have remained unchanged."

"True," Bardazel replied, "but if you had not returned, I would not have discovered the outlander's deception."

"What did you discover?" Skealfa's voice mirrored his concern.

"I have spoken of this to no one," the king began furtively. "The outlander returned to the palace last night, unseen and in secret. He appeared to me when I was alone in the treasure hold. Suffice it to say that his account of events was contradictory to your own."

"I have no doubt. What did he tell you?"

"He told me of your journey through the forest and into the canyons. He further described entering the tower and finding his way to the very gates of the unknown realm. I would have had a difficult time disproving his account of events had you not returned, because in his version, you made it to the tower with him. He further claimed that you were trapped there along with my son."

"Why would he have returned to spin such a tale?" Skealfa mused. "His sole intent has been to move beyond the tower in order to claim the power he seeks, removing himself from further involvement with our kingdom entirely."

"I believe he did not have a choice in the matter. It stands to reason that he *did* enter the tower as he claims, but he lacked an additional key that was required to pass beyond it. The item he sought was within my treasure hold. It was much like the first one I allowed him to take."

"That was surprisingly short-sighted for one who claims to be a such learned scholar," Skealfa interjected smugly. "I would have thought he would have been aware of the necessity of such a thing."

"It would seem that way," Bardazel agreed. "He did have knowledge that the artifact was within the treasure hold. He told me he noticed it when he was first there. I am sure if he had known it would be necessary for his purpose, he would have concocted some well-crafted reason to claim it, despite my limitation of taking only one item." Bardazel seemed thoughtful for a moment. "I do not think he realized he would need it at the time. I am not sure why he is encountering such seemingly excessive challenges in order to move through the tower, but I believe it is not as simple as we might think."

"Why would he beseech you to give him the artifact?" Skealfa puzzled. "You say he arrived unseen; surely, he could have used stealth to simply take the artifact, unnoticed."

"I wondered the same. The reasons he gave were clearly lies, but whatever the truth is, I would wager that he could not just steal it, or he surely would have. It appears he is bound by restrictions that dictate his actions. I have been pondering this since your return." Bardazel rubbed his chin as he considered the outlander's motives. "He claims to have seen the horizon of the unknown realm. He also claims that my son is trapped beneath the tower, tethered somehow to it. It is possible that both or neither of these things are true, but there are two things I am sure of. First—the artifact he took is an essential component in order to achieve his goal, and second—he does not want my army to interfere with his design. He made a point of insisting that only one person could approach the final gate or else all would be lost and the way to the hidden realm would be closed forever. I do not believe that is the case. Whatever his plan, he strives to reach the final gate before we can overtake him, but who is to say that anyone holding the artifact could not unlock the gate? Perhaps you or I could have achieved what he already has if we had but known about the tower. I will no longer allow him to manipulate affairs to further his selfish ambition. It is time to regain control of my kingdom's future and unlock the hidden realm myself." Bardazel regarded the battle-lord skeptically. "Are you *sure* you are well enough to lead my army in this pursuit?"

"I am well enough to follow the outlander into the depths of hell!" Skealfa declared fervently, his fists clenched in rage. "I owe him a debt of pain and suffering for the lives of my fallen brothers."

The king nodded with satisfaction. "I am also eager to see a full accounting for his myriad misdeeds against our kingdom. Do you think you can find your way back to the place where he slipped away?"

"I can," Skealfa replied confidently. "I was able to memorize the path we took through the canyons so finding my last position will not be an issue, and I believe we were in the vicinity of the tower when we were set upon. It should be possible to divine its location once I have returned, but it will be treacherous leading the entire army through the narrow corridors. Our forces will be stretched thin, removing the ability to defend our position in numbers. However, under the circumstances, it is a necessary risk.

"Then resume your station at once. You will see to the final preparations of the army. Relieve General Scorthis from the task and instruct him to return to his position as second-in-command. I will make the royal proclamation within the hour. Today, we march on the tower and lay claim to the hidden realm ourselves!"

"As you command, highness." The battle-lord responded enthusiastically with a bow before excusing himself and quickly striding from the chamber, vengeance burning in his heart. The king had finally unleashed him upon the outlander whose mockery and manipulation he had been forced to endure for far too long. He was anxious to turn loose his fury, barely noticing his wounds as he made his way to the barracks. He knew he would have to push the army hard through hostile territory if they hoped to catch the old man. It was also likely they would have to contend with the Grohldym as well as the vicious cliff dwellers along the way. *"Let them come!"* Skealfa thought to himself, grinning wickedly. *"I will send them all to oblivion in pieces!"*

Once Lord Skealfa was reunited with his men, he explained where he had been and what had transpired in his absence. After receiving the full account of events, they understood the critical nature of their cause and were eager to set out. Final preparations were completed expeditiously, and soon, every able-bodied soldier in the king's army had amassed themselves in the abandoned part of the city where they would soon depart.

The governors of the various regions had also accomplished their directives with haste, preparing the people for the delivery of the king's proclamation. It was not long until all citizens of the kingdom were gathered in and around the palace courtyard. Those who could not find room in the over-crowded square spilled out into the surrounding streets of the marketplace. Some perched atop rooftops, while others leaned precariously out of windows, anxiously awaiting the royal proclamation they had been unexpectedly summoned to attend.

King Bardazel stood high atop the pinnacle of the palace keep ready to deliver an announcement that would change the fate of his kingdom beyond imagining. There were growing murmurs of concern throughout the crowd at the absence of the king's soldiers atop the battlements where many would surely be stationed in attendance of a royal proclamation, but before the crowd was able to become overly anxious, the king's voice resonated throughout the walls of the city, amplified by the concave surface of the towering cliffs behind the palace.

"Good citizens attend to my words," he began. "I know there have been rumors spreading throughout the kingdom of late—whisperings of secret undertakings by the throne, unknown to the council of governors. There have also been concerns by some, that I have gone mad in pursuit of my obsession. I have also heard it surmised that the great battle-lord, Skealfa, has fallen in one of these rumored campaigns and that the army has crumbled into disarray. I am sure their absence today has etched these rumors into your minds as fact. I have brought you all together so you may know the truth." The king paused. "There have indeed been secret exploits conducted by the throne, and they have yielded fruit." Shocked gasps and mutterings of wonderment drifted among the people as Bardazel continued. "Today is the day I fulfill the promise I made to you all when I was crowned as your king." The crowd quieted. "As your ruler, I have tirelessly sought to discover a way beyond the confinement of these lands. Many have given their lives in that pursuit. Fathers, sons, and brothers have fallen in their efforts to liberate us from this land that holds us captive to the whims of the Grohldym whose vicious exploits have plagued us since the dawn of time. It has not only been your men who have fallen victim to violent and unknown ends; wives, mothers, and daughters have also been claimed by their cruel appetite—No longer! The time of our deliverance is finally at hand! It has been a strange fate that has revealed a path to an unknown realm, beyond what we have all come to accept as the limits of our world. Today, I tell you all; I have found a way beyond the horizon!" A palpable hush fell over the crowd. "As I have said, many brave men have paid the ultimate price in order to make this day possible, and we are all in their debt, but not everyone who sacrificed has fallen. Behold, your battle-lord, Skealfa!"

From the back of the pinnacle, unseen by the crowd below, Skealfa stepped forward to stand next to the king. Thunderous cheers shook the walls of the palace at his appearance. Bardazel knew the sight of the kingdom's cherished hero would raise the people's spirits and rally their support, and he would need it when he presented the next portion of his announcement which would be the hardest for them to accept.

When the cheers began to subside, the king's address recommenced. "Lord Skealfa has been instrumental in forging a path to this new horizon. He will be the one to lead the army who now stands ready in the ancient part of the city, and I will be at his side as we press through hostile territory and lay claim to this new land. Your governors have received instruction on seeing to the safety of the city during our absence."

Worried murmurs floated through the courtyard with growing fervor.

"Fear not, my people!" Bardazel shouted encouragingly. "My army will strike at the Grohldym as we depart should they show themselves, drawing them away. This will eliminate the possibility that they might attack the city. You will be safe within these walls while your governors and their agents attend to your well-being." The king raised his hand in an attempt to appease the crowd's growing unrest. It took several moments to achieve the desired effect, but he managed to calm them enough to offer further inspiration. "Each of us has a role to play in this if we are to have any chance of success. You have all proven yourselves to be brave and strong throughout the years, and you must accept your duty to stand together and hold fast until our return. This is what I must ask of you as we forge a new era for our kingdom—an era free from our oppressors—an era of peace and prosperity! Will you do your part to see this though?"

King Bardazel's unrelenting resolve and enthusiasm had its desired effect. Scattered shouts of approval were quickly joined by additional voices, and soon the majority of those gathered were showing their support with applause and cheers that echoed throughout the streets. Bardazel raised his fist triumphantly, stirring enthusiasm from even the most reserved members of the crowd who could not help being swept up in the infectious show of unity. The roar of the crowd was deafening as the king gave a final wave and departed with Lord Skealfa at his side.

With the necessary spectacle of the formal announcement behind him, Bardazel wasted no time returning to the to the interior of the palace keep and entering a secret corridor that would take him and the battle-lord directly into the ancient part of the city where they would join the waiting army.

CHAPTER 27

Czarstostryx was leading Prince Nieloch and his son through the canyon labyrinth when the unnerving stillness was finally shattered. The sound of crashing thunder boomed throughout the canyons with deafening force, sounding as though a hundred storms had been simultaneously unleashed from the heavens. Czarstostryx froze in his tracks, peering at the canyon walls high overhead. Nieloch and Mecursto crouched reflexively, shielding their heads with their arms, half-expecting the walls to crash down upon them. It was difficult to know for certain which direction the noise had originated from, but it seemed to be growing louder with each passing moment.

Nieloch noticed Czarstostryx's face briefly shift from his normally unreadable countenance to a look of deep concern, causing fear to grip his heart. Throughout everything they had endured, he had never seen the outlander react in such a way. He quickly forced the worry from his thoughts, hoping his son would not become alarmed at his reaction, but

Mecursto had noticed. *"What is it, father? What is happening?"*

Nieloch could feel his son's fear radiating through his mind, but it was clear that Mecursto was doing his best not to succumb to panic. Nieloch understood the impulse and was impressed at the boy's composure considering the circumstances. The prince did his best to steady his nerve as well, looking to the outlander for an explanation as the thunderous racket grew steadily louder. Czarstostryx had to raise his voice in order to be heard. "Something has roused the Watchers!" he exclaimed while doing his best to keep his voice subdued.

"Are we in danger?" Nieloch asked in alarm.

The outlander said nothing. Even if he had tried to answer, his voice would have been drowned out by the overwhelming noise. Instead, he motioned for them to get down and stay silent. He quickly extinguishing the phantom flame as they did so. The group pressed themselves against the canyon wall, crouching as low to the ground as possible, huddling in total darkness. Within moments, the ground began to shake from the relentless impact of the cliff-dwellers moving directly above them. A gust of wind swept against them, generated by the swift movement of the creatures as they rushed in the direction the group had just come from. As the procession continued, the three remained frozen on the canyon floor, tension mounting as time dragged on. It was impossible to say how many of them there were considering the disorienting nature of the echoes. To Nieloch, it sounded as though many hundreds had moved past them before the cacophony began to subside, though it still resonated in the distance.

As soon as the threat passed, Czarstostryx stood and produced his phantom flame, motioning for the others to get back to their feet as well. "Quickly!" he said harshly. "We must hurry!"

Nieloch and his son rose unsteadily, bracing themselves as they regained their rattled senses. They quickly fell in behind Czarstostryx, continuing their journey with renewed vigor.

They were exhausted by the time they reached the tower. Czarstostryx had kept them moving at an accelerated rate until the massive tower was looming before them. The sounds of the cliff-dwellers' movements still echoed menacingly in the distance. The commotion had not ceased as they traveled, giving them added incentive to maintain their rapid pace, but no matter how quickly they moved, it still seemed they were unable to put distance between themselves and the thunderous booming. Nieloch could tell that Czarstostryx was troubled by it as he continued to push them hard around the sweeping contour of the tower, moving nearer to the far side where they would enter the door he had unlocked.

When they arrived at their destination, Czarstostryx came to an abrupt halt. The doorway he had opened earlier was no longer there. Instead, there was a stairway rising up and out of sight as it wound its way around the tower like a massive serpent.

"Where is the doorway?" Nieloch asked in confusion.

Czarstostryx seemed to consider for a moment, then he instructed them to follow as he quickly began to stride up the stairs.

The stairway was easily wide enough for all three of them to climb side by side, but the prince and his son chose to ascend single file, keeping close to the tower wall as they climbed. It was not long before they had left the ground far below. The sheer drop off the edge of the steps was unnerving to Nieloch, but Mecursto did not seem to be bothered by the dizzying height. Czarstostryx also seemed unphased as he continued to move unrelentingly upward.

The tower was massive, and even though they climbed with haste, it would still take a fair amount of time to reach the top. Nieloch realized as they climbed that the thunderous echoes seemed somewhat diminished when the tower was between themselves and the entrance to the gorge, but each time they made a complete orbit and returned to the point where they had escaped the canyons, the tumultuous uproar persisted, growing louder each time they passed. By the time they had climbed halfway to the top, there was no mistaking it; whatever moved through the canyons was getting closer. It seemed to be following them. Even from the vertiginous heights, the disturbance below had reached an alarming intensity. Soon, they would discover the identity of what it was that pursued them.

CHAPTER 28

When Skealfa and King Bardazel emerged from the seldom used corridor that connected the palace to the ancient ruins of the palace outskirts, they found the deployment of forces well underway. While Bardazel had been addressing the city, General Scorthis had been repositioning the army from the abandoned streets into the forest through the access gate Skealfa had set out from days earlier. Moving thousands of heavily armed soldiers was time consuming, but Scorthis was expediting the transition into the forest as efficiently as possible. The soldiers jogged through the narrow gate and quickly reformed their ranks in the forest just outside the city walls. Over half of them were in position as Skealfa and the king joined the general near the gate. Scorthis bowed to the king as he approached, but he addressed Skealfa first. "Insertion of troops into the forest is going well. Our full number will soon be in position and ready to march in force."

"What of the Grohldym?"

"There has been no sign of them, my lord," Scorthis said tentatively. "The stillness in the forest remains. Nothing moves. There is not even a breeze to stir the leaves. I have never seen the like."

"Indeed, it is strange," the battle-lord agreed, "but I believe it will serve our purpose." Skealfa continued firmly. "I will take my position at the head of the ranks and lead the army to the tower. King Bardazel will remain with you near the center of our forces until we get closer to our destination."

"As you command, my lord," Scorthis replied, motioning for the king to take his place beside him.

Bardazel reluctantly took his position with General Scorthis, though he had originally insisted he should accompany the battle-lord at the head of the army; after all, it had been his life's ambition to liberate his people, so it only made sense for him to lead from the front. Skealfa had managed to convince him, after some deliberation, that it was critical for him to stay well protected on such a perilous journey. He explained that the best protection would be afforded near the center of the formation since an attack would most likely come from the front or the rear. Skealfa had also argued that it would not serve the king's purpose if he fell before they made it to the tower, and he assured him that once they reached the tower, he could claim his position at the head of the army, assuming the most imminent danger was truly behind them. Skealfa told the king that he anticipated a positive outcome if they took such precautions, and Bardazel could not argue with the logic, so he had grudgingly agreed, and the matter was resolved.

With the king in position, Skealfa took his place at the front of the army to finalize the transfer of troops into the forest which continued to go exceptionally well. As the battle-lord advanced the forward portion of the army, the ranks at the rear were quickly replenished by the remaining soldiers passing through the gate. In due course, the entire army moved as one, resembling a massive snake moving through the forest with deadly intent.

The sheer number of men the king had set to purpose was a tactic that had never been employed before. Typically, the main body of the army's forces would remain within the city to safeguard against attack if its forces were to be divided, but the current state of affairs was far from typical and called for an unprecedented strategy. Rank after rank of seasoned, well-armed soldiers and novice recruits alike, marched with grim determination, crashing through the forest with no regard for stealth. The full force of the king's army shook the ground as they moved through the home of their enemy, daring its inhabitants to try and stop them.

The battle-lord welcomed the thought of opposition. He was anxious to catch up to the outlander, but he still hoped the Grohldym would be foolish enough to get in his way. His blood boiled. He longed to deal death to his foes but knew full well that his thirst for vengeance would never be satisfied.

Skealfa had been given many opportunities to seek out the Grohldym over the years, but their elusive nature made it virtually impossible to track and kill them at will, so his clashes with them were usually the result of raids on the city which made the outcome much harder to predict. In the case of Czarstostryx, it was invigorating to finally have a foe whose whereabouts were known. It would give him a rare advantage when engaging the outlander. Skealfa knew he would be able to follow the course the old man had taken without difficulty, and though he had not actually seen the tower, he was certain he would be able to locate it; he *had* to if he wanted to serve justice to the vile miscreant.

Skealfa found it fortunate the king had finally seen the old man's true nature revealed. The battle-lord had always been aware of the outlander's devious intent, but as a loyal soldier it was his duty to serve the will of the king, not to question his judgement. His spirits soared at the thought of finally being free to crush the arrogant old man to dust beneath his heel.

The entire army seemed to be feeding on Skealfa's feverish anticipation as they trampled through the underbrush of the forest leaving a wide swath of devastation in their wake, and even though they made excellent time marching unopposed, nighttime was upon them by the time they reached the entrance to the canyon labyrinth.

Skealfa considered the lead the old man had achieved, doubting they would be able to overtake him before he reached the tower; he only hoped he could catch him before he gained access beyond. Skealfa knew that locating the tower would be challenging, but tracking the outlander through an entirely unknown region might prove impossible. *"One task at a time,"* he told himself.

Skealfa slowed the army as they approached the canyon entrance then brought them to a halt as he came to stand before the obscure crack in the cliff wall. "Runner!" he called out.

A young soldier in light armor immediately appeared at his side. "Yes, my lord?"

"Inform the king that we have reached the canyon entrance. He is to maintain his position in the middle of the formation as we move forward. Remind General Scorthis that we will need to slow our pace as we enter the canyons, but once we are inside, we must avoid spreading our ranks too thin in case we encounter opposition."

"As you command," the runner said before quickly bowing and racing away.

Skealfa knew the narrow canyon entrance would only allow the passage of one man at a time, but the labyrinth itself was much wider. Most of the paths he had seen would allow them to travel in a formation of six abreast once they reassembled beyond the entrance. It would be the transition where they would be most vulnerable, and he wanted to move through it as quickly as possible.

Before setting out, the soldiers had been well briefed regarding the execution of Skealfa's pursuit strategy through the unusual landscape, and so far, everything was going smoothly. Raising his torch high above his head, the battle-lord slowly waved it back and forth, triggering a chain-reaction of more torches imitating the signal down the ranks. "For vengeance and freedom!" the battle-lord roared to his men. "Forward, with haste!"

Plunging into the blackness, Skealfa prepared to deliver a viscous attack. He half-expected to find himself face to face with the monstrous cliff-dweller that had cast him from the labyrinth, but there was nothing. The looming darkness of the narrow path stretched before him, stagnant with unnatural silence. It stood that way for but a moment before the sound of heavy footfalls began striking against the stone floor, ringing loudly through the corridor. The noise quickly filled the canyons, echoing with increasing volume as the army reformed itself, filing into ranks of six men abreast spaced two paces behind the row in front of them. Row after row of soldiers steadily moved forward as Lord Skealfa led the way.

Torchlight began to fill the canyons as growing numbers of soldiers crowded into the narrow passages. The men kept their ranks tight, but there was just enough room to maneuver should they find the need to engage in combat. For every row of six, there were two men who carried long spears pointed skyward in anticipation of an attack from above. The soldiers had been warned of the nature of the cliff dwellers' attacks and kept a wary eye above them as they made their way deeper into the canyon labyrinth. They had also been informed of the thunderous crashing that accompanied the cliff dwellers as they moved, but as growing numbers of soldiers gathered in the canyons, it was less likely they would be able to take advantage of that fact. It would only be a matter of time before discerning the Watchers' movements from their own would become nearly impossible.

From the mid-point of the procession, King Bardazel was considering that very thing. After an extended, painstaking process, the well-organized army was once again marching collectively. The sound of their swift passage was deafening, but the king's concern over the matter dissipated as he passed the cave Skealfa had described to him where Toric had been consumed by flames. He became giddy with anticipation, beholding firsthand one of the wonders of the newly discovered region. After countless centuries of believing one truth about the land surrounding them, it was exhilarating to finally see those beliefs shattered. He was on an uncharted road leading to an unknown realm. It was something he had always believed in, but now, it was more than just a dream.

The king felt the urge to race past the soldiers in front of him and join Skealfa at the head of the procession so he would be able to witness any new discoveries for himself. So far, he had followed his battle-lord's advice and remained in the center of the formation, but it seemed that the dangers Skealfa had warned of were not going to be a concern after all. The forest had been silent in the absence of the Grohldym, and they had been traveling inside the canyons for hours without incident. Only the sound of the army's crashing footfalls echoed in the towering corridors.

Bardazel could wait no longer. He was determined to be present when the events shaping his kingdom's future unfolded; he was the king after all! Just as he was about to command General Scorthis to clear the way for his advancement, something caused him to hesitate. Whatever had given him pause also affected the troops surrounding him. There was a noticeable ripple throughout the ranks as something unseen made an impact on the army. Looks of confusion passed among many of the soldiers as they continued to march.

"What just happened?" The king's voice was filled with concern as he posed the question to his general. Before he had an answer, blaring horns began to relay from the front, signaling the army to come to a halt.

"Something shifted," Scorthis replied slowly. "The stillness is gone."

Bardazel suddenly realized that his awareness of the unusual phenomenon had diminished as they traveled. The army's clamorous movement, and his excited state of mind, had masked the stillness from his perception almost completely. Now, as the army stood motionless, the silence around them should have been impossible to ignore, but strangely, it was not.

The king had only been exposed to the maddening effects of the Forest of the Grohldym a few times in his life. He had on rare occasion accompanied Lord Skealfa and his elite soldiers into the forest during dormant periods to become more familiar with the lands surrounding his kingdom. Skealfa had been impressed that he exhibited a high level of resistance to its effects, but Bardazel still recalled the nauseating feeling of mental unbalance and the effort required to maintain control of his will. He was having the same experience again, only much stronger; it was quite unnerving. His mind swirled in a vortex of confusion that resonated loudly, making it hard to concentrate. Many of the soldiers around him seemed to be experiencing something similar if not more intense, considering what he saw.

Some of the men clutched at their helmets with their hands while others shook their heads as if trying to clear their thoughts; still others stared blankly, weapons hanging loosely in their grip. A few of the soldiers scattered throughout the ranks showed less of an impact from the sudden, radical shift in the air. General Scorthis was one of the few maintaining all of his faculties. He began bellowing orders, commanding the soldiers to gather their wits and stand fast. Many of the men began to collect themselves as years of deeply ingrained discipline and training took hold. It appeared as if they were waking from a dream, compelled to regain their readied stance with weapons held tightly. There were, however, an alarming number of soldiers who remained confused and disoriented.

"Get me to Lord Skealfa at once!" Bardazel snapped as he grabbed General Scorthis' arm. "I must find out what is happening!"

Scorthis immediately moved to comply, knowing that something was terribly wrong. He did not even consider trying to convince the king to await Skealfa's command. With the sudden decline in the army's efficacy, Lord Skealfa's sword would be the most capable of defending the king's life.

BOOM! BOOM! BOOM!

The abruptness of the thunderous crashing was a startling contrast to the relative silence left in the wake of the army's sudden halt, and the temporary composure General Scorthis had managed to instill in the troops was shattered in an instant as chaos descended upon Bardazel's army.

At the head of the formation, Skealfa was doing his best to counter the effects of madness that suddenly afflicted the army. He was all too familiar with the power it had over the minds of most individuals from his experiences in the Forest of the Grohldym, but within the canyons it held an even greater influence. He had managed to rally a good portion of his soldiers when the madness was unleashed, much as Scorthis had, but as the thunder heralded the approach of the cliff dwellers, he knew that no amount of coercion would return all of them to their senses. "All who can still reason, stand ready!" he roared to his men.

Most of the soldiers held their weapons at the ready, peering intently into the gaping chasm overhead. The thunderous approach of the Watchers grew steadily louder until its deafening roar was directly above them. Skealfa gripped his sword tightly as he prepared to launch his attack, but to his amazement, the procession continued to move down the canyon in the direction they had come from, toward the rear of the army.

Having been in multiple battles with the Grohldym, Skealfa had developed an instinct for countering their unusual tactics in battle, but he had only recently encountered the cliff dwellers. He had no way to anticipate what they might be planning. Regardless of their intentions, he knew one thing for certain; the king was vulnerable, and he had to move quickly if he wanted to have any chance of protecting him.

Skealfa yelled out to the nearest, ranking soldier. "I must get to the king! Do what you can to keep the men organized and moving! We cannot allow ourselves to get boxed in! If you reach a junction before I get back to you, hold your position!"

The soldier gave a salute of acknowledgement and sounded the signal horn to spur the army's advance. Repeated signals were relayed through the ranks, but they fell short of the precision registered only moments earlier. The desired result was achieved, however, and the army resumed its advance.

Skealfa began to work his way back through the ranks in search of the king. He noticed as he pushed his way through the formation that most of the troops marched with faltering steps, inspiring those from the elevated ranks to shout encouragement. It was painfully obvious that he would have to return to the front of the formation as quickly as possible in order to keep things moving. If he did not return in time, the army would have to stop, imperiling them to a much greater extent. It would also allow the outlander to further distance himself from his grasp. He could afford neither outcome. Frustration gripped the battle-lord as he continued to force his way through the shaken soldiers, but his consideration of outcomes was cut short as the horns once again began to sound.

The piercing report came from the rear, heralding the attack. Skealfa knew he had a lot of ground to cover before he would reach the king's position, and he could see that the continued break-down of morale was going to impede his progress. "Keep moving forward! Stay in formation! Maintain your discipline!" Skealfa bellowed as he waded through the troops, closing the distance between himself and King Bardazel.

Skealfa had made a fair amount of progress when he began to hear the din of battle echoing through the canyons. He did his best to gauge the sound, trying to determine where the cliff-dwellers were making their attack. The army had been stretched out over a great distance, so it was difficult to know for sure, but Skealfa believed the sounds of battle were somewhere beyond the king's position. If that were true, then he might still be able to reach him in time.

Overwhelmed by the urgency of the situation, Skealfa's concern for the well-being of those in his path became secondary to a higher purpose. Startled and confused soldiers were knocked aside as the mighty battle-lord bulled his way through the throng to reach his objective. The sounds of clashing steel and screams of pain grew louder with every step gained through the tide of soldiers rushing against him, but Skealfa was still far removed from the battle, and he could only guess at the details of the conflict from what he heard.

Based on his recent experience with the Watchers, Skealfa knew the army would be at a serious disadvantage against the foes residing in the high cliff walls. The cliff-dwellers used the unusual terrain to accelerate the force of their attacks, delivering a virtually unstoppable impact of devastation, but the troops had been briefed on the most effective method conceived to defend against their attacks. Soldiers armed with long spears would target the creatures as they descended, bracing the butts of the spears against the ground in order to use the Watcher's own force against them. If the creatures impaled themselves on a quickly positioned spear, the swordsmen might have a better chance of finishing them off. It would take precise timing and nerves of steel to combat them; unfortunately, each moment the army spent under the influence of madness made it less likely a counterattack would be successful.

Skealfa could not help being impressed by the discipline shown by the army. Despite the sounds of chaos behind them, and their deteriorating mental state, the men continued to march forward as commanded. Their restraint would certainly benefit him in getting to the king more quickly, but if he were to ensure King Bardazel's survival, he knew that simply reaching him would not be enough; he would need to see what the army faced firsthand. He hoped he would reach the king before that question was answered.

The battle-lord was well over halfway to reaching the army's center when he was surprised by the sight of General Scorthis and the king pressing toward him. "Did your position fall under attack?" Skealfa asked Scorthis as he met him in the middle of the surging army.

"No. The enemy was not in our proximity," Scorthis replied.

"I ordered him to take me to the head of the army's ranks when the stillness ended," Bardazel explained as he joined them. "I must lead alongside you in this endeavor. It is my legacy, and I will not hide among my soldiers out of fear for my own safety any longer!"

"Well, it seems your timing on the matter has served both our purposes. It appears the enemy has fallen on the rear of our formation, so the further you are from it the better." Skealfa then addressed General Scorthis. "Take the king to the front of our lines and keep the army pushing forward. I must fall to the rear and see what is happening. I will return to your position as soon as I can, but I have to know what we are dealing with. If you reach the next junction before I join you, take the path to the right. I did not make it far beyond that point, but I believe the tower was nearby." Looking once again at Bardazel, he continued. "If you encounter another fork beyond what I have described and I have still not returned, then it will be up to you to choose the path. Should that happen, it truly *will* be your decision that determines the fate of the kingdom as you have so often hoped. Now hurry, both of you!"

King Bardazel and General Scorthis nodded resolutely and began to press through the ranks toward the front of the formation.

Skealfa turned his attention to the ever-increasing sounds of fighting and continued to force his way through the tide of soldiers, intent on reaching the source of the conflict as quickly as possible. The sounds of battle became deafening as he closed the distance on his objective which seemed sooner than expected. He estimated that he still had a fair distance to travel before reaching the end of the army's ranks, but as he rounded yet another turn in the winding corridor, he reached his destination. The army was under attack just ahead of him.

It was not Skealfa's intention to engage the enemy in a futile battle, but if there was a chance of defeating them with a flurry of force, it might make sense. His first objective was to see what the army faced and strategize accordingly. Ideally, his forces would be able to eliminate the threat before it compromised the success of the mission, but it was imperative that they overtake Czarstostryx before he escaped. It was also necessary to ensure Bardazel's safety and keep the army moving forward.

As the battle-lord pushed toward the fray, all of his mental planning vanished from thought as he beheld a horror even he could not have prepared for.

CHAPTER 29

Nieloch could not ignore the fact that something was seriously disturbing his son as they climbed the tower. It was certainly understandable that the boy would be uneasy; his whole world had recently been turned upside down, but it was not as simple as that. Ever since entering the canyons, the prince could sense growing feelings of dread emanating from his son, despite Mecursto's best efforts to mask them.

Nieloch was amazed at the boy's mental fortitude, and he also could not help being impressed with his physical attributes. Mecursto's well-muscled form shown plainly through the thin robes the outlander had provided him with, and as they traveled, he had shown few signs of fatigue. Now, climbing the seemingly endless ladder of stairs, he continued to move effortlessly while the prince struggled to keep pace. In the dim light of the outlander's flame, Nieloch also could not help noticing the way his son's golden curls bounced upon his shoulders with every step, painfully reminiscent of his lost love. Pride and admiration filled his heart. He would never be able to fathom how the young man had grown so quickly in such a short time, and it was upsetting that it seemed he had missed so much of his son's life.

He turned his mind from the thought. Soon, they would be able to make up for lost time under a new horizon. Who could say what they would discover beyond the confines of his father's kingdom? What grand cities and civilizations might await? Nieloch's fanciful thoughts were interrupted by another unmistakable pang of apprehension radiating from his son.

"What is troubling you, son?" Nieloch reached out to Mecursto's mind with his thoughts as he had grown accustomed to; he also did not want to alert Czarstostryx to his son's growing unrest.

"I am not sure. This place seems so familiar. I am certain I have never been here, but I feel like I have. There is something horribly wrong with this tower—something that makes me feel as if I cannot breathe. I do not know what it is, but somehow, I do. I am frightened. We should turn back."

"Try to calm yourself." Nieloch did his best to offer encouragement while managing his own apprehension. *"I know this place is frightening. It is unlike anything I have ever seen. I am terrified by it as well, but we are so close to finding what your mother had hoped for us. Is it not worth finding out what waits above?"*

"I do not want to find out, father. Could we not simply return to the forest and live there instead? I know how to avoid the monsters, and I know a safe place where we can stay, or perhaps we could go to my mother's home if you would rather not return to your father's palace. I do not need a new horizon. Everything is already new since I found you. I am content with that."

Nieloch's heart swelled at the sentiment. Even though he had only discovered him recently, the love he felt for his son was immeasurable, and he was finding that the moments he spent with him offered a kind of peace and contentedness similar to that he which he had experienced during his time with Glithnie. Perhaps, it was not necessary to go to such extreme lengths to seek out what already existed for them.

The prince began to slow his pace as the realization sank in. Finding a new world was the king's obsession, not his, and Glithnie had only thought of seeking it out so they could live a happy life together as a family—away from his father's control. As Nieloch thought about it more, he saw no reason why the king and his army could not enter the unknown realm on their own once the path was open to them. It held no relevance whether he and Mecursto entered at all, and it seemed likely that once the king's ambition was realized, his concern over the choices he made concerning Mecursto's future would be less consequential. It was doubtful he would even care what he did in the shadow of such a monumental event.

"Why do you falter?" Czarstostryx paused to look back sternly at Nieloch who was standing motionless on the stairs pondering his revelation. Mecursto had also stopped, looking hopefully to his father whose thoughts were clearly reflected in his own eyes.

"Do not stop!" Czarstostryx snarled. "We have almost reached the top!"

Nieloch looked up and saw the summit of the massive tower. Roughly one hundred steps further and they would be there. Looking down, he saw the canyon floor had long since disappeared. He realized that even if he wanted to turn back with his son, they would never be able to negotiate the course through the canyon labyrinth; he did not even have a torch. It was

Czarstostryx who had guided them through the darkness, and the prince knew there was no way he would be persuaded to take them back.

As the hopelessness of the situation sank in, Nieloch noticed the shadows below beginning to writhe and shift. He thought he was imagining things but quickly realized he was not. Sinuous, black figures were climbing the sheer face of the tower below them, rising like tendrils of smoke escaping a dying fire. From the periphery of the dull light emanating from the outlander's staff he could see hundreds of strange figures emerging from the darkness below, climbing higher with each passing moment.

"There is no time for hesitation!" Czarstostryx shouted. "Hurry!"

Nieloch felt as if he had just been woken from a dream by a hard slap in the face. He stumbled forward, pushing Mecursto up the steps as they both gathered speed, trying to keep pace with the old man. The three of them raced up the remaining stairs, finally reaching the tower's apex.

The top of the tower was a massive expanse of smooth, nondescript stone lying just below the crest of the canyon walls encircling it. The light from Czarstostryx's phantom flame had been replaced by the strange illumination of a new horizon which was no longer hidden by the high canyon walls. "This way, quickly!" Czarstostryx urged, as he hurried toward the center of the expanse.

"*I do not trust him!*" Mecursto's thoughts cried out.

Nieloch looked back over the edge, still seeing the twisted creatures drawing ever closer to where they stood. "We have no other choice now. We must put our faith in Czarstostryx to take us the rest of the way."

Mecursto looked around frantically, resembling a fish struggling to escape a net.

"Please, my son!" Nieloch grasped Mecursto's arm. "If you do not believe in him, believe in me! We will make it! All will be as it should."

Every fiber in Mecursto's being screamed out for him to vanish and flee, but as he looked at his father and saw the hope and desperation in his eyes, he could not leave him. His father had not given up the search when he was lost, so he would not abandon him. Together, they would discover what lay beyond the tower. Mecursto gave a resolute nod to his father and the two of them raced to the center of the expanse where the outlander had stopped to kneel.

As they approached Czarstostryx, they could see strange symbols deeply etched into the stone where the old man knelt. The symbols were connected to others on the floor creating a large, triangular pattern that stretched out around him. "Enter the protective barrier of this triangle," he instructed.

Nieloch and his son looked at one another uncertainly but did as they were directed and stepped into the confines of the pattern on the ground. Once they were all within the triangular perimeter, Czarstostryx reached into his robes and brought forth the artifact he had retrieved from the palace treasury. Holding the artifact firmly in his grasp, he positioned it directly above a hidden opening near the point of the triangle opposite from where they had entered. In the next instant, he slammed the artifact into the small opening with violent force.

The tower began to shudder, and the floor within the triangle began to slowly sink. Nieloch and his son exchanged worried looks as Czarstostryx stood and faced them. "Do not be alarmed. The tower is making its final alignment. We three must also be properly positioned for the final gate to open. We are standing upon a large counterbalance within this triangle. Each of us is required to stand in a corner in order to activate the mechanism. "Quickly, Prince Nieloch, take your place upon the circle of runes in the far corner and have your son to do likewise over there." Czarstostryx directed them to their positions with haste and took his place as well.

All three of them stood in the prescribed arrangement facing the center of the triangle when the slowly sinking floor came to a jarring halt as it settled into its final position. The tower's activation sounded like the tolling of an unimaginably large bell, absorbing all other sounds that echoed through the canyons. The impact was deafening, and Nieloch and his son were stunned as its reverberation penetrated their bodies and minds, holding them frozen where they stood.

After several moments, Mecursto's voice filled Nieloch's mind, louder than the aftershocks that continued, unabated. *"I cannot move!"*

Nieloch attempted to go to his son's aid, realizing with horror that he too was unable to move. He was being held fast by a powerful, unseen force. The prince felt completely paralyzed and was unsure if he would even be able to speak. To his relief, he found that he could as he called out to Czarstostryx. "Why can we not move?"

"All will be made clear presently," the old man said, smiling as he strode to the center of the triangle where a large, circular pattern of runes on the floor began to emit a sickly green glow. Czarstostryx stepped into the circle of illumination, and the light radiating from the runes began to gather intensity. As the light grew, the resonating of the tower's activation began to fade, leaving the trio bathed in blinding, green light, and utter silence.

"You have done well."

Upon hearing the unknown voice speaking to the old man, Mecursto's mind became frantic as fear and panic welled up inside him. Long-dormant memories washed over him, emerging from the hidden recesses of his mind—memories of being held captive in total darkness, unable to break free—memories of blinding light and pain. Peering through the dazzling, green light surrounding Czarstostryx, he finally recalled the glowing green eyes—the first thing he had ever seen!

He could no longer control his instincts. He was trapped, and there seemed to be no escape. Reflexively, his mind told him to be gone. He felt the unusual tingling sensation upon his skin that occurred whenever he vanished from the sight of others, but he did not disappear.

"Yes, young one," Czarstostryx cooed. "Summon your strength; its potency will add to my own."

Again, Mecursto tried desperately to escape, to no avail. Tears of frustration began to stream down his face as he realized the strange, old man was too powerful to overcome. He was helpless against him and whatever he had in store.

Mecursto turned his attention back to his father whose mind was in a state of panic and confusion as thoughts of regret and sadness poured from him. Mecursto scanned his surroundings, knowing he had to find a way to save both himself and his father as he desperately searched for anything that might help them escape.

Suddenly, he saw movement on the canyon wall behind Czarstostryx. Two men appeared on a small outcropping just below the ridge line of the cliffs surrounding the tower. They were heavily armored and covered in blood. He recognized the giant man brandishing a huge sword but not the other who was older and wore a gleaming crown upon his head.

"Look father!" Mecursto's thoughts cried out to Nieloch. *"There are men on the cliffs behind the old man!"*

Nieloch focused his gaze beyond Czarstostryx, fervently peering through the glaring light, trying to locate the small outcropping where Lord Skealfa and King Bardazel stood.

CHAPTER 30

S kealfa bore witness to the ghastly carnage at the onset. Even with the might of the army's entire fighting force, they never stood a chance against what they faced. The battle-lord knew engaging the enemy within the narrow canyons would be inherently perilous, so he had prepared his soldiers with weapons and tactics that might reasonably withstand an assault from the cliff dwellers residing there. Considering the haste in which the army was deployed, it was the best that could be achieved, and it might have proven effective had the opposition not taken an unexpected turn against them.

The army was at a disadvantage before the attack began, becoming psychologically compromised by the mind-altering effects within the canyon when the stillness ended, but they had done their best to rally as the Watchers amassed themselves near the rear of the army's formation and descended upon them with lethal precision and cunning. The creatures avoided the troops armed with spears and engaged the soldiers carrying swords instead. The swordsmen were easily overcome by the speed and force of their attacks which allowed the cliff dwellers to impale and carry them to the shadowy heights overhead. Shortly after ascending, the heavily armored victims began falling from high overhead, crushing, and confounding the troops below. Each time a captive was released from above, no less than two men on the ground were either killed or gravely wounded. As their brothers-in-arms rained down upon them, the army broke at last.

Panic set in as the out-matched soldiers scrambled to find a way clear of the relentless barrage. There was not enough room for the soldiers to move past the forces in front of them, so they had no choice but to hold their ground as bodies piled up around them. As more soldiers near the rear of the formation came under attack, they were forced to cease any attempts of forward progress turning instead to engage their attackers, but they were met with the same outcome. The cliff dwellers continued to impale and collect soldiers, taking them to the heights to send them plummeting to the earth again, and again. Bit by bit, the army was picked apart, slowly decaying from the rear as it was eaten away toward the front.

Skealfa continued to force his way through the surging press that was moving against him with increased urgency. All around him panicked soldiers clambered among the dead and dying, desperately seeking escape. Some sought to flee by returning the way they had come since the corridors behind them were empty. Climbing over the bodies that blocked their path, they raced toward the shadows. At first, it looked as if they would make good on their escape, but in the next moment the Grohldym began to emerge from the darkness, stopping them dead in their tracks.

Skealfa's blood boiled at the sight of his most hated enemy. He had begun to think that he would not get a chance to slay any of the foul creatures on his quest, but it seemed they had arrived just in time to prove him wrong. He gripped his sword with anticipation, pushing hard to close the distance to make his attack.

The first soldiers encountering the Grohldym stumbled to a halt and began to back away as the beasts materialized unexpectedly from the blackness, but it was too late to escape the grasp of the lightning-fast creatures. Skealfa expected the unfortunate souls to be quickly dispatched, as the Grohldym had no finesse when it came to eliminating their enemies. Their killing technique was brutally savage and simple. They typically clutched their victim firmly within their taloned grip utilizing all of their arms, then with an explosion of force, ripped the captive to pieces, sending their body in all directions.

To Skealfa's surprise, the creatures did not carry out their standard method of execution; instead, the men who were being held in their unbreakable grip were hoisted from the ground as the beasts stood tall. The Grohldym's necks arched so their faces were positioned within a hair's breadth of the terror filled eyes of the soldiers. In the next instant, the scissor-like mandibles opened wide then snapped shut, cleanly severing the men's heads from their bodies. The Grohldym continued to hold the headless bodies close as blood jetted high into the air, spraying all over the canyon walls. Again, the great mandibles opened wide, revealing a long, black stinger emerging from the throat of each one. With a violent, stabbing thrust, the stinger was driven deeply into the gaping neck of each of the hapless soldiers and then retracted. The headless corpses were then cast aside as the Grohldym quickly set upon others who were attempting to flee or else found those lying injured on the ground to victimize. Over and over the grisly procedure was repeated.

Troops who had thought to follow the lead of the first unfortunate few, turned in fear, adding their numbers to the inexorable surge of bodies pressing against Skealfa. The battle-lord began to lose momentum against the insurmountable tide as the growing force of heavily armored soldiers became too much for him to overcome. He witnessed continued attacks from above and below as he was swept along the canyons with the rest of the soldiers, unable to reach the fray, but as the number of soldiers opposing him dwindled, he knew it would only be a matter of time before he would regain his leverage.

Nearly half the troops impeding his progress had been methodically slaughtered when he began to feel an ebb in the press of bodies. Soon, the enemy would feel the bite of his sword, but he knew his chances of defeating the hoard were remote. The cliff-dwellers were easily dispatching the army's ranks, overwhelming them with far fewer numbers. Now, the addition of the Grohldym made even the prospect of survival doubtful. Skealfa smiled grimly, contenting himself to send as many of them to hell as possible before they took him. Gripping his sword eagerly, he plowed through the rest of his ill-fated brothers, dodging the cliff-dwellers and avoiding the endless rain of falling bodies. Maniacal laughter filled his throat as he finally reached the loathsome Grohldym.

Skealfa's sword swung in a wide arc, too fast for the eye to follow as he engaged the first Grohldym he came upon. The head of the beast flew from its shoulders just as it finished the bizarre impalement of another soldier's headless form. The battle-lord continued his assault with the ferocity of a man possessed. His sword was a blur amid his battle frenzy, cleaving his enemy into pieces as they diligently continued to cull the broken soldiers left in the wake of the Watcher's harvest.

Skealfa had slain no less than ten Grohldym before realizing they were not trying to defend themselves against him. They only seemed to be interested in infecting the fleeing or fallen. It was the cliff-dwellers who were killing and injuring the soldiers, leaving the dead and dying for the Grohldym to gather for their savage rite. *"Why?"* The question echoed in Skealfa's mind as he slaughtered increasing numbers while they continued to decapitate and inject bodies, unphased by his violent intervention.

Whatever reasoning drove the Grohldym to ignore his attacks mattered little to Skealfa as he continued with his butchery. Perhaps, this would be his opportunity to eliminate their entire race once and for all. No one knew for certain how many of them there were, but by all accounts, there had never been more than fifty seen in the same place at the same time. If he survived long enough, he may yet discover their true number, but it would be a monumental undertaking considering there were always more Grohldym emerging from the darkness to replace those he had slain. He could see that he was slowing their progress but quickly realized that as he reduced their numbers, they were eliminating his own forces in kind. Even at his frenetic pace, he would not be able to keep them from their purpose.

The odds he faced were overwhelming, and although the mind-altering effects of the canyons had served to increase his own fighting prowess, the morale of the army had been destroyed, which was allowing the Watchers to decimate them. The span of broken bodies left in their wake continued to grow longer, but Skealfa knew if he chose to engage the Watchers instead, the number of Grohldym would surely swell. One way or another the army would be destroyed.

It was a certainty that the soldiers wounded by the cliff dwellers would die if the Grohldym took them, so Skealfa concluded that his best chance to save at least some of his men would come from stopping the Grohldym. He had to destroy them all. Firmly deciding on how he would face his end, Skealfa set his jaw and continued to eradicate his nemeses, but ultimately, the choice would not be his to make.

Darting between the hulking beasts, he hacked and slashed with unrelenting determination to rid the world of their kind. The effects of the madness grew in him as he raged on, increasing his strength, and sharpening his senses. The awareness of his surroundings was keenly focused, allowing him to avoid the inordinate number of dangers assailing him, and it also alerted him to subtle movements among the headless bodies lying in heaps along the canyon floor. At first, he thought it was merely shadows being cast by flickering torches that lay scattered among the bodies, but it was hard to tell; the Grohldym also threw menacing shadows as they swarmed from the darkness, and blood was continually spraying throughout the corridors from endless decapitations and dismemberments, making it impossible to see clearly amidst the carnage.

It was when one of the headless bodies lurched to its feet that Skealfa knew he had not imagined what he had perceived after all. Disengaging from his attack, he paused briefly, pressing his back against the canyon wall. His blood ran cold as the mystery behind the Grohldym's unusual incentive materialized before him.

The headless body that stood was badly broken within the crushed armor it wore. Skealfa noticed the exposed skin was a dull, grey hue, and black ichor oozed from many gaping wounds. Balancing on unsteady legs, the body began to shudder violently, and its chest began heaving as if taking in huge gulps of air. The soldier's arms began to elongate impossibly until they nearly touched the ground. Needle-like talons tore through the tips of its human fingers and the flesh tore free, revealing grossly misshapen hands. The headless soldier slumped forward clutching its chest, presenting a clear vantage that allowed Skealfa to see something beginning to emerge from the stump of its neck. He immediately recognized the contour of a head being forced through the opening, emerging as the face of an unknown demon glistening black in the wavering light. Suddenly, the taloned grip clutching the soldier's chest grew tighter, piercing armor and flesh alike. With an explosion of force, both were torn away as one, and a new abomination stepped from the discarded husk of the soldier to confront the astonished battle-lord.

The creature appeared to be formed from some kind of exotic stone that had been polished to a high luster, but somehow, the being was able to move with fluid grace. Its smooth body was pitch black with streaks of deep, vibrant green running through it, much like the massive columns located in the most ancient parts of the city. It had the semblance of a man, but its legs were shorter and its arms much longer. The lanky, lean muscles spoke of incredible agility and endurance. It slouched forward, supporting much of its weight upon its long, powerful arms. Its short, squat legs seemed secondary to its mobility.

The creature moved lightly between the battle-lord and the Grohldym, blocking him from advancing on them while they continued their bizarre procedure upon the fallen men. Skealfa could see that more bodies of mutilated soldiers were rising to their feet and making the same gruesome transformation, and he knew he would have to move quickly in order to avoid being overwhelmed as more of their numbers began to emerge.

Skealfa's battle-frenzy was at its height, infusing him with unmatched strength and fury. He towered over the newly born enemy standing before him, and he was confident that he would be able to easily destroy the naked, unarmed being. With a roaring battle-cry, he leapt at the creature with his sword raised high, bringing it down with full force as he landed directly in front of it. The aim of his stroke was precise and should have easily sliced the creature in two, but his sword was deflected from the top of the creature's head as if it had been smashed against solid rock. The sound of the ricochet was lost in the din of the cliff dwellers' endless attacks as Skealfa sprang away from the creature, poised for another attack. His hands stung from the impact of the blow, but it was a mere annoyance. Still, it was cause for alarm. Already, several more of the stone demons were advancing on him with additional numbers rising by the moment to join them. They were creating a wall between themselves and the Grohldym. Skealfa faced their growing numbers warily with his back to his own retreating army.

The span of dying soldiers that lay between the battle-lord and the front of the army's formation had grown significantly. While the soldiers desperately pushed through the canyons, the cliff dwellers kept pace and continued to pick them off as they fled. Skealfa guessed at least half of the army had already been dispatched by the Watchers, and half of those had been poisoned. It would not be long before the entire army was transformed, and there seemed to be nothing he could do to stop it.

Desperately, the battle-lord lunged at the advancing wall of newly spawned forces, slashing at them with his sword. Each time, his attempts were deflected by their stone-like flesh, causing no damage whatsoever. As they drove him through scores of his dying brothers, Skealfa could see that the Grohldym would remain out of his reach, especially with the stone demons' ranks growing larger. Rage filled his heart as he realized his vengeance against the Grohldym had been cut short, but perhaps he still had time to take his revenge on the outlander and save the king. There could be no hesitation if he hoped to have a chance. Committing to a new plan of action, he turned from the stone demons and sprinted the way he had come, hurdling the bodies of the dead and dying.

It took longer than Skealfa expected to reach the front of the formation, and there were only a handful of soldiers still fighting when he arrived. They had reached the final fork in the path and had been forced to make a stand in order to protect the king. The surviving troops were comprised of those most resistant to the maddening effects of the canyons, and Skealfa was relieved to see they were still being led by General Scorthis.

The cliff dwellers had made short work of Bardazel's army, but the few remaining soldiers continued to fight fiercely against the Watchers who relentlessly dove at them from above. General Scorthis had rallied the soldiers, utilizing the long spears against the creatures with some success. Several of the beasts had been impaled and were slowly pulling themselves back up the walls, but there was no evidence any had been slain.

Skealfa could see that the soldiers would not be able to protect the king for much longer as he hurled himself along the final stretch running as fast as his legs would carry him, dodging attacks from above. Ten more soldiers fell in the time it took to for him to cut the distance in half, and he knew the rest would fall before he got to them. "King Bardazel, run!" Skealfa's bellowing voice rang out through the canyon, reaching the king's ears.

Bardazel could not believe it! His battle-lord was still alive and would soon be at his side. The fear and despair that had filled him since being overwhelmed by the Watchers was instantly replaced by a spark of hope. With newly found inspiration to survive, the king turned and took off like a shot into the unknown darkness of the left fork, narrowly escaping the final wave of cliff dwellers and a barrage of falling bodies.

Skealfa dove into the fray, but the creatures leapt clear of his sword, returning to the heights with their victims. Only one of the Watchers lingered. General Scorthis had managed to impale it but was met with the same outcome. The creature held him pinned to the wall as it flailed against the spear being wielded against it, struggling to tear it from the general's grasp. It was all the time Skealfa needed.

With a brutal chop, Skealfa severed the limb that held Scorthis, and with whirlwind speed, spun and delivered a lethal strike to the elusive head of the brute, nearly splitting it in two. Without a moment's hesitation, he tore the dismembered limb from Scorthis' chest and picked him up like a sack of grain.

He then snatched a burning torch from the ground and charged after the king into the darkness. Sprinting along the unknown path, he caught up to Bardazel quickly, and upon reaching him, pressed him to keep moving as he handed him the torch.

"You cannot expect me to go alone!" Bardazel protested as he took the torch.

"Fear not. I will be close behind, but I must cover your retreat. Now go!" Skealfa spun the king by his shoulder and shoved him roughly on his way, allowing no further debate.

Turning his attention back in the direction of the threat, the battle-lord kept his eyes sharply focused on any sign of movement from above. His body tensed as he listened intently for sounds of pursuit, but the thunder of the cliff dwellers and the crashing of bodies had subsided. There did not seem to be anything closing in on them at the moment.

"You must leave me here," Scorthis said weakly.

Skealfa took a moment to set the old warrior on the ground, propping him gently against the canyon wall. Having witnessed the violent attack, Skealfa knew the general was gravely injured, but he could not see the extent of the damage in the quickly fading light.

"I can get you out of here," Skealfa said, with conviction.

"Indeed, you could, but burdening yourself with my corpse will serve no purpose. Stay with the king and get him to the tower. Find the hidden realm, if it truly exists, and see that the outlander pays for his deception!" Scorthis' body shook with effort as he forced his words to be heard, then he slumped against the wall. A low, gurgling sound escaped his lips as the final breath left his body.

Skealfa rose from the revered warrior, pausing briefly for a moment of solemn regard before turning to race after the diminishing glow of Bardazel's torch. As he ran, the last words of his fallen mentor echoed loudly in his mind.

CHAPTER 31

Skealfa and King Bardazel skidded to a halt, narrowly avoiding a lethal fall from the sheer drop-off as the path they had been climbing ended abruptly. It was the first impasse encountered since their mad flight from the canyon labyrinth below where chaos had consumed Bardazel's army. The path the king had chosen led to a vantage point with an unusual perspective. On a small perch, just above the lofty heights of the tower, they stood in awe as they beheld what they had been seeking at last. It took them several moments to comprehend the sight before them. After the attack, they had not been certain they would make it to the tower, but they assumed if they did, it would be looming high above them; instead, they found themselves looking down upon it.

A blinding, green light emanated from the center of the tower's apex, casting dark shadows around its perimeter which stood out in stark contrast to the writhing darkness along its circumference. Within the light, three figures could be seen standing motionless. Two of them were facing in the direction of Skealfa and the king. One, they recognized as Prince Nieloch, and the other was a youth with a flowing mane of golden curls who they had never seen before. The third figure stood with his back to them, but Skealfa immediately knew it to be the outlander. His jaw clenched in anger as he beheld the devious old man who was responsible for so much destruction.

The battle-lord was quick to formulate a plan. The edge of the tower was just below the ledge he stood on, but it was a stone's throw away. It was far too great a distance for someone to simply leap across, but Skealfa's attributes greatly surpassed that of a normal man. His enormous size and strength had allowed him to perform incredible feats throughout his life, and in his heightened state, he had no doubt he would easily clear the distance in order to crush the vile deceiver. Since the old man's back was to him, Skealfa surmised he would be able to set upon him before he could use his powers to stop him.

"I have him now." Skealfa spoke quietly to the king as he prepared for his attack.

"Wait!" Bardazel hissed. "It appears he has advanced his plans to unlock the tower just as he said he would. I may not understand the workings of his magic, but I am sure he will accomplish what he set out to do. He is on the threshold of unlocking the hidden realm. Do not strike!"

"I fear something is amiss," Skealfa replied gravely. "You cannot trust the outlander. What of the prince?"

"If my son needs help, he will alert us. Wait until he has finished. You can dispatch the outlander once the way is clear."

Skealfa's anger boiled, but he held his position…

"Who are they, father?" Mecursto's distress translated clearly in Nieloch's mind.

"It is my father and the battle-lord, Skealfa—the mightiest warrior in the kingdom!" The prince's thoughts were filled with hope.

"Will they help us?"

"I am not sure they can." Nieloch wished he had the answer his son hoped for, but he was still confused by what was happening, and he was afraid to call out and give away the position of their potential saviors until he had some idea of what was going on.

"Why are we being held?" Nieloch again demanded of Czarstostryx. "Explain yourself!"

Czarstostryx no longer heard the pleas of the prince as he stood in the presence of the one he had summoned.

It was apparent to the prince that the old man was mesmerized by something powerful and unseen. In the brilliance of the light surrounding him, the outlander was being steadily lifted from the floor by an invisible force. As he rose, the light engulfing him slowly began to fade while somehow growing brighter. It appeared that the sickly green luminescence was being absorbed by the old man, becoming filtered and redistributed through his eyes which began to glow brighter.

Nieloch's thoughts were blurred as the intensity of Czarstostryx's eyes began to penetrate his very soul. Feelings of dread and panic dissipated as he was held in the burning gaze. He had a vague sense of someone trying to wake him—as if from a dream—pleading for him to save them, but he could no longer think clearly.

Mecursto felt his father slipping away. His mind screamed out to him—warning him of the approaching danger. The boy recognized the power that was manifesting itself within the old man and realized the peril that was upon them. *"Father, we need help! Call to the battle-lord!"* It was no use. Nieloch's mind was enslaved just as his body was.

There was nothing Mecursto could do. He looked desperately to the men on the cliff who stood motionless, watching, then he returned his gaze to the old man who was radiating with immense power. Again, he frantically tried to vanish but remained firmly fixed to his position, unable to escape.

Mecursto had no choice but to watch in horror as Czarstostryx slowly raised his arms over his head and brought them down in a quick, slashing motion. The prince howled in anguish, and Mecursto's eyes shot back at his father whose arms were falling to the floor, severed at the shoulder by the outlander's immeasurably heightened focus. Blood sprayed wildly, covering Mecursto and Czarstostryx who was again raising his arms and crossing them over his chest this time. With a violent sweeping movement, he slung his arms out to either side at a sharp downward angle, and Nieloch's legs were lopped off at the hip. Prince Nieloch's tortured screams continued unbroken as he fell to the stone floor, toppled to lie facing his son. Mecursto looked into his father's eyes and was overwhelmed by the sadness and regret he saw there. Nieloch's senses had returned as the pain of dismemberment wracked his body. The stark realization of how he had been misled washed over him, and he was filled with despair as he looked upon his son for the last time. In the next moment, Czarstostryx thrust his arms high overhead, brutally tearing Nieloch's head from his shoulders by sheer force of will.

Mecursto stared in horrified disbelief at his father's dismembered body laying before him. The vicious transformation had been almost immediate, making it difficult to register what had happened. An unnatural amount of blood poured from the pieces of Nieloch's corpse. Somehow, the tower's activation served to amplify the production of the precious resource to accommodate the demon-lord's appetite. Pooling blood rapidly began to fill the triangular depression where Mecursto stood, trapped...

King Bardazel was having a difficult time processing what he had seen. In one moment, his son was standing calmly before the outlander, in the next, he appeared to crumble in a heap at his feet. It was hard to tell for sure what had occurred since the brilliant light faded just before the prince fell, making it tricky to interpret from his vantage point.

"What is happening, Skealfa?"

"Prince Nieloch has been slain! The final deception is exposed! It is time to end this madness!"

Skealfa moved to make his attack, but Bardazel grabbed his arm in desperation. "You cannot know for sure what has happened! The shadows are deceptive. Perhaps what we have witnessed is a part of the final ritual. We must not intervene! The way will soon be open. I can still lead my people into the unknown realm!"

"Are you blind?" Skealfa seized Bardazel by the shoulders. Frustration and outrage blazed to life as he tried to make his king see reason. "There *is* no unknown realm! We have been misled. Everything the villain told us was a lie! His only purpose was to achieve his own diabolical goal at the peril of our kingdom." The battle-lord angrily shook the king. "Your son is dead! The army has been decimated, and your kingdom now stands unprotected from whatever evil is being unleashed. This must end now!"

Bardazel struggled in Skealfa's iron grip. "I have not been misled! All is as it should be! The way to the unknown realm will be revealed, and I will be the one to set us all free!" Skealfa could see the madness in Bardazel's eyes. The effects of the canyons, combined with the fervor of his life-long obsession, had provoked an unstoppable mania that had clearly devoured his mind.

Skealfa understood the futility of his efforts as the king continued to struggle—the futility of his *life*. He had given his loyalty and service to a megalomaniac who cared nothing for the lives of others in his own pursuit of personal glory. All he had lost—all he had suffered—everything had been ripped away and there would be nothing to justify any of it! Blinding rage gripped him. No more would he be bound by misguided loyalty! No more would he be controlled by the will of another!

The battle-lord's grip on King Bardazel's shoulders grew tighter, and his hands crushed the king's armor as he lifted him from the ground. There was a flicker of shock in Bardazel's eyes as Skealfa flung him from the ledge. As the king plummeted into the darkened depths still clutching the torch in his hand, Skealfa glimpsed the multitude of writhing figures clinging to the sides of the tower just below him. Bardazel's transformed army swarmed in the shadows beyond the ledge where he stood, assuring the battle-lord's demise should he interrupt the outlander's grisly proceedings.

Skealfa laughed at the thought. The only thing he had left to live for was ending the old fool's miserable life and destroying all he had hoped to achieve. He would welcome death as long as he took Czarstostryx with him.

Skealfa distanced himself from the ledge, allowing the necessary space to generate enough speed to make the leap to the tower. Crouching low, he sprinted from his position with all the force his powerful legs could muster and launched himself from the ledge. The battle-lord sailed through the air, easily clearing the span between the ledge and the tower, and landed with acrobatic precision, tucking, and rolling as he hit the stone surface, greatly diffusing the sound of impact made by his armor while maintaining his momentum without breaking stride. Czarstostryx remained with his back to him, but there was still a fair span to cover before Skealfa would reach the center of the tower where the outlander was kneeling above the fallen prince ...

Mecursto struggled violently against the invisible bonds holding him as the old man dropped lightly to the floor and moved to his father's body where he began to re-arrange the pieces of his corpse.

"Stay away from him!" Mecursto's thoughts pierced Czarstostryx's mind with vicious intent.

"Ah, you break your silence at last," Czarstostryx replied mockingly as he continued without pause. "You need not have bothered. That which I seek is within my grasp, and you will play your part just as your father has."

Again, Mecursto attempted to vanish, fighting desperately against the barrier that shielded him from his abilities. Sweat beaded his forehead under the strain of his efforts as he continued trying to unravel the forces holding him. He recognized the power the old man possessed; it was familiar, but he did not fully comprehend its true nature. Czarstostryx, however, was able to manipulate it at will with deadly purpose. Mecursto had paid close attention to the way the outlander channeled his powers as they traveled and had gained a vague understanding of its mysterious design—enough to warrant his unbroken efforts to overcome it. Focusing his will with deliberate and unshakable intent, he pushed relentlessly against the old man's steadfast restraint. For a brief moment, he felt the invisible bonds that held him, slip, ever so slightly. Czarstostryx felt it too. Out of the corner of his eye, the outlander noticed the boy's head shift, then he saw a twitch of movement in his hand as well.

Having completed the reconstruction of the prince's body, Czarstostryx stood to face Mecursto. "Impressive!" he marveled. "The raw power you possess is truly immense. Had you been given the time to understand its full potential your abilities would have surely rivaled my own." Refocusing his energy on Mecursto's confinement, the outlander slowly stepped backward to return to the position within the triangle where he would repeat the killing ritual. He could feel the boy's surging, emotional energy challenging his control well beyond what he expected, but he maintained his unwavering concentration. Stepping back upon the glowing runes, Czarstostryx was again bathed in the radiant, green light which seemed to burn even brighter than before. The light was quickly absorbed by the old man as he slowly began to rise into the air.

Even as Mecursto continued to gain leverage against the invisible bonds, he knew he had run out of time.

Out of nowhere, the giant man who had been standing on the cliffs, leapt from the shadows, and crashed to the ground behind Czarstostryx like a meteor from the heavens. His sword screamed through the air in a downward arc, delivering a colossal blow intended to slice the old man in two, but Skealfa missed his mark. Czarstostryx flitted forward like a moth avoiding a flame, narrowly dodging the unexpected attack as sparks flew from the ground where Skealfa's sword struck the etched symbol above which the old man had been hovering. Undaunted and without hesitation, the battle-lord followed up his attack, slashing at the outlander who narrowly managed to dart from the path of the whining blade as he floated lightly above the surface of the stone floor. Again, Skealfa swung his sword with a viscous lateral slice intended to cut down the old man, but his sword was denied purchase as it struck a shimmering barrier that suddenly enveloped the outlander. The air around Czarstostryx crackled with blue flashes of electricity, wrapping him within a maelstrom of lightning, preventing Skealfa's sword from reaching him. Skealfa ceased his barrage momentarily, slowly circling the old man.

"I must admit, I am surprised to see that you still live. You are remarkably resilient to have made it here. A pity you have come so far only to fail." Czarstostryx's words dripped venom as he scrutinized the imposing battle-lord who seemed to have materialized out of thin air, interrupting his most critical proceedings.

"You are the one who will fail wizard! All of those you have betrayed and murdered will be avenged on this day!" Skealfa's fury was effusive as he stepped into the blood-drenched triangle and lunged at the outlander, driving the point of his sword with all his might straight at the old man's heart, but he was stopped mid-stride as his sword struck the impassible barrier and was rejected with the force of a lightning strike.

The blast knocked Skealfa to the ground and sent his sword clattering to the floor as the paralyzing attack dislodged it from his grasp. Skealfa fought to find his breath as he frantically blinked his eyes, attempting to restore his vision which had been stolen by the brilliant flash. He searched blindly for his sword, but quickly located it as he tracked the sound of its impact. Gripping the blood-slicked sword firmly, he scrambled to his feet to face the shadowy silhouette of the outlander hovering before him—relieved to discover his blindness had only been temporary.

Skealfa understood the old man possessed great power, but as he realized its true depths, he knew his chances of defeating him were slim. If he could not find a way to get past his guard, it would be impossible. As his sight came into sharper focus, he saw blood trickling from beneath the robes of the outlander. Skealfa smiled grimly. He knew the old man had dodged the full force of his first attack, yet he had not avoided it entirely. It would only be a matter of time before blood loss would claim him. "Your time is at an end old man!" Skealfa growled. "Your tricks will not save you from the vengeance I have wrought. Your death awaits!"

"Fool!" Czarstostryx hissed. "You cannot stop me. My power has grown exponentially upon the completion of each ritual. I have seen what it is to be a god and rise above this mortal coil! Your interference is inconsequential. Nothing will prevent me from fulfilling my destiny!"

As his tirade ended, the old man ceased to hover and dropped to the floor of the triangular depression, but the barrier around him still swirled electric with all the energy of a lightning storm. The moment his feet met with Nieloch's pooling blood, the bolts of energy surrounding him were conducted through it. Electricity crackled and hissed as the battle-lord's blood-soaked armor drew in the current. As blue, cold fire tore through him, Skealfa crashed to the floor, writhing, and contorting in the blood of the fallen prince His mind did not have a chance to register what had happened. All thought stopped the instant he was struck by Czarstostryx's shield of lightning.

Czarstostryx reveled in the power coursing through him as he focused his will upon the destruction of the fallen battle-lord. He had not yet completed the ritual that would unlock the full potential of promised power, but he was far mightier than ever before. Excitement gripped him at the prospect of what he would soon become once he finished off the bothersome warrior.

He was mere moments away from the fruition of his life's endeavors when his reality was shattered. Without warning, all the power coursing through him was severed, and he was slammed back to his point of origin within the triangle. Shock and dismay stunned the outlander as he tried to grasp what had happened. Frantically, he looked around for the answer. Skealfa's crumpled body lay near the prince's remains, but the boy was no longer upon his pedestal; he was stepping down into the blood of his father.

Mecursto stared intently at the old man. His eyes were filled with fury as he slowly approached Czarstostryx who was now being held by his will. The giant warrior's attack had given him the opening he needed to free himself while the old man was distracted. Now, he held the outlander within his own web of magic, forged from powerful emotion and instinct.

Czarstostryx's face grew ashen as he realized what had happened. His conflict with Skealfa had drawn him away from maintaining his hold on the boy whose resistance to his power had been growing increasingly difficult to manage. He found himself restrained in much the same manner he had employed, but the boy's design was primitive and raw, and he could not see a way to undo it.

Mecursto was not entirely sure what he had done to sever the old man from the source of power they both shared or how exactly he was holding him captive. He had acquired a reasonable sense of manipulating the energy and was doing his best to imitate what the old man had done to him and his father. Compelled by the force of grief and rage, the power flowed through him without thought.

As Mecursto drew closer to the outlander, he found himself stepping over the runes in the center of the triangle. Unexpectedly, he began to rise from the ground, and the sickly green light began to fill *him* with its brilliance. Soon, his eyes burned brightly—filled with the fire of unknown mysteries.

"*You have returned to me as I always knew you would.*" The demon-lord's voice echoed loudly in Mecursto's mind. The words came as if he were being spoken to, but at the same time, it felt as if they were his own thoughts. *"Czarstostryx played his part well bringing you here. He chose you and your father for the final sacrifice because only the spilling of royal blood can unlock the final gate. He sought to reach the hidden realm in order to gain mastery of the source of limitless power residing there. It is a power he has partaken of throughout his life but only in small portions. It is what allowed him to acquire the skill and knowledge necessary to seek me out. You, however, have been imbued with that power since the day you were born. You have grown stronger without having to learn how. Now that you have immersed yourself in its radiance upon my tower, your full potential has been unlocked, making you more powerful than Czarstostryx whose ambition was only to achieve power to rise above others, but it can also be used to benefit the world. See through my eyes and understand the power of creation."*

As Mecursto's mind became one with Kkrolszerogg, the shared perception of the eternal demon-lord was intoxicating, and it granted understanding of limitless possibilities. Mecursto experienced what it felt like to be a god, rising above the restrictions of humanity. The veil of the world around him was lifted, exposing its potential as well as its vicious and cruel nature. He was bestowed knowledge of what it was to wield unmatched power that could destroy life as well as give it. He also realized there were very specific laws and intricate requirements demanded by the demon-lord in order to attain such heights as a mortal. The spilling of blood was compulsory for those who would partake in the power that was offered.

Mecursto considered how Czarstostryx had brutally sacrificed his father and would have done the same to him in order to achieve mastery over the world, but Mecursto realized if he acquired such power for himself, he could undo what had been done—he could bring his father back! He could even do the same for his mother who he had never known. He could take them with him to the unknown realm to live the life they had hoped for—a life that would be safe, and peaceful, and filled with love.

The power to resurrect his family was within his grasp, but Mecursto knew he would have to complete the ritual if it were to be so. The old man would pay for what he had done to his father. *His* would be the blood that would satisfy the demon-lord's demands! Mecursto raised his hands in the same fashion the old man had. Power surged through his entire being as he focused his fury. Czarstostryx did not have long to consider the unexpected turn of events as Mecursto's quick, concise motions rendered him into six, severed parts which spouted blood in all directions.

After dismantling the outlander, Mecursto settled to the floor and stepped forward to reassemble the pieces. Focusing on the gruesome mandate, his mind once more became his own. As he set to work, the writhing figures in the surrounding darkness began to close in around him. The wait was over for the stone demons.

Creeping from the outer rim of the tower, the creatures crowded around the edge of the triangular depression and began hungrily lapping up the pooling blood that Mecursto was immersed in. As soon as one took its fill, it moved back, allowing another to take its place. Hundreds gathered to feed and then recede into the shadows as Mecursto continued to reorganize the fragments of the outlander.

Upon the completion of his grizzly task, Mecursto found himself restricted by the stone demons as he stood in their midst. He was unable to leave the triangle and had no choice but to wait for them to become satiated. The blood grew shallow sooner than expected, and before long, it was completely devoured. Once the depression was emptied, the demons pulled Mecursto from its confines and began funneling him through their numbers—pushing him to the outer edge of the tower. When he reached the edge, Mecursto realized he was directly across from the small outcropping where he had first seen the giant soldier and the king. He watched with morbid fascination as the demons began to link themselves together, forming a bridge with their twisted bodies that began to stretch toward the cliff top above the outcropping. As the makeshift walkway lengthened, the demons continued guiding him along its span, until he was finally deposited atop the cliffs to stand at unparalleled heights.

Mecursto scanned the bizarre landscape. In every direction were deep crevasses shattering the expansive plateau. The outcropping below him was too far removed to reach safely, but he saw before him a gently sloping trail leading away from the tower. Looking back over his shoulder, Mecursto considered how he had narrowly escaped the fate of his father, but once he reached his destination, he knew he would be able to set things right. Perhaps, he could do the same for the giant soldier who tried to help him. He hesitated at leaving them behind. It did not seem right, but he had little choice in the matter since returning was no longer an option. The bridge was already shrinking away behind him as those who formed it regrouped upon the tower.

Mecursto could see the creatures in the dim light of the new dawn. Thousands of them writhed on the tower, intertwining with one another, obscuring the smooth surface of the massive expanse. The triangular depression, and the bodies contained within, became covered as well, leaving no trace of the unholy ritual. Mecursto thought his eyes were playing tricks on him as the light of the rising sun cast its dull light upon the tower. The tangle of bodies covering it seemed to shimmer and melt into one another until the surface once again gleamed smoothly, reflecting the light as if it were an enormous onyx mirror.

Mecursto never expected any of this, but as he turned his back on the tower, he knew his path was set. He would complete the journey his father set out on. He would reach the unknown realm and claim the power that awaited. Then, he would make everything as it should be. With hope in his heart and implacable determination to succeed, Mecursto set off along the descending trail that would take him the rest of the way to the unknown realm.

CHAPTER 32

Mecursto moved briskly along the trail, trying to rid his mind of the brutal images of his father's murder. He focused his attention instead on his surroundings, trying to keep the dark thoughts at bay.

When he first set out from the high clifftops surrounding the tower, the sloping path had been quite narrow, much like the canyon corridors leading to the tower, but as he descended, it began to widen. Eventually, it led him beyond the towering mountain range into a low-lying region well beyond his father's kingdom.

The sun continued to climb high overhead as Mecursto traveled, providing a bit of welcome warmth. He was pleased he would no longer be forced to endure the bone-numbing chill and perpetual shadows of the canyon labyrinth, but even in the full light of the midday sun, the brightness remained noticeably diminished and tainted somehow. He also noticed how quickly the landscape was changing. The stark confines, frigid darkness, and lifeless rock of the canyons were replaced by clumps of sharp-edged grass and small, twisted trees covered with hanging moss.

A warm, damp breeze wafted from the unseen depths of the increasingly foreboding surroundings, carrying with it the stench of ancient decay. Mecursto stopped abruptly as the familiar smell overwhelmed his senses. He felt it creeping into the very core of his being. Somehow, he knew where he was; it was a place he was sure he had been before. He struggled to recall something tangible that might give him a clue as to how he was familiar with the unusual surroundings. The answer tickled his memory, but try as he might, he could not grasp it. He decided not to let it trouble his thoughts unduly, perhaps it would come to him as he traveled.

As he pressed on through the strange landscape, the vegetation continued to grow denser, eventually turning into a murky marsh. The trees crowded around him, obstructing his view, allowing him to only see a short distance in any direction. The light of the sun had become heavily diffused by a low-lying haze that further altered its illumination, filtering it into a sickly greenish hue. The combination of the haze and the restricted line of sight would have made navigation impossible if not for the clear path of hard-packed earth meandering through the clumps of grass. It had remained constant ever since leaving the tower, guiding him unfailingly toward his destination.

The fetid stench grew stronger with every step, carried on the warm, gentle breeze surrounding him, daring him to remember its origin yet managing to elude him. He suspected it would only intensify as he drew closer to his destination—the place the demon-lord, Kkrolszerogg, had shown him upon the tower—

the place where he would complete the final ritual and have the power of a god bestowed upon him.

After walking for most of the day, Mecursto knew he was getting close. The sticky dampness in the air no longer clung to him as it had earlier. The warm breeze was arid, and it reeked with the foul stench of death. The clumps of grass were stark and lifeless, crouching among the snarled, brittle branches of misshapen trees. It appeared as though the lush decay of the marshy bog had been drained of all moisture in an instant, transformed into a withered imitation of its former self.

It was not long before the trail came to an end, delivering Mecursto from the murky tangle of trees into a large clearing. At the center of the barren expanse were crumbling, ancient ruins. Some of the ruins lay beyond the clearing and were hidden from sight, obscured by the pale wisps of moss hanging dryly among the interwoven branches. Broken fragments of other parts of the ancient structure could be seen within the perimeter of the clearing, coming to rest near their toppled counterparts. The massive pieces of several broken obelisks formed a disorganized circle around the source of the oppressive breeze.

Mecursto walked into the clearing, cautiously approaching the ring of broken stones. The familiarity of the place was overwhelming. The foul stench, the strange breeze, the sickly green light, all of it bombarded his senses with each step he took. He began to grow light-headed, feeling as if he floated in a dream. Passing between two of the broken stones, he entered the inner circle to behold with his own eyes what he already knew would be there.

A pile of human bones lay in a heap, arranged in an unusual manner. It was similar to the way Czarstostryx had organized his father's remains, but it was much more complicated. It was not necessary for him to interpret the unknown arrangement; he only had to re-assemble the bones in the original configuration of human design in order to achieve what he had been promised. His hands seemed to work of their own accord as he knelt before the ancient bones, reconstructing the demented figure into that of a human skeleton.

In due course, he finished, and the final step of the ritual was at last complete. Mecursto rose slowly to his feet, unsure what would come next. The demon-lord had shown him all that was required to unlock the source of power but not how the transition would manifest itself. He looked up from the skeleton lying in the dust and noticed shadows gathering among the twisted trees. The air grew cold, and the breeze disappeared, leaving everything still and silent. Mecursto looked around nervously.

An unexpected clattering sound at his feet quickly drew his attention back to the skeleton which began to shudder. He took an involuntary step backward as the skeletal remains began to twitch and convulse violently. Slowly, the skeleton sat up and began to fastidiously transition into a standing position. It reached out to Mecursto to gain balance on unsteady legs, grasping his arm and then his shoulder within its bony grip, pulling itself closer as it stood.

Mecursto found himself face to face with the newly risen abomination, looking straight into the empty eye-sockets of the grinning skull. The fear rising within him quickly turned into terror as the dark sockets began to glow with strange light, pulling him into their terrifying depths. His head began to swim as he struggled to find his breath, fighting against the relentless scrutiny of the glowing, green eyes that held him fast.

He remembered! He was in the land of his birth, and once again, he was trapped!

Mecursto felt an irrepressible urge to escape, but he could no longer move. He felt weak and afraid, just as he had on the day he was born. Without warning, the skeleton released him from its grasp, and Mecursto fell to the ground, unable to catch himself. He realized something strange had happened; it was beyond anything he had ever experienced. He could see and hear, but he could no longer feel his body. He was completely disconnected from it, yet it continued to hold him firmly in place, trapping him within flesh that grew colder with each passing moment.

Mecursto lay on his side where he had fallen, filled with dismay. Behind him, he could hear the sound of crunching footfalls. He surmised they must have originated from the steps of the skeleton as it departed, but he could not know for certain. The view he had been afforded when he fell was that of several large, broken stones directly in front of him. There was a gap between them which allowed a clear line of sight into the murky tree line beyond the clearing; other than that, he had no way of knowing what transpired around him. Mecursto noticed there was something stirring in the shadows among the trees. He could feel eyes upon him, but whatever lurked within the gloom remained hidden—watching—waiting. So, lying there trapped within a lifeless shell, he had no choice but to do the same…

Mecursto had no idea how long he lay there before realizing that aside from the shifting shadows in the trees, nothing around him was changing. The sun should have set long ago, but the tainted daylight had not been altered. The surreal, greenish cast of the dimly lit surroundings remained constant. Maybe it was imagined; maybe less time had passed than he realized. He doubted it, but he really could not be sure.

Mecursto contemplated the unanticipated events that had transpired since completing the ritual. His assumption had been that he would simply embrace the promised power, but something had gone wrong, or maybe something had been concealed. Panic began to rise as it occurred to him that even though he had partaken in the shared consciousness of the demon-lord, he really had no way to interpret the experience with certainty; he had never been subjected to anything so foreign and unexpected, so how could he? The terrifying thought that he had been misled just as his father had, haunted him as he lay in the dust.

Time crept by slowly in the unchanging surroundings. Eventually Mecursto came to accept the fact that he was imprisoned within his own corpse and would linger there. Powerful memories flooded his mind, bringing vivid clarity of similar sensations he had experienced. He recalled feelings of being restricted and held in total darkness. He also remembered a constant, rhythmic beating. It was a memory before thought—a thing of the past he should not even be aware of, yet as he pondered his current state, he realized that despite the exchange of blindness for sight and sound for silence, he was exactly where he had been once before. He felt like screaming. He was truly and utterly bound. The power that had always been within him was out of reach, and the power he had been promised remained unattainable. He tried to rationalize what had happened. Had he really died, or was he lost in a dream? Was this part of the ritual, or had Kkrolszerogg misled him? He knew there was nothing he could do about it in either case. Try as he might to reach his inner power, he could not connect to it. The link between his flesh and spirit were the same—detached.

Mecursto lay there for what seemed like days, then weeks, with nothing to mark the passage of time. He could not see the sky from where he had fallen, but he knew there had been no sunset or sunrise. The sickly green illumination remained stagnant. The only stirrings were of shadows moving under the cover of the trees. The swirling, shifting shadows were a welcome distraction from his thoughts with their mesmerizing effect, and with nothing else to draw his attention, he watched them constantly, but their hypnotic swirling could not pacify his troubled thoughts indefinitely.

As time dragged on, he wondered if he would ever discover the source of movement in the shadows. He did not care if the unseen presence meant additional misfortune as long as the unbearable monotony was broken. He felt as if his sanity were unravelling. Oppressive thoughts continued to plague his troubled mind. Images of his father's death tormented him. Unfulfilled promises of power to undo it all taunted him. Madness began to claim him as he struggled to endure the unbearable prison of his own demise.

Mecursto did his best to keep his focus on the shadows. They had a calming effect that seemed to help him remain tethered to his sanity. He had been focused on them for so long that he had not noticed the subtle changes of his flesh or the exquisite stench that he was somehow able to perceive. Something was happening that was impossible to ignore.

The way he had fallen allowed him a view of his own hand and a bit of his wrist beneath the robes he wore. Now, he realized the significance of what had so languidly drawn his attention. The flesh of his hand and wrist had swollen a great deal. He had not paid much attention to the insidious swelling as time slowly passed, but now he found morbid fascination in the idea of watching the skin fall from his bones. He was thankful for the distraction. He had been finding it increasingly difficult to keep his reason from slipping away completely.

As Mecursto watched the tissue of his hand distend and slowly change color, he knew time was indeed moving forward. He had not been entirely sure before, and he was still not certain how much time had actually passed since his body died, but now he realized, several days had gone by. The thought terrified him; it felt like much longer. He tried not to think about the prospect of being held in such a state indefinitely, but at least for now, he had something to engage his thoughts. He watched in wonder as the swollen flesh of his hand changed from a greenish hue to a dark red color. Eventually, the nails on his fingers began to drop off one by one, and the tissue began to liquify. It all seemed so surreal.

Mecursto's thoughts inevitably returned to the events leading to his current state, all stemming from his decision to help his father. The tortuous memories of his father's death flooded his thoughts. The demon-lord's unfulfilled promise of power enough to undo his death, mocked his reason. His sanity continued to crumble, and his will to resist ebbed. *"Let madness take me,"* he despaired. *"Why should I fight against the inevitable? I was a fool to hope! I am undone."*

Overcome by grief and misery, Mecursto resigned himself at last to the sanctuary of insanity when unexpected movement from the edge of the clearing subjugated his anguish. Within the surreal climate, however, he was not immediately convinced he had actually seen anything. In the next moment, he realized that what he thought he had observed was not imagined. There were shapes emerging from the shadows of the trees, but it was hard to tell exactly what it was he was seeing. It appeared as if curling tendrils of smoke were gathering at the edge of the clearing near the woods. The sinuous shapes quickly advanced on him, revealing their true identity as they descended on his fallen corpse. *"What new horror is this?"* Mecursto wondered as several of the hideous beings attached themselves to his rotting cadaver.

The creatures were not very large. It took several of them to envelop his hand and arm. Many more began covering him from head to toe. They appeared to have no bones in their bodies as they writhed into position with unnatural flexibility. Their multiple limbs oozed from a central point where he could see black eyes glistening—sparking an unexpected hint of recognition within him. Snaking limbs compressed upon his flesh, shrouding it completely beneath their interwoven bodies. As each one established a suitable position, it began to pulsate quickly, causing the thinly draped flesh of the creature to slowly swell. As they became engorged, the pulsing slowed and eventually ceased altogether; then, the strange creatures detached themselves and slowly withdrew, crossed the clearing, and returned to the shadows of the surrounding trees.

Mecursto recognized their purpose when his hand and arm were revealed. Tissue had been removed, exposing the underlying bone. It seemed the creatures were feeding on his rotting flesh. He watched as several more of them returned to the forest moving much more slowly and awkwardly having indulged themselves with his putrescence. As they departed, others emerged from the shadows to take the place of their satiated counterparts, repeating the cycle. He watched the bizarre procession with detached interest, finding a modicum of comfort in their presence. He was not sure why. *"What does it matter?"* he thought. *"This is just another horrific event in a sequence of unimaginable and pointless experiences."*

He was having difficulty recalling his recent optimism about his future. His mental state was reaching its breaking point, trapped in the shell of his former self, watching as it was slowly stripped to the bone. Time became meaningless as he drifted through the unrelenting nightmare, abandoning all hope. He heard his own, hysterical laughter echoing in his mind as he teetered on the precipice of insanity…

Eventually, the saprophytes extracted all the rot and decay. Mecursto barely noticed when the parade of parasites came to an end, and he found a moment for solitary consideration of his transformation. His freshly denuded bones gleamed dully in the unwavering glow of his surroundings. The robe he had worn had also stripped away as cleanly as his flesh. From his limited perspective he could see the entire length of his arm reduced to bone and assessed it as a valid representation of what he could not see.

A sound in the distance pulled him from his thoughts. Something large was moving through the trees. The sound of snapping limbs echoed loudly through the haze, hailing the approach of something massive and powerful. It was moving quickly and getting closer by the moment. The heavy footfalls of the unseen caller drew near, and Mecursto instinctively tried to summon his power, desperately searching for a means of escape, but his link remained severed while *he* remained firmly tethered to his bones. He was vulnerable and exposed, and even though he did not believe there was anything left to lose, he was unable to suppress his burgeoning fear as he studied the tree line with nervous anticipation. Resigned to his fate, he waited.

Mecursto watched in awe as the beast emerged from the shadows. The tops of the twisted trees barely reached its waist. He immediately recognized the demon-lord, Kkrolszerogg. Although he had been in the presence of the mighty being upon the tower, Kkrolszerogg had not manifested in the flesh. Beholding its physical form filled Mecursto with potent, supernatural dread. The demon-lord strode toward Mecursto, spanning the clearing in just a few steps. The silver skin of the entity reflected the sickly green light, making it difficult to fully comprehend the demon's reality. Mecursto's vantage point from the ground increased his disorientation, further masking the being's true form.

Mecursto was cast into darkness as the light was blotted out by the shadow of Kkrolszerogg kneeling over him. His line of sight shifted unexpectedly as the mighty being dismantled his skeletal remains and began to deftly reassemble them in a way nature had not intended. Mecursto was unsure what was happening to his bones since his consciousness was firmly rooted in his skull. Everything he witnessed originated from that perspective, so it was difficult to see as the demon-lord went about its task and obscured his sight. It was not long before everything became still once more, and he saw the face of Kkrolszerogg directly before him—green eyes glowing fiercely—piercing his soul. There was a flash of blinding light and intense pain; then, there was nothing…

When awareness returned, there was no sign of the demon-lord. Slowly, Mecursto regained his senses and absently wondered what had become of the towering demon. Recalling his last moments of clarity, he noticed an odd sensation. He could not believe it! His bones and soul were one—connected as they had been in life. An immense power surged through him as he rose from the hard-packed earth. His movements felt strange, arisen in a new form, but what he had been promised was his at last!

CHAPTER 33

Mecursto was ecstatic. It seemed he had escaped a fate too terrible to imagine, and now, he held the promised power. It was something he had never sought for himself; that had been the dream of another, but fate had chosen him. He would use the unexpected gift to undo all the evil wrought by the old man. He had seen through the eyes of Kkrolszerogg and knew that all he hoped to achieve was possible, although at the time, he was not sure how. Now, he understood. He had been reformed in an ancient and forgotten way that was beyond human conception. It was a perversion of the natural design which allowed god-like energy to flow through the body of the host without destroying it. Being altered in such a way was inconsequential to Mecursto if it meant he would be able to restore the life of his father and mother, and he knew that eventually he would have the ability to return to his original form; however, in order to do either, he would first have to return to the tower and link its energy with his own as he had been shown.

Mecursto recognized that the brief moments he had seen through the eyes of the demon-lord were fractured. As he lay rotting, he had tried to recall everything he had been shown, looking for clues that might explain what was happening to him, but the vastness of the demon-lord's reasoning surpassed all human comprehension, and much of what he glimpsed was beyond his understanding. When he tried to recount fragments of the experience, they dissolved as a fading dream. He was not surprised that he could not fully interpret the mind of such a powerful and ancient being, but he was also aware that Kkrolszerogg had not granted him full sight; there were things that had been intentionally shielded from him. Despite not having a full grasp of the phenomenon, Mecursto was able to interpret enough to know that the demon-lord had not lied about being able to bring his parents back from death, and much had also been revealed about the world around him.

Mecursto now understood the true nature of the tower. It was a holding cell for the souls of the dead, and Kkrolszerogg was a caretaker of sorts, collecting and re-distributing the souls of the fallen. It had been so since the time of its creation many eons earlier when it was built by the will of the demon-lord. The architecture allowed a means to unlock the spark of creation, granting the ability to generate life. Kkrolszerogg saw the light of creation as a source of incredible power—one that could be harnessed and used for his own purpose, but mastering the formation of life was incredibly complex even for one as powerful as the demon-lord. He was limited by the numbers he could spawn in the beginning. Still, he was able to generate a modest population of creatures to inhabit the canyons, forests, and wastelands. It took centuries, however, to discover the design of human souls and how to incorporate them successfully into living flesh. Once he did, the few became many with the help of nature, and the city that had been constructed was filled.

Mecursto had no idea to what extent the demon-lord controlled the tower, or the souls gathered within, but he knew what must be done in order to restore his parents to the land of the living; he had to return to the tower. Committed to a course of action, he scuttled across the inner shrine toward the clearing, but as soon as he reached the outer edge of the stone ruins, he was stopped in his tracks by excruciating pain and a blinding flash that knocked him back into the circle. Unsure of what had happened, he slowly righted himself and moved to exit the shrine again. As soon as he reached the outer edge of the circle, he was met with the same outcome—being painfully struck and unceremoniously deposited back to the center. He began to worry. There was an invisible barrier preventing him from returning the way he had come. He considered that perhaps he needed to depart some other way, maybe from a different direction. He decided upon exiting to his immediate right instead. Moving cautiously to the edge of the circle, he reached out toward the threshold of the barrier and was immediately sent sailing through the air—struck by a powerful, unseen force. Anger welled up inside him. He had been held against his will too often to ever allow it to happen again! It occurred to him that maybe it was some kind of test—one final rite of passage to overcome; if so, he would not fail!

Mecursto felt the newly acquired power surging through him. The god-like strength was beyond comprehension just as the demon-lord had promised.

Surely, he could use the energy he possessed to escape the shrine and return to the tower. Picking himself up from the ground, he again approached the perimeter near his original point of entry and focused all of the power within him. Confidently, he moved to cross the barrier, and again, he was repelled by a shocking blast that launched him back to the center of the shrine. Fear began to take hold as he righted himself. He decided to try exiting opposite the way he had entered, away from the tower. As he moved toward the invisible boundary, he felt a glimmer of hope. He was just able to perceive a minute indication that the barrier leading away from the tower was not as strong. Harnessing all his surging power, he approached the edge of the perimeter, willing himself to be free from the shrine. Still, he was met with yet another stunning power surge that violently rejected him and cast him back to the hard packed earth.

Panic assailed him as he rose from the ground and threw himself toward a different path with the same result. Desperately, he hurled himself again and again against the barrier, despite the blinding pain of each failed attempt. Anger turned into white-hot rage as the promised power coursed through his bones. It was an unimaginably potent magic containing the very spark of creation, but what good was it if he could only unlock its full potential while standing upon the tower? *"What if I cannot reach the tower?"* The thought crept into his mind like poison.

Mecursto did not desire the power so he could dominate others as Czarstostryx had; he had not even sought it. All he ever wanted was to be safe and belong somewhere that made sense—the way he had felt with his father—the way he would surely feel with his mother. It was all within his grasp, yet he could not reach it! Frustration and loss overwhelmed him, becoming too much for him to contain.

A deafening howl of lament erupted from Mecursto as he expelled the full force of raw power that had been building inside him, slamming it against the barrier in a blinding flash of rage. The magnitude of its impact shook the earth and traveled far beyond the prison of the shrine, but the barrier remained unbroken. He continued his unrelenting assault with increasing ferocity, causing the force of will that he projected to rebound within the circle, creating a vortex of incredible, destructive energy that spiraled high into the sky. On and on, he raged, feverishly trying to break free from the unyielding barrier. Unbeknownst to him, the culmination of his fury was having a devastating effect on a grand scale.

The clouds high overhead began to converge, growing black and heavy. Lightning cracked and heavy winds blustered. Torrential downpours channeled through canyons and ravines, causing flash floods and landslides. The earth rumbled and split apart, waking long-dormant volcanoes that sprang to life, belching ash and molten lava. Ill-begotten fires battled against the rain, seeking to devour all life.

Far away, the people of Bardazel's kingdom scrambled in the streets, looking for sanctuary from the devastating storms that suddenly appeared. They had been living in fear since the king and his army had abandoned the city, leaving them to wait in dread anticipation of the unknown. The city's leaders had done their best to keep the people calm in their absence, promising them that all would be well, reminding them that the king and his army would soon return, but as days turned to weeks, it became more difficult for them to believe their own reassurances.

Their tenuous encouragement finally turned to dissolution as panic-stricken masses screamed in terror while the heavens and earth unleashed devastation upon them.

Burning rock, rained fire from the mountains surrounding the city, igniting the trees of the Forest of the Grohldym. Towering flames rose high into the air, filling the city with heavy smoke that choked and blinded the unfortunate multitude. Flood water rushed through the marsh road, spilling over the banks of the swollen twin lakes, destroying the outlying villages, and drowning those within the city who could not reach higher ground quickly enough. The ones who did manage to find refuge within the high city walls fared no better as earthquakes shook the foundations, splitting the rock of the ancient stronghold and burying those within under tons of broken rubble. There was no safe haven to be found as high-born and low-born alike met their demise within the crumbling walls of the flooded city.

The devastation of Bardazel's kingdom continued long after the last of its people had perished. The forest was consumed by fire and the lakes were poisoned with ash. The walls of the city fell, and only the most ancient parts of the mountain palace that were built from the cliffs themselves remained.

Back in the ancient shrine, Mecursto's fury began to subside. He had no idea how long he frenzied. The flow of power had been intoxicating, making it all but impossible to release, but despite its potency, the outpouring of primal rage had done nothing to weaken the barrier. It seemed impossible to Mecursto that such a massive surge of force would yield no result, but he was entirely unaware of its impact beyond the shrine. The cries of the dying had gone unheard. He did not know that the shrine amplified the power he had set against it, spreading it throughout the world, even to unknown lands far beyond the kingdom of his father. As the force of its devastation had been magnified, so too had its duration. The world shook as all manner of disaster took life on a grand scale. The hearts and minds of men became twisted and cruel under its influence, creating further carnage through the guise of war and murderous violence.

Mecursto was oblivious to the devastation he had released in his attempts to free himself. He was only considering the things the demon-lord had shown him, not the things that remained hidden. He came to the bitter realization that although the power he possessed was vast, it could not be used to free himself from the shrine or the prison of bones that held him, and he also understood that death would not reach him. With no other option left, he resigned himself to discovering something he may have overlooked—something that might yet hold the key to his escape…

Time passed slowly as Mecursto pondered his fate. Years turned into decades, then centuries, yet he was no closer to freeing himself than he had been since he first set foot inside the shrine. He tried countless times to escape throughout the years, shaping the magic in every way imaginable. He threw everything he could against the barrier, without success. Despite all that he tried, he could see no impact from his efforts, but the rest of the world did. Each time he attempted to escape, more of humanity suffered.

In due course, Mecursto submitted to failure and fell into overwhelming despair and hopelessness. Positioning himself in the center of the shrine, he gazed in the direction of the tower, longing for things that might have been. Unexpectedly, he found that spending long periods in quiet contemplation seemed to improve his ability to endure his fate in a profound way. Extended meditation allowed him to travel beyond the restraints of his physical limitations to a place where he could plumb the depths of his subconscious. Since rage and desperation had failed to serve him, he decided to seek answers through calm, focused tranquility.

As the years gradually crept by, Mecursto became increasingly adept at maintaining prolonged states of calm awareness, suspending himself in a trance-like state for weeks at a time, then months, and eventually, years. He began to detect the elusive answers he sought, hidden in the void of his meditations. He discovered that if he maintained his subconscious mind-state long enough, revelations began to materialize, but they were murky and tedious to grasp. He finally realized the key to his salvation would be to sustain an indefinite state of undisturbed consciousness. The prolonged stillness would allow his energy to grow like the sapling of a mighty tree, eventually reaching a potency that would surpass the barrier's resistance. Determined to accomplish the seemingly impossible undertaking, he set to the task.

Despite his best efforts to endure the exceptional requirements, he would occasionally succumb to his despair and break his focus to lash out in a furious rage, using the pent-up energy of his meditation to assail the barrier exponentially, but it was never enough to break through. Time and time again, he was forced to begin the process all over, slowly nurturing the energy through quiet meditation. Long years passed as he mastered the extreme technique. Eventually, he entered an unbroken state of will that he was sure would set him free.

Centuries drifted by as he held his meditative state, and the power inside him grew beyond anything he had previously achieved. The discipline required to hold it was perpetually tested as he resisted the impulsive urge to unleash it, fearing it would still not be enough to escape, so he remained frozen, not daring to try...

And so, it came to pass in a mental landscape devoid of time that the subtle sound of approaching footsteps stirred conscious reasoning to awaken from its endless slumber. Mecursto had been in the timeless embrace of his mind for so long that it was unusual to garner perception attuned to the physical world around him, but as he regained his connection to his physical form, he knew that what had disturbed him was real. He clearly heard the sound of approaching footsteps coming from the direction of the tower. Mecursto fixed his gaze upon the swirling mists of the surrounding trees and soon saw the source of the disturbance. He was immediately filled with a powerful feeling of deja vu when he saw the young man emerge from the shadows. He appeared to be about the same age Mecursto had been when he discovered the hidden shrine so many years earlier. The young man strode confidently into the clearing and continued walking toward the center of the shrine where Mecursto waited, motionless.

He watched intently as the youth crossed the invisible barrier and came to stand directly in front of him. The young man knelt before Mecursto, reaching for him eagerly. Mecursto's first impulse was to resist the probing hands of the unexpected visitor, but he had a sudden realization that gave him pause. He had done the same thing! He recalled that when he reassembled the bones belonging to that of another, he had taken its place. He remembered hearing the footsteps of its departure while he lay frozen on the ground. This is how he would escape!

It was a strange sensation to have his bones dismantled so they could be reassembled into his long-forgotten human form, and it was unexpected that each time a piece returned to its original configuration, a part of his consciousness linked to the mind of the demon-lord who had abandoned him. Piece by piece, he began to see through Kkrolszerogg's eyes as he had upon the tower, but the final part of the ritual was no longer hidden. The configuration of form Kkrolszerogg had designed for him made it possible to contain immense power and develop it without being destroyed, but its full potential had to grow within the shrine. All the suffering he had endured *and* inflicted upon the world were part of the price the demon-lord demanded in order for him to be as one with the gods. Mecursto had persevered, and the power he had been promised would be his! Once he was re-created, as Kkrolszerogg had devised, he would be freed!

Excitement and hope long forgotten washed over him. It was hard to imagine that he would finally be able to restore his family and find the peace and happiness he had always dreamt of.

As the last bone was put into place, Mecursto was struck by a magnificent pulse of power as his true potential was finally realized. He felt like leaping from the ground and escaping the shrine straightaway, but he knew the ritual was still not complete; he had to exchange places with the young man who stood cautiously regarding him.

Mecursto slowly began to rise from the ground. The young man took an involuntary step back but remained close. Mecursto reached for him as he stood, gripping him firmly by the arm, then the shoulder. Once he had gained his footing, he collected the other shoulder in his grasp and pulled the young man close, gazing deeply into his eyes. Mecursto could feel the will of Kkrolszerogg taking over his mind as his consciousness became one with the demon-lord. He felt the life-force of the young man being drawn into his bones, once again establishing his connection to the land of the living.

The ritual, at long last, was complete. Mecursto released his hold on the young man and allowed him to fall to the ground, knowing he was finally free to leave the shrine. All he had endured was truly at an end! He resisted the urge to run toward the tower in his elation, remembering the weak spot he had perceived at the opposite edge of the shrine. He did not doubt that he could cross the barrier, but after everything that had happened, he decided not to risk it and chose instead to exit as the last denizen had— opposite the tower. Turning from the fallen corpse, he approached the edge of the barrier. He shook off a sudden feeling of apprehension, then took the step that would take him past the invisible barrier.

A warm, gentle breeze greeted him as he walked unopposed into the outer perimeter of the clearing, steadily approaching the trees of the decaying forest. He had done it! His mind exulted in triumph. He was free at last from the inner shrine! His spirits soared as he approached the tangle of trees and turned in the direction of the distant tower. Eagerness to reclaim his stolen life overwhelmed him as he began to run through the low-lying brush.

He only managed a few strides when he was stopped dead in his tracks, overcome by pain—white-hot—searing—all consuming—suddenly gone...

EPILOGUE

Mecursto's lifeless bones lay in a crumpled heap amidst the brambles and underbrush of the murky forest where they would remain along with many other such piles lying unseen on the outskirts of the ancient shrine. It was not the first time he had fallen beneath the swirling mists of Kkrolszerogg's interment, but it would be the last. The time had finally come for the demon-lord to reap what he had so meticulously sown.

Glossary

Bardazel - **bär'• du • zel´**

Brilldagh - **bril'• däg**

Crel - **krel**

Czarstostryx - **zar • stä'• striks**

Glithnie - **gliŧh'• nē**

Grohldym - **grōl'• dim**

Hreydol - **rā'• dōl**

Kkrolszerogg - **krä'• sʉr • räg´**

Mecursto - **mə • kʉr'• stō**

Nieloch - **nī'• läk**

Scorthis - **skōr'• ŧhis**

Skealfa - **skel'• fu**

Toric - **tor'• ik**

Varthaal - **var • ŧhäl'**

Servants of the End Series

Book One: Servants of the End

Upcoming titles

Book Two: Skealfa

Book Three: Czarstostryx

Book four: Mecursto

Book Five: Kkrolszerogg

Book Six: The Grand Scheme

For news on upcoming books in this series or for more information about Servants of the End, go to servantsoftheend.com or follow Shawn Finn's author page on Facebook.

Made in the USA
Middletown, DE
27 September 2023

39552597R00198